PETER CH|
DARK WANTON

REGINALD Evelyn Peter Southouse Cheyney (1896-1951) was
born in Whitechapel in the East End of London. After serving
as a lieutenant during the First World War, he worked as
a police reporter and freelance investigator until he found
success with his first Lemmy Caution novel. In his lifetime
Cheyney was a prolific and wildly successful author, selling, in
1946 alone, over 1.5 million copies of his books. His work was
also enormously popular in France, and inspired Jean-Luc
Godard's character of the same name in his dystopian sci-fi
film *Alphaville*. The master of British noir, in Lemmy Caution
Peter Cheyney created the blueprint for the tough-talking,
hard-drinking pulp fiction detective.

PETER CHEYNEY

DARK WANTON

DEAN STREET PRESS

Published by Dean Street Press 2022

All Rights Reserved

First published in 1948

Cover by DSP

ISBN 978 1 915014 31 3

www.deanstreetpress.co.uk

CHAPTER ONE
TANGO

LADIES and gentlemen, I present to you Vincente Maria Jesu Callao.

The business of a personal introduction seems necessary because he was the spring—however unconscious—that set in movement the rather peculiar actions of most of the people concerned in the business of the Dark Wanton.

A relatively uninteresting person, he becomes interesting, not for what he was, but rather for what he was not. Callao was born in Andalusia in 1913. There appeared to be some doubt about his parentage—a matter which repercussed on his mother, who was adequately catered for by her husband with a seven-inch Spanish sailor's knife five days after the birth of the child. His education was nondescript, but with the passage of years he developed certain attributes, many of which made him attractive to women. He developed little else except perhaps the one sincere thing in his life—an honest love of music and the making of music.

When he was sixteen he was playing the trap drums in a three-piece amateur syncopated orchestra. By the time he was eighteen he was a superb guitarist. At twenty-five he was an expert musician with a flair for controlling the unruly Latin temperaments of a small rumba band—a semi-professional affair which he directed.

Four years later, financed by a woman who thought she knew what she wanted, he had a good rumba band in New York. At the beginning of 1948 he descended upon London with a ten-piece rumba band which was, to my mind, the best of its kind.

Vincente was the type of man that all normal men consider in their secret hearts to be an utter bastard. Normal men thought about Vincente like that first of all because they were entirely unable to understand him and secondly because they thought he looked like that. He seemed to be—and probably was—everything that a normal Englishman or American—or any other man for that matter—dislikes. There was a certain sinuosity—a feminine grace—in his movements; a suggestion of leopard or puma in his walk and the way he put his feet on the ground. His wrists and ankles were slender and well shaped, although very strong. He was well made. He had slim buttocks, a thin waist, a deep chest and fine shoulders. Incongruously enough, his neck was inclined to shortness and thickness. His round, olive face was jowled but his nose was well shaped and sensitive. His mouth was one of those mouths which give women who are interested in men's mouths a good deal to think about, and the curved line of his short upper lip was accentuated by a pencil-line black moustache. His eyes were large; sometimes soft, sometimes very hard and cynical, and his hair of the sort you would expect to adorn such a type—black, patent-leather hair, very well-kept, with a decided, immaculate parting.

Beyond these things there was little to him except his voice, and that deserves especial mention. Vincente possessed one of those strangely attractive voices which seem to thicken almost imperceptibly during talking or singing. A peculiar husky note dominated his vocal cords. At first you thought that this annoyed you, but after a little while you found yourself rather liking it. Most women began by being fascinated by his voice, which led them on to a consideration of his other qualities of appearance. Usually, when they arrived as far as that they were utterly lost. Because very few women escaped from Vincente without leaving something desirable in one form or another behind them.

His attitude towards them was peculiar. At first, after he had made a small success in the United States, he was surprised and amused by the interest which they took in him. Afterwards, and by the time he arrived in England, he had become satiated, and almost bored with women ("choosy" he called it), but used to them in very much the same way as a brandy drinker goes on drinking brandy, not because he gets any of the original kick out of the business, but because he is used to the process of drinking brandy and because he thinks that one day, by some happy chance, he may discover a brandy that tastes better.

Vincente always saw himself in an important light. But he was clever enough to conceal this attitude of mind. In speaking and in his general behaviour he usually produced an effect of humility and diffidence—almost of modesty—which was delightful and which made females believe that in no circumstances could he consider doing anything that was not correct and charming. The incongruity of the quiet sadism and more blatant physical toughness which he eventually showed them was possibly fascinating to ladies who, by the time they became aware of this part of his character, were usually too far gone to be able to do very much about it, even if they had been able to do anything about it.

And in these days, because of the way things are, there are many women who are prepared to be fascinated too quickly by men like Callao. The experience of many young women in the war, their bravery, initiative, their heightened instinctiveness, the result of the part they played, has left its effect, I have been told, on their post-war mentalities. Because they were used to taking one sort of risk some of them seem prepared nowadays to take other chances. The idea appeals to them. As abnormal risks seldom come the way of women in peace time, those of them who are emotional, appreciative of male attraction, lonely or unhappy, often delude themselves into a belief that, in some extraordinary way, or because of some attribute peculiar to their character which they imagine themselves to possess, they may be able to excite and hold the passion of a man like Vincente Callao. Women, even if they are very intelligent in other things, are sometimes, in affairs of the heart, particularly stupid.

After all, nobody can prevent an ostrich from burying its head in the sand, a process which everyone knows is quite stupid—everyone, that is, except the ostrich.

Callao fascinated women. Even those who were sensitive enough to become aware of the danger of Vincente were often too intrigued or interested or curious to go whilst the going was good.

He seldom lost his temper with them. If he had kept it during his quarrel with Kiernan he would, in all probability, be alive to-day, singing those attractive songs set to good rumba music and accompanied by the deadened tom-tom with which his expert trap drummer accentuated the perfect time of that delightful dance; looking with his soft brown eyes at the couples who danced on the small but crowded floor of the Cockatoo; allowing himself to be persuaded (he always allowed himself to be persuaded) to take some lady to his apartment in Clarges Street to see his Mexican art collection.

In his own profession he was important. And, at this time, in the early part of 1948, his rumba band was engaged on a year's contract at the Cockatoo—probably the most fashionable night club in London.

Perhaps I should also say that he had been co-respondent in no less than five divorce cases, in all of which he had really not the slightest interest in the unfortunate women, each of whom lost most of the things which women like to have for something which she thought she would like to have.

I do not think an apology is necessary for this lengthy dissertation on the characteristics of the late Vincente Maria Jesu Callao. As I said, the introduction seemed necessary because the background of the man who was drawn into curious but very vital contact with such persons as Quayle, Frewin, Ernest Guelvada, Aurora Francis, Kiernan, Kospovic and the Practical Virgin, should be made plain from the start.

So much for Vincente. Let us imagine him stepping on to the band platform at the Cockatoo on the evening of Thursday, the 29th January, smiling his own small, diffident, smile at the faces expectantly raised to greet his appearance, bowing with the quick, jerky inclination of the head peculiar to him. And let us think as well of him as we can. We know that he had not long to live, but to him death was a thing unknown and unthought of. Vincente did not like things to last too long. And death is so very permanent that the idea of it would not have appealed to him. It would have made him feel sick, as women who tried to be permanent made him feel sick.

FRIDAY

If Mr. Everard Peter Quayle presented the picture of a normal successful business man of fifty years of age, it is probably because he wished to present such a picture. He could look like other things. He could also be all sorts of things except a business man—which he was not. Quayle spent most of his time sitting in a large office in the International Export Trust Company, which existed purely for the purpose of providing him with a façade behind which he could carry out those rather peculiar activities which caused so much consternation to all sorts of people during the war years and which, it must be admitted, still continue to cause a certain amount of trouble to ladies and gentlemen who have decided inclinations to interfere with the peace of the world for sinister motives best known to themselves.

Quayle was burly and bald. An active-minded person, his thoughts were continuously ahead of the matter he was considering at any given moment. Secretive—as was necessary—to a degree, it was said of him that he never let one hand know what the other was doing, and that, in his particular profession, was perhaps a good thing.

At eleven o'clock on Friday morning he pressed a button on his desk. After a moment a woman secretary came in. Quayle asked for the files on Roumania. When they were brought he sat for an hour, turning over the pages, studying the papers in the folders, making mental notes. It was just after twelve when he sent for Frewin.

Frewin came into the room, shut the door quietly behind him and stood leaning against the wall opposite Quayle's large mahogany desk.

Quayle thought that Michael Frewin was an odd bird. He thought, simultaneously, that it would be strange if he were not. He thought too, with an interior grin, that anybody who rated as being his—Quayle's—principal assistant must, of necessity, be an odd bird.

Frewin was tall, lithe, wavy-haired, very well dressed in a manner which was entirely his own, and apparently lazy. Looking at him, Quayle thought that Frewin spent a whole lot of his life thinking about clothes. He wondered why. Then he thought that after all a man must think about something. Clothes certainly appeared to take a decided part in the mental peregrinations of his assistant.

There was a reason for it. Frewin, as Quayle knew, was a man intelligent enough to hide a direct and peculiarly vibrant and sensitive mentality behind a mask of appearances. These carefully calculated appearances deluded most people—as Frewin intended they should be deluded—into believing him a poseur, a dilettante, a well-dressed executive who did his work satisfactorily and spent his leisure hours in the most futile, tortuous or artistic pursuits possible.

Quayle, however, who had seen Frewin kill four men in difficult circumstances with the utmost indifference, realised exactly what went on under the sometimes cool, sometimes apparently emotional exterior. Frewin must have known this. He had been working with Quayle too long not to know it. But it made no difference. Even when, in intimate and secret conversations with his chief, Frewin still maintained one or other of the many poses which had become second nature to him. Quayle was never for one moment deluded.

Frewin wished people to think of him as being lazy, quasi-artistic and vaguely intelligent. Quayle knew him to be clever, quick-thinking, sensitive to every influence and, if occasion demanded, damned dangerous. One other person was to discover these attributes during the Dark Wanton business; Miss Antoinette Brown was to realise the efficacy of Frewin from quite a different angle and with quite different results.

Quayle said: "Michael, I had a telegram at home last night. Those damned lists haven't got to Roumania yet."

Frewin raised his eyebrows. He took a cigarette case from his pocket and lighted a cigarette. He seldom stopped smoking.

He said: "That means that somebody is still trying to negotiate them; that the job hasn't been done; that they're not actually sold yet."

"That's what I think," said Quayle. "I'm going to do something about it."

Frewin said nothing. He continued to lean against the wall and smoke.

Quayle went on: "I've got an idea that Kiernan's coming to England. I thought we might use him in this."

Frewin asked: "Why? You know he finished after Nuremberg. He got a gratuity, and that was that!"

Quayle grinned. "I don't think he was very pleased with the gratuity. I'm rather inclined to agree with him that it wasn't worth the work he'd done. He took an awful lot of chances in the war, you know."

Frewin nodded. "You feel you want to use him?"

Quayle got up. He walked over to the window and stood looking out. He asked: "Why not? Kiernan's got all the qualifications. He's tough, tenacious, very intelligent."

Frewin said: "All right. I think he's on holiday in France. You want me to let you know when he arrives; where he is?"

Quayle nodded. "Just let me know when he gets here and his whereabouts. I'll do the rest."

Frewin pushed himself lazily away from the wall. He asked: "Anything else?"

Quayle said: "Yes. Can you remember off-hand any women who worked for us in the war—one or two? People who would rate as first-class?"

Frewin smiled reminiscently. "There's one," he said. "You remember her? She was pretty good, that one—Antoinette Brown. I think she's more or less got everything you want."

Quayle said: "I remember her vaguely. Isn't she doing some sort of job in a Government office somewhere?"

Frewin nodded. He knew that Quayle knew perfectly well just where she was and what she was doing.

He said: "Yes. Do I get her?"

"Yes," said Quayle. "Arrange that she has leave of absence. Let her come here and work for a bit. Have you anybody in your mind for a second string?"

Frewin said: "No. Most of the girls we used in the war who were lucky enough to come out of it decided they'd like a quiet life. Most of them are married or doing some normal sort of job. I might think of somebody."

"Well, think about it," said Quayle. "I'll think too. We'll compare notes. But you'd better arrange this Brown transfer as soon as you can." He went on casually: "If I remember rightly, she was rather a nice girl."

Frewin opened the door. He looked over his shoulder. He said: "Very nice. I believe they call her the Practical Virgin."

Quayle said: "No! Why?"

Frewin shrugged his shoulders as he went out. "I don't know," he said in his affectedly quiet voice. "I suppose because she's practical and a virgin."

He closed the door.

Quayle lighted a cigarette and began to think about the lists. He realised grimly that for the six years when the war was on and even now, when it wasn't supposed to be on, he had been thinking in terms of lists. Lists of agents, parachute Intelligence details, lists of espionage and counter-espionage details, lists of people who were too dangerous to everybody to go on living, lists of people who were so valuable to everybody that they must be kept living. He sighed.

Now there were two more lists. Just two. One containing seventeen names, the other four names. Twenty-one names in all. Two lists that had been collected after a comb-out search by one of the best mixed Allied Intelligence details in operation immediately after the war. Two lists that had got as far as the G.I. office in Nuremberg and had then disappeared into thin air. Two pieces of paper which silently revealed the identity of twenty-one individuals who were very badly wanted for all sorts of nastiness. Twenty-one individuals who were being hidden away in some place in some country so that, at some time or other, they could use their own special techniques for the purpose of starting some more trouble.

Quayle stubbed out his cigarette. He began to map out a plan of campaign.

There might be a development at any time now. Why not?

He went out to lunch.

On that afternoon at four o'clock a telephone call came through to Quayle. When the voice came through he listened, drawing easily on his cigarette, his eyes quietly regarding the blotter before them. After a few minutes he hung up the receiver. Then he got up; began to walk about the office impatiently. Now vague ideas began to take shape in his mind.

Quayle's secretary came into the room. She was a tall, thin girl. She appeared dull and uninteresting. To look at her you would find it difficult to believe that she had been parachuted behind enemy lines seven times during the war.

She said: "A Miss Brown to see you. Mr. Frewin said you'd see her."

Quayle nodded. "Ask her to come in. And bring some tea."

She went away.

Antoinette Brown came into the room. She was quietly dressed in black with a smart black hat, and her shell-rimmed glasses had slipped a little on her nose.

Quayle grinned at her. "There'll be some tea in a minute. Sit down and smoke a cigarette if you want to."

She sat down placidly. The secretary came in with the tea.

Quayle went back to his chair. When the secretary had gone, he said: "You worked for me during the war, Antoinette. You did very well."

She said: "Thank you, Mr. Quayle."

He went on: "Something's turned up in which you can help. I asked Michael Frewin to get in touch with you and get you away from that department where you've been so efficiently working at an uninteresting civil service job"—he smiled at her—"because I think that I've got something that's a little more up your street."

"If you say so I'm sure that's right, Mr. Quayle," she said.

Quayle flipped open the folder on his desk. He asked: "When you were in Nuremberg you met Anthony Kiernan, didn't you—that would be about two months after the war ended in Europe? You knew what he was doing of course?"

She nodded. "I assisted him in a secretarial capacity for a little while. I knew he was one of your principal agents, Mr. Quayle; he carried out four or five important assignments whilst I was there."

He asked: "Did you like him?"

"Yes, I always try to like the people I work with. It's so much easier. And Mr. Kiernan was quite a pleasant person."

Quayle grinned. "He never made a pass at you?"

She shook her head. "No."

He went on: "Kiernan's going to do a job for me. You'll be helping him in a rather indirect way. I thought I'd get you to come here this afternoon so that I might have a general talk with you about it, because there won't be any necessity for you to be seen in or around this office while this particular work is in progress. Do you understand?"

She said: "I understand."

"You'll get your instructions through Michael Frewin," said Quayle. "He'll contact you outside."

She said: "Oh!" There was something in her voice.

Quayle grinned again, "You don't like Frewin?"

"No, Mr. Quayle . . . not very much. Not that that makes any difference."

Quayle said: "Exactly." He went on: "I'll give you an outline of the business. We're looking for two lists—mixed lists of secondary war criminals and enemy agents. The two lists were made in the first place by one of the Allied Investigation teams that went into Europe looking for these men. There were no duplicates. The lists went to 21 Army Group Headquarters in Nuremberg and disappeared. There could be only one reason for their disappearance. Somebody was looking after the people whose names were on those lists. They're being hidden somewhere in Roumania or the Russian satellite countries. Somebody feels that some time they might be useful for something or other, Understand?"

She said: "Yes."

Quayle continued: "I've got good reason to believe that the lists were stolen so that somebody could make quite a piece of money out of them. It would be worth a great deal of money to conceal the identity of the men whose names were on those lists. Somebody knew that, but as far as I know—and I have no reason to believe to the contrary—the lists are still in existence." He smiled a trifle whimsically. "Possibly," he said, "because the man or the woman who stole them is holding out for a lot of money."

He lighted a fresh cigarette. "I want those two lists," he said. "I want them badly. I want them before the sale is completed and they are handed over to the purchaser. I haven't very much information but I have a little. And I have decided to use Kiernan in this matter. He is, as you know, tough and extremely intelligent. There's another reason that I have for wanting to use him. He was supposed to finish with us over a year ago. He's been on holiday ever since. I think he's in France at the moment. The fact that he's left my own particular organisation will certainly be known to people who may be interested. That's going to make it easier for him if this thing is played the way I want it played. Understand?"

She said. "Yes, Mr. Quayle."

He smoked silently for a few moments; then: "I'm probably going to want to use another woman. I asked Frewin about it this morning. He couldn't think of one"—he smiled at her—"not of one who had the necessary qualifications. Can you think of one?"

She said: "No, Mr. Quayle."

He went on ruminatively: "Actually the second woman doesn't matter an awful lot. One might almost say that she matters very little. Tell me, Antoinette, when you were in Nuremberg did you know any of Kiernan's women friends? Was there anybody that he was fond of—someone who might be expected to be seen in his company to-day?"

She thought for a moment; then: "Mr. Quayle, there was a woman. I met her. I rather liked her. I think that Mr. Kiernan seemed rather fascinated by her. She was doing some work in Germany under the Control. Her name was Aurora Francis."

Quayle asked: "Do you know where she is?"

"Yes. I had a letter from her the day before yesterday. She's finished her job in Germany, She's coming back to England to-morrow."

She smiled. "She's a fearfully attractive person." There was a pause; then: "Mr. Quayle, are you thinking of using her in any confidential capacity?"

He said: "No." He grinned at her. For a moment his expression was almost mischievous. "Why did you ask?"

She shrugged her shoulders almost imperceptibly. "Only that I think she is fearfully attracted to men. Don't misunderstand me, Mr. Quayle. She's very efficient and awfully good at any work she does. She's well educated. She's good-looking, but I think she's too much interested in men generally all the time."

Quayle asked: "Exactly what do you mean by that?"

She said vaguely: "I don't really know. I suppose I meant just what I said."

Quayle sat drumming quietly on the blotter with his fingertips. After a long silence he said: "Where are you living?"

She told him.

Quayle said: "You'd better leave there on some pretext or other. Go and stay at some good second-class hotel, some place where you'll be on your own and which you could use as a headquarters. You can arrange that to-day. Come back here in about an hour's time and see Frewin. You'll find him in his office. I shall have had a chance to talk to him before then. You'll get your further instructions from him. He'll arrange about money and a banking account for you. He'll tell you just what you have to do. Understand?"

"Yes, Mr. Quayle." She got up.

Quayle said: "Thank you, Antoinette."

She adjusted her glasses. She smiled a small, vague smile. She said: "Thank you, Mr. Quayle."

She went out.

Quayle lighted a cigarette. He thought to himself that in any event he had started something which must, of necessity, lead somewhere or other. The thing to do was to get started.

He began to think about Antoinette Brown. He grinned. He told himself that one day Antoinette was going to make a lot of trouble for some man. One day . . . when she began to get wise to herself . . .

At six o'clock Quayle sent for Frewin.

Frewin came into the office; closed the door quietly behind him; stood in his usual indolent manner, leaning against the wall.

Quayle asked: "Have you talked to Antoinette?"

Frewin nodded.

Quayle said: "The position's clarified a little. Now I know more or less what I'm doing." He told Frewin about the telephone call he had received in the early part of the afternoon.

Frewin said: "I see. . . . So it's like that. Did you think it was like that—before you had the call, I mean?"

"I've always had the idea more or less," said Quayle, "but nothing much to support it." He went on: "You can carry on from there." He grinned. "I think this is one of those things that you'll handle very successfully, Michael. You know what must happen?"

Frewin nodded. "I know what you mean."

Quayle said: "I'll be going away for a few days. I'm going to Germany. I may be away two days; I may be away a week. I don't know. But I'd like this thing cleared up quickly."

Frewin smiled. He asked: "How do I clear a thing like this up quickly? All sorts of things will have to happen."

"Maybe," said Quayle. "But I have no doubt you'll make them happen."

Frewin said: "All right. Tell me something . . . why are you using this girl Brown on this thing?"

Quayle cocked one eyebrow. "You suggested her, I didn't. It was you who said she rated as one of our best operatives."

Frewin said: "I know. But I didn't understand the implications of this job then."

Quayle lighted a cigarette. He settled himself back comfortably in his chair. He smiled almost benignly at his assistant.

He said: "You don't like Antoinette Brown, do you, Michael?"

Frewin shrugged his shoulders. "I suppose I don't. But that doesn't mean that she's not a good operative for normal work."

Quayle asked softly: "Why don't you like her?"

Frewin shrugged his shoulders again. "She's either too good to be true or she's one hell of a hypocrite. And I don't like women who are hypocrites."

Quayle's smile broadened. "Do we care," he said; "provided they do their job as efficiently as Antoinette Brown does, and keep their mouths shut as tightly as she always has? But tell me why she's either too good to be true or a hypocrite, Michael."

Frewin said: "It's her general attitude towards life. I've watched her for quite a while—especially during the Nuremberg days. She doesn't seem at all interested in any of the things that interest a normal woman. But she's too uninterested. No ordinary normal woman can be as uninterested in the things that make people tick over as she is, without either being slightly mental or fearfully hypocritical."

Quayle said: "You're talking about sex of course, aren't you, Michael?"

Frewin nodded. "Of course I am. Everybody in the world thinks somehow—sometime—about sex except, apparently, Miss Brown. Yet, if she wants to produce some feminine attribute that's going to get her some place in her job she can produce it."

Quayle asked quietly: "Then why worry?"

Frewin frowned a little. "I'm not worrying," he said.

Quayle knocked the ash from his cigarette delicately into the ash-tray in front of him. "Well, so long as the job's done, your likes and dislikes don't matter. In point of fact I think when people are doing the sort of work that you and she will be doing a little dislike doesn't hurt." He grinned mischievously. "She doesn't like you a lot," he concluded.

"I know. The fact doesn't keep me awake at night."

Quayle said: "I thought it wouldn't."

"And," continued Frewin, "I'm not interested in what she does or she doesn't think, because she's not working with me; she's going to do what she's told."

Quayle nodded. "Precisely," he said.

Frewin asked: "Anything else?"

Quayle said: "About the other woman, something interesting has turned up having regard to that telephone call. If you want anybody to use as a stooge—if you know what I mean—it seems that Kiernan was attracted to a woman called Aurora Francis who worked under the Control in Germany when he was out there. Brown told me that. It seems that Francis is coming back to England to-morrow. Now, if it's of any use to you, and you feel that you'd like to use her as an unconscious contact, do so."

Frewin said: "I'll remember that."

Quayle got up and stretched. "Good luck, Michael," he said. "Keep it as clean as you can. And I'd like it all tied up in three or four days whichever way you have to do it."

Frewin moved away from the wall. He asked: "Even if it's the hard way?"

"Even if it's the hard way," said Quayle. "Life's hard anyway."

Frewin nodded. He went out.

Quayle sat down at his desk; lighted another cigarette.

The Mordaunt Hotel is a very good hotel of the second class sort. An old-fashioned family hotel, its suites are comfortable and the service still good and respectful in days when suites are usually small and stuffy and service exists when you can get it—if you can.

At seven-thirty Antoinette Brown was looking at herself in the cheval mirror in her bedroom on the first floor. She was wearing an attractive black evening frock. She thought she looked "very nice." She came as near to feeling annoyed as she ever did when the telephone rang and reception told her that Mr. Michael Frewin wanted to see her.

She asked that he should be sent up to her sitting-room; then she powdered her nose; put on her glasses; looked at herself in the mirror; took the glasses off; went into the sitting-room.

When Frewin came in she was sitting demurely in an arm-chair reading a copy of the Tatler. He closed the door behind him; put his hat on a chair.

He said: "Good evening. I hope I'm not disturbing you. But it was important to see you."

She got up. "If you say so, it must be important, Mr. Frewin."

He wondered for a moment whether there was a hint of sarcasm in her voice.

She went on: "Please sit down and I'll get you a cigarette."

Frewin said: "Thanks. I'll smoke one of my own." He took his case from his pocket; lighted a cigarette. He went on: "I had a talk with Mr. Quayle this afternoon. It seems that you told him that a woman named Aurora Francis who knew Mr. Kiernan in Nuremberg would be arriving to-morrow afternoon at Victoria. Is that right?"

She nodded.

Frewin said: "I haven't quite made up my mind exactly what action I'm going to take, but in the meantime I think it would be a very good idea if you confined yourself to some general tactics without particularising too much, and you can report to me all the time. When the situation hardens—if it does harden—I'll be able to give you more definite instructions."

"Very well, Mr. Frewin." Her voice was efficient.

He took a sheet of closely-typed quarto paper out of his pocket. He said: "I've made some notes here. Some general notes of what's in my mind. Some notes on what one might call the opening gambit in this business. I want you to read them, memorise them; then destroy the paper. Really, everything's rather vague at the moment. I can't help that. I don't suppose it'll be vague for very long." He smiled at her.

She said: "I don't suppose so, Mr. Frewin. I've noticed in any operation where you've been concerned, everything is inclined to be very definite."

Frewin thought there was something in her voice that he didn't like. He said: "I don't know that I'm particularly interested in what you notice or don't notice. All I'm interested in is that you do what you're told."

"Quite. I always do, don't I, Mr. Frewin? In any event, I've never had any complaints from Mr. Quayle about the methods I've used in my work. I've often wondered . . ." Her voice tailed off into nothingness.

Frewin asked: "You've often wondered what?"

"I've often wondered why you are so unnecessarily unpleasant. One would have imagined that in our sort of work a normal co-operation would have been much more desirable than the sort of armed neutrality"—she smiled quickly at him—"which you always manage to bring into any working association with me."

For some reason which he didn't know Frewin found himself rather angry. He thought that Antoinette Brown was rather like an eel—something that you could never quite get hold of.

He got up. "I'm sorry if you don't like working with me. But that's how it is. We've got to work together, and things being as they are you'll work in my way."

She said quietly: "If you say so, Mr. Frewin."

He asked: "You don't like me, do you?"

She said softly: "No, Mr. Frewin."

He picked up his hat. "If you have anything to-morrow night you'd better ring through to my apartment. You've got the number. You've got all the places where I'm likely to be at any time during next week. Good-night."

She said: "Good-night."

Frewin went out. In the corridor, for some inexplicable reason, he felt a sense of frustration and annoyance. He wondered why.

SATURDAY

It is doubtful if any one would have noticed Miss Antoinette Brown sitting at the corner table in the refreshment room at Victoria Station. But there are not a very great number of people extraordinarily sensitive to the auras of young women who used the refreshment room at Victoria Station at four o'clock in the afternoon.

If it is difficult to give a picture of Antoinette it is because she was a difficult person to describe. In the office of the Civil Service department to which she had been attached until the day before, she was nicknamed, as Michael Frewin had told Quayle, the Practical Virgin. The reason for that nickname was obvious. Antoinette was practical and she was a virgin.

She was practical because she possessed a quiet analytical mind and an extremely active brain. She knew a lot because she liked knowing things and if she didn't know anything about any given subject she looked it up. In this manner one may acquire a great deal of extraneous knowledge; a certain philosophy of life. I am not suggesting for one moment that Antoinette Brown's philosophy of life was even plausible, but it was definitely hers and she liked it.

Women liked her because they trusted her, because she was honest—or seemed to be honest—and because she never attempted to steal their men. But, in fact, this was not a virtue on her part, because her attitude towards men was somewhat strange as we shall see. I do not mean that she disliked men as a sex. She merely disliked sex.

This might lead you to believe that men were entirely uninterested in Miss Antoinette Brown. If you believed this, again you would be wrong—very wrong! They were interested in her for a diversity of reasons. Some of them thought that she was a little cocky and prone to over-value herself in her office capacity. Some of them disliked her because she had a flair for discovering their mistakes, and even though she would point out the discovery to them personally and in a most charming way, they didn't like it. It made them feel a trifle inferior and no man likes to feel like that. The more clever men with whom she came in contact in the course of her work—men who did not make mistakes; men whose jobs were sufficiently important to enable them to regard Antoinette in her secretarial capacity as a relatively unimportant person—were often annoyed because when, in a moment of (as they afterwards thought) mental aberration, they asked her to lunch or dinner, they found that her reactions were not what they thought they would have been. And for any attempt at familiarity—a stolen kiss in the taxicab, a surreptitious arm about the waist or the straying hand which seeks the solace of a feminine knee—she had the sting of a wasp.

Then there were men who frankly admitted to themselves that they admired her in a rather nebulous way; and men, on the other hand, who realised quite clearly that there was something definitely attractive, even magnetic about this young woman. Frewin himself, in spite of the lazy and indolent air he affected, knew perfectly well that he had a distinct yen for Antoinette.

During the day, plainly-dressed, with a pair of horn-rimmed spectacles on a well-shaped nose, the Practical Virgin exuded sweet nothing. She was interested in what she was doing to the exclusion of all else.

But in the evening, if and when she went out, she looked definitely very attractive. She had a good sense of clothes, a slender but rounded and beautiful figure. And she never wore her glasses in the evening. She was a perfect dancer, moving with something of the quiet abandon of the best Spanish dancers. Then lots of men looked at her; wondered about her.

She was a vexing person to dance with. She held herself six or seven inches away from her partner—almost at arm's length. And she gave him the impression that she was only dancing with him because it was done to dance with a man and not alone.

Actually, no one—except Quayle—knew a great deal about her. She lived with another girl in a small, well-kept flat in Knightsbridge. Her people lived in Sussex.

She was one of those people whom you liked rather in spite of yourself; whom you missed in spite of yourself. In fact, all the people who met her in the course of her work in the office never realised how much they could miss her until she went to work for Quayle on the night of Friday, the 30th January. But the next morning it seemed that her department was strangely empty. Everybody walked about telling everyone else what a shame it was that Antoinette had gone and asking why? Except that they never called her Antoinette—they always referred to her as the Practical Virgin. She knew it, of course, and rather liked the nickname.

It was ten minutes past four when she got up from her seat at the corner table in the refreshment room at Victoria, paid her bill and went out. She walked slowly across the main platform as the Continental Express came in.

Aurora Francis stepped out of the train at the very moment when it came to a complete standstill beside the platform. She was like that. There was a precision and timing about her every movement that was fascinating to watch.

She was just over middle height, alluringly curved, with dark brown hair. Her skin was like cream. Her features regular; delicately chiselled. Her nostrils were sensitive. She had a seductive mouth. She was a charming woman and she knew it.

She was dressed in a grey coat and skirt with a beaver coat over it. Her small brown brogue court shoes set off a beautiful foot and ankle.

She told the porters about her luggage; walked slowly down the platform towards the barrier.

As she passed through the barrier Antoinette Brown crossed the platform. Aurora saw her first; called: "Antoinette!"

Antoinette Brown hurried towards her. The two women kissed affectionately.

Aurora said in her deep, lazy voice: "You know, my dear, I had an idea you'd be here to meet me. It's charming of you."

Antoinette said: "Much as I'd like you to believe that, Aurora, I must tell you I am here quite by accident. I'd some work to do at the local Government office and came in here for a cup of tea. Also I thought you weren't arriving until Monday. I must have misread your letter."

Aurora said: "It doesn't matter what you thought, darling. It's nice seeing you. You don't know how much I've got to tell you. And I'm so glad I've finished my job in Germany."

Antoinette nodded. "So you said in your letter. What are you going to do now?"

"I don't know," said Aurora; "but I've quite a piece of money saved. I'm going to buy some very nice clothes and just laze about for a bit."

Antoinette said admiringly: "You look marvellous! But then you always do. You're quite lovely, Aurora."

The other woman laughed. "You're too sweet, Antoinette. You're pretty good yourself, you know."

Antoinette shrugged deprecatingly.

"Listen," said Aurora, "I'm going to have dinner at the Cockatoo to-night. I've promised myself that I would dine there on my first evening in England. Will you come?"

Antoinette said: "Of course, I'd love it. But weren't you going with someone else? Surely you weren't going to dine there alone?"

"Why not? I love going to places alone." Aurora's eyes narrowed a little as she smiled. "You never know what's going to happen, my dear," she said archly.

"I can see you're just the same sort of person, Aurora. You haven't changed."

"No," said the other. "I'm just the same . . . still seeking romance."

"And finding lots of it," said Antoinette. "But here's your porter with your luggage, and it looks as if they've actually found you a cab. It's marvellous the way you organise things, Aurora."

"I don't know about that," said Miss Francis. "Possibly I'm just lucky. Now don't forget, Antoinette. Meet me in the restaurant at the Cockatoo to-night at nine o'clock."

"I'll be there," said Antoinette. "I'll wear my prettiest frock. I'll try not to disgrace you. Good-bye, dearest Aurora."

"Good-bye for the moment, darling," said Aurora. "We'll have a lovely talk to-night. I've so much to tell you. And you're always so sweet. Such a good listener."

Antoinette Brown watched the cab drive away. Then she walked to the telephone booths in the booking office. She dialled Frewin's office number.

When he came on the line she said: "I'm dining with her at the Cockatoo to-night at nine o'clock, Mr. Frewin."

Frewin said: "All right. You'd better ring me afterwards and give me what you can. Find out when she saw Anthony Kiernan last and if she has any arrangement with him to meet him again. Find out what her plans are. Understand?"

"Perfectly," she answered.

She hung up; went away.

SATURDAY NIGHT

At five minutes to nine Antoinette Brown arrived at the Cockatoo. She was wearing a close-fitting black dinner frock cut very simply but with that sort of "line" that comes only from haut couture. Her hair was dressed softly about the nape of her neck and she was not wearing her spectacles. Whilst she was powdering her nose Aurora arrived.

Aurora looked superb. She had dressed carefully to bring out every point of her unique personality. Antoinette thought, quite dispassionately, that she looked an eyeful and a lot more. She wondered just what was in Aurora's mind, because there had to be something. No woman, thought Mr. Quayle's operative, dressed like that to dine with another woman. Somewhere in the offing there had to be a man.

They talked for a few minutes. Aurora said they would have cocktails in the restaurant, and not in the cocktail bar. Her eyes were a trifle too bright and there was almost an air of suppressed excitement about her.

She wore a red chiffon frock with a tight bodice and a full skirt which, in spite of its fullness, gave more than an indication of her shape and the grace with which she moved. Her dark brown hair was caught straight back from her head and dressed in a bunch of soft curls that fell about her neck. She wore a collar of pearls. Most of the men she passed on her way to the restaurant stopped to look at her. Antoinette thought Aurora liked that.

The maître d'hôtel who showed them to the table which Aurora had reserved was inclined to be passionate about women. He thought that Aurora was definitely something. Then he looked at Antoinette and realised that she was also something. He pondered the matter during the few seconds that it took to traverse the floor between the entrance and their table and, as he seated them, concluded that he would prefer Aurora but would if necessary settle for Antoinette. Afterwards he thought he was not so certain and spent the following Sunday afternoon considering the matter.

Aurora looked at her wrist-watch. She said: "It's five minutes past nine. Vincente Callao's rumba band plays at nine-fifteen. It's a fearfully good band."

Antoinette smiled. "If you wanted to dance why did you ask me?"

Aurora sipped her cocktail. Her eyes narrowed a little. "I'll tell you," she said. She began to talk.

At this moment Kiernan paid off his cab outside the Cockatoo and went into the cocktail bar. He went into the cocktail bar because he thought that if Aurora Francis were, by some chance, in England, and if, by greater chance, she was dining at the Cockatoo—a place which he knew she liked because she had told him so—she would go into the cocktail bar before dining.

So he went there. If he had not I should not be writing the story of the Dark Wanton.

*

At half-past nine Kiernan still stood at the end of the curved cocktail bar drinking a dry Martini and listening to the rather hoarse but quite attractive voice of Vincente Callao who was singing a rumba in the restaurant. The music and the voice were filtered before they reached Kiernan's ears because the sounds had to penetrate the atmosphere of the corridor that led from the restaurant to the cocktail bar; to make themselves felt above the subdued hum of conversation.

Kiernan thought about Callao. He thought, in the hard, direct way in which he thought about everything, that Callao was a bastard—one of those people. Albeit an attractive bastard—at least as far as women were concerned. Kiernan thought that as far as men were concerned attraction meant very little. Men weren't attracted. They liked. Which is the essential difference between men and women. Or is it? thought Kiernan. He wondered what the hell it mattered anyway. At the right time, in the right place, Callao might be useful—one never knew. . . .

He finished the drink; ordered another one. His mind came back to Callao and that brought him to the Cockatoo and then to Aurora because, he supposed, she had told him that she liked the Cockatoo; that the atmosphere fascinated her; that the place "did something to her." He wondered if, by any chance, Aurora was interested in Callao. . . .

That, he thought, in the circumstances, would be very funny. Or would it?

He was experiencing a peculiar sense of well-being, for which he could find no adequate reason. He tried to analyse it. Was it because he was back from Germany, more or less at a loose end, with some money in his pocket? And the prospect of as amusing a holiday as England could hold out to any one. Was it that? Was it because he thought there was a chance of meeting Aurora? . . .

He thought that might be it. There was something about her, he thought, that he went overboard for. She certainly had an allure—a thrilling and powerful allure. And she dressed well, spoke delightfully. Aurora had a certain quality even if she was inclined to reduce it occasionally by being or appearing to be—he wasn't quite certain which—a trifle promiscuous where men were concerned. Or maybe she was merely curious. Kiernan thought that might easily be—that she was curious. She'd said that. That she liked to know about things; that if she were interested in something she had to know about it. Well, she was interested in men. She hadn't told him that but several other people had. So, logically, if she were interested in men she would want to know all about them. And, thought Kiernan with a grin, there was only one way of knowing about a man. As he finished the second Martini, he wondered just how much she was interested in him . . .

As he put the glass down on the bar he looked up. His eyes widened a little in surprise as he saw Nielecki at the other end of the bar. Nielecki looked like he always looked—like exactly what he was. He was short and stumpy and his overcoat fitted badly round the collar. His hat—one of those peculiar green Homburg hats which are only produced in the depressed areas of occupied countries—was worn perfectly straight on his head with its brim at the same angle all the way round. He was drinking lager beer and he carried his mouth towards the glass mug instead of raising the mug. His small eyes were still tired and shifty behind the horn-rimmed spectacles. Nielecki finished drinking; raised his head; saw Kiernan. He started.

Kiernan grinned at him. Always, when he met Nielecki; when he'd met him in Germany, in Roumania, in the other places where he'd seen him previously Kiernan had possessed the same sense of power and authority—the power which a special agent who is sure of himself feels for one who, when all is said and done, and in spite of his background and education, is nothing but an informer—a rather indifferent and badly paid spy, as Nielecki was. Kiernan thought that they came in droves. Here to-day in 1948 you could see them walking about London, looking exactly the same, behaving in the same quietly argumentative manner, trying to prove some theory which they were paid to try and prove wherever they went. Groups of frightened, sometimes vicious, and occasionally clever men, employed by even more stupidly vicious people for the purpose of stirring up wars and rumours of wars. Some of them had once been decent. Some of them had been honest, European lawyers or farmers, business men, professors. Now, with the old classes, moral and attributes flattened out of existence, they crept about the world working for whoever frightened them most.

Kiernan beckoned with his finger and Nielecki, carrying the glass mug in one hand and the inevitable document case in the other; came quickly round the bar until he stood by Kiernan's side.

Kiernan said: "Well, how's it going, Nielecki? Are things good with you?"

Nielecki shrugged his shoulders.

Kiernan continued with a grin: "Who are you working for now? Which group of so-and-so's is paying you to find out what's going on? And how many pups have you sold them?"

Nielecki said in his quiet, stilted voice: "I don't know what you mean by that thing . . . the pup? . . . What does it mean to sell a pup?"

"To sell a pup means, in your case, to sell somebody false information," said Kiernan.

Nielecki said: "I don' give nobody false informations."

"You're a bloody liar," said Kiernan cheerfully. "When you get frightened you tell 'em anything to keep them quiet and so that they won't cut your expense account."

Nielecki stiffened. Kiernan thought casually that Nielecki seemed to have acquired a modicum of courage from somewhere or other.

After a few seconds the Pole said: "Mos' of the time I speak the trut'. When I am paid for it I always speak the trut'." He looked sideways at Kiernan. "Perhaps you always speak the trut'?" he said.

Kiernan ordered another large Martini. He told the bartender to make it very dry.

He said: "I tell the truth when it suits me. And don't be rude, Nielecki; otherwise the next time I meet you in one of those unoccupied territories I'll hurt you like I did once before. Remember?"

Nielecki's shoulders dropped a little. "I remember." He looked up quickly. The vestige of a smile crossed his face so quickly that Kiernan wondered if it had ever really existed.

Nielecki said: "I have a piece of interesting news for you. I heard from one of the people on the Control in Germany—a high-up person—that there is a lot of trouble about some missing lists of secondary war criminals who have quietly disappeared."

Kiernan grinned. "That wouldn't surprise me. At the end of '45 and in '46 everybody was so keen on finding the big boys—the Himmlers, the Goerings, and their high-up assistants—that they didn't worry too much about the second and third-class war criminals, who were just as dangerous as the other ones—possibly more so. Why should they be surprised if, when they did get around to them, lots of them had disappeared?"

Nielecki said: "Somebody must have helped them to disappear."

"You're telling me," said Kiernan. "Somebody did. I bet you've helped a few of 'em in your time." He laughed. "How much money have you taken to smuggle some of those boys into Romania where they're sitting pretty?"

Nielecki said: "Why should any one want to smuggle them into Romania or anywhere else?"

"Search me," said Kiernan. "Evidently, somebody thinks they'll have a use for them sometime."

Nielecki shrugged his shoulders. "I see," he said. "So," he went on, "I heard also that somebody had a thought who the person was who'd taken the lists."

Kiernan said: "Yes? I could make ten guesses myself. Any list of wanted war criminals would only be useful if it were a new list, before it had reached one of the registries. I should think there were quite a few people who were prepared to take a bribe to 'lose' a list, especially if they were shown some real money."

Nielecki said: "Possibly. But in this case the information was definite."

Kiernan began to drink his third cocktail. "I know," he said. "I know that definite information. I've spent a long time checking on definite information. When you get down to hard tacks you find it's usually gum bubbles."

Nielecki sipped a little more of the beer, which had remained in the glass mug so long that it was flat. Kiernan thought that flat beer meant nothing to Nielecki; that probably he liked it. Anything was good after the dirty water of a concentration camp.

He said: "So the information was definite. Does that mean you brought it in?" He grinned amiably.

Nielecki said: "No, I didn't bring it in. But I had it direct."

Kiernan lighted a cigarette. He was almost not interested.

He asked: "Who did you hear it from, Nielecki?"

Kiernan thought quickly for a minute. "That sounds phoney to me," he said. "Presumably you've heard this fairly recently. I heard you hadn't been out of England for six months."

Nielecki nodded. "That's right. I heard it in England." He went on: "I was in the country. I was staying at some place—what you call . . . a guest house—called 'The Rambling House,' near South Brent in Devonshire. I went there because I was unwell—my chest got himself bad in the concentration camp in '43." He looked at Kiernan with a surprised expression on his face. "One evening I was in the little bar drinking beer, and I looked up and Kospovic came in. He had only then arrived. He said to me he was going to stay there permanently. His chest was bad like mine. He said to me he had a little money from somewhere and he was being paid by some European organisation to do some work. He said to me that he liked it there; that the air was good for him. Then he told me of getting some knowledge about the one who was responsible for the disappearance of those lists."

Kiernan said: "Which lists were they, Nielecki?"

Nielecki looked into the remains of the beer as if he were reading the future. "They were the lists of the Roumanian people— the war criminals who never came out of Roumania because from the first they were hidden. People who were supposed to be handed over after the Armistice and who weren't handed over because somebody didn't want them to be handed over. They could have got them if they'd had the lists. The allies could have insisted, but those two particular lists disappeared and there weren't copies because they were the original investigation team lists. Kospovic said all this he knew."

Kiernan grinned. "If Kospovic knew so much it was a pity he didn't come up to London and tell somebody in the Special Branch about it."

Nielecki shrugged his shoulders. "That's what I said to him. But Kospovic said it didn't matter; that he was tired; that he would not embroil himself in something."

"You mean he had the wind up." Kiernan laughed. The idea of a man like Kospovic having some real information and not trying to get something out of it amused him.

"No," said Nielecki. "No. I don' mean that. Kospovic had not the wind up, as you say, but he was very tired. Maybe he's been kicked about a lot, you know. Mos' of us were. Maybe he thought that he would wait until he was better. I think he is a fool. I think he ought to tell somebody about what he knows. I told him so. I told him that if they found out that he knew and had said nothing they would kick him out of England. They would send him away and that wouldn't be at all good for him."

"You're telling me," said Kiernan. "What did he say to that?"

"He said to me that he thought it good to wait. He would wait until his chest was better. He did not want to leave this place in Devonshire where the air was soft and he did not cough so much. He said when he was better he would think again. I think he is a fool. I said that to him."

Kiernan said: "You're a strange bird, Nielecki. You don't like Kospovic, do you?"

"No." Nielecki shook his head. "I don' like Kospovic, I don' like a lot of peoples. I don' think I like you very much."

Kiernan laughed. "Thank you for nothing. You ought to be very fond of me."

Nielecki held out his left hand. There was a deep indentation right round the base of the first finger. He said: "Why do I have to like you, please? You did that to me. You did that to me in 1945 with a piece of red-hot telephone wire."

Kiernan said: "I know. You wouldn't talk. I had to persuade you."

Nielecki looked at him. There was a malicious gleam in his eyes. He said: "Well, I still didn't talk even after the telephone wire, did I?" The gleam in his eyes deepened. "Bu I'm talking now. That's because maybe I've forgiven you."

Kiernan said in his quiet casual voice: "That's very nice of you."

Nielecki picked up the glass mug. His fingers were trembling a little. He finished the beer.

He said: "I have to be going away. It's time I went back to my work."

"Just a minute," said Kiernan. "You know, I don't dislike you, Nielecki. I think you've been pushed around a bit the last ten years or so, haven't you?"

Nielecki's shoulders drooped again. "My God . . . have I—?"

Kiernan said: "What were you before they started pushing you around—before the concentration camp?"

"I was a lawyer," said Nielecki. "I had a wife. I was happy."

Kiernan asked: "What happened to your wife?"

Nielecki answered in a flat voice: "I don' know."

"Are you getting enough to live on?" asked Kiernan.

Nielecki said: "I have my work. I'm doing some work for the Central Eastern Refugee Committee. I get enough to live on. Life is never very easy."

Kiernan put his hand into the breast pocket of his coat. He produced a thick bundle of bank notes. He peeled off ten five-pound notes.

He said: "Go buy yourself a drink sometime, Nielecki."

Nielecki picked up the money; put it into his overcoat pocket.

He said: "In spite of the fact that you burned me with a piece of telephone wire I'm not a bad friend to you."

He walked out of the bar.

Kiernan lighted a cigarette. He ordered another Martini. He stood there relaxed, listening to Vincente Callao singing another rumba song.

In the restaurant Antoinette Brown finished her coffee; put the cup down; looked at Aurora.

She said: "So you'd heard about Callao?"

Aurora looked towards the band platform. Her cheeks were a trifle flushed; her eyes too bright. Antoinette saw that her friend's eyes were narrowed—a habit she had when thinking of some men.

"I'd heard about him," said Aurora. "He's a poppet, isn't he? You can see exactly what he is—very good looking and Latin and sleek and dangerous. Rather an interesting type."

"Are you really curious about him, Aurora?" asked Antoinette.

The other nodded. "Awfully curious. So much so that in a minute I'm going to send him a note and ask him to play a special rumba for me. Then we'll see what happens."

"What do you think will happen?"

Aurora shrugged her shoulders prettily. "I don't know, of course. But I should think that he might come over here and say something about it. They tell me he often does—especially if he's attracted to a woman."

"And if he does?" queried Antoinette.

"I believe"—Aurora smiled, showing her white teeth—"that the next move in the game is to ask the lady if she's interested in Mexican art, and if she says yes to offer to show her his collection."

Antoinette raised her eyebrows. She looked a little scared. She managed this very well. She really did look as if she were scared and not as if she were pretending to be scared.

She asked breathlessly: "But would you go, Aurora?"

Aurora nodded. "I'll try anything once!"

There was a pause. The waiter refilled their coffee cups.

Antoinette said: "You ought to have been born a man."

"Why?" demanded Aurora. "I think I like being a woman. Am I so difficult to understand?" She smiled deliciously. "But perhaps you're too nice, my dear. I think you have an awfully nice mind."

"I often wonder," said Antoinette. "But you are a little difficult to understand, aren't you? One never quite knows what you're getting at; what you really want. You're not in love with this Vincente Callao, are you?"

Aurora laughed. "Don't be silly, Antoinette. Of course I'm not in love with him. I'm merely curious about him."

There was another pause; then Miss Brown said demurely: "You know, the reason why I'm surprised at your attitude about this"—she waved her hand towards the band platform—"is because when we were in Nuremberg I thought you were awfully interested in Mr. Kiernan. Remember . . . Anthony Kiernan?"

Aurora raised her eyebrows. "But I was . . . and am. Very much interested."

"Are you curious about him too?" asked Antoinette.

Aurora shook her head. "That comes into a rather different category, my dear. Callao looks to me like a very interesting and dangerous play-thing. Kiernan is definitely a man with a capital 'M.' You know what he did in the war?"

"No," said Antoinette. "I know very little about him. I knew he'd done some rather special work of course, but I never asked what it was, and he didn't volunteer any information. I worked with him, as you know, for a little while, but that was only in a secretarial capacity just before the Trials started."

Aurora said: "I see. . . . Well, I'll tell you something. Anthony Kiernan was one of our best secret agents in the war. He was dropped many times behind the enemy lines. He speaks three languages perfectly. He's got the nerve of the devil. That man, I think, could get away with anything." Her eyes glowed. "The Gestapo had him twice. He talked himself out of it once and escaped the second time."

Antoinette said: "You're really fond of Kiernan?"

Aurora considered the matter; then: "Yes . . ." she said a little dubiously. "But I wouldn't say I was in love with him. I'd say that I have an intense admiration for him and a great curiosity about him; that I'd like to know him really rather well and keep on knowing him. Is that difficult to understand?"

Antoinette looked vague. "It is a little. I still don't understand the category—as you call it—into which you put Anthony Kiernan."

Aurora said: "My dear, if you want it straight I'll give it to you. I'd like to have Kiernan as a sort of 'steady'—someone who was always there; someone on whom one could rely; someone to whom one could return after—"

"After you'd satisfied your curiosity with any one else who came into your orbit?" asked Antoinette.

"That's about it," said her friend. "Do you think I'm a very shocking person, Antoinette, because I'm not fearfully good and demure and sweet like you?"

"I don't know," said Antoinette. "But I think you're a very straight person. I think you have the gift of entire honesty of mind, which is something, isn't it?"

There was a silence; then the band started and Callao began to sing a Spanish rumba. He put it over wonderfully. His eyes—large, soft and brown—wandered slowly round the ring of tables at the Cockatoo, hesitating for a moment here and there before moving on. They stopped for a long time at Aurora's table.

She asked the waiter for a piece of paper and a pencil. She wrote a note; told him that when the song was finished she would like it taken to Mr. Callao. The waiter nodded and went away.

Antoinette began to talk about Nuremberg; about some of the things that had happened. Her voice was soft and relaxing. Aurora thought she liked listening to her. She thought that Antoinette was a nice child, but rather stupid to allow life to pass her by. She thought that Antoinette was a person whose mind had not progressed with her body; that she was still about sixteen years of age. Which goes to show that even Aurora had a lot to learn.

The song was over and the music stopped. The waiter unobtrusively went round the outer circle of the tables; passed the note to the guitarist at the end of the platform. The guitarist, who was Spanish American and looked it, rolled the note into a ball; flipped it with his forefinger and thumb into the air towards Callao, who caught it deftly.

Callao looked at the note. He put it into the pocket of his tuxedo, He gave the band the name of the number. They began to play it. Callao turned round and faced the dancers. His eyes moved slowly towards Aurora; stopped at her.

Antoinette said: "I must be going, Aurora. Because while I stay I don't think he'll come here, and you won't get what you want." She smiled at Aurora. "And I've such a lot to do. When shall we meet again?"

Aurora said: "I'm living at the Berkshire apartments in Lowndes Square—No. 21. You'll find the house telephone number in the book. Ring me up to-morrow and come and see me."

Antoinette said: "Perhaps by then you'll have even more to talk to me about." She picked up her handbag. "Do you expect to see Kiernan? And do you think he'd be pleased if he knew what was in your mind about Callao?"

Aurora said: "My sweet, I don't have to tell him, do I? Yes . . . I expect to see him. I told him that I used to come here a lot. If and when he arrives in London I expect he'll come here and look for me."

"And if he does, and if he finds out about Callao . . ." Antoinette hesitated. "Don't you think there might be a little trouble if Kiernan is such a man with a capital 'M' as you say he is?"

"I think there would be a lot of trouble," Aurora answered. "But sometimes a situation like that can be very amusing. But you wouldn't think that, would you?"

Antoinette got up. "Possibly not. But then my opinion isn't necessarily right. Good night, Aurora. I'll telephone you to-morrow."

She threaded her way through the tables towards the exit. By the time she got there the lights had been subdued. The room was in half-darkness when the band began a slow tango. In the curtained doorway Antoinette turned; looked towards the platform. She saw Callao make a gesture to the violinist to carry on. She saw him step off the edge of the platform and move round the shadowy walls towards Aurora's table.

She turned, passed through the curtains and began to walk down the corridor that led to the entrance. Halfway down she stopped. She moved down the short passage-way towards the closed door of the cocktail bar. She looked through the door. She saw Kiernan at the end of the bar drinking Martinis. She thought that life was a little extraordinary.

She walked back to the main corridor; arranged a strand of hair that was out of place; put on her spectacles; stood for a moment, thinking. Then she turned; went down the passage-way into the cocktail bar.

There were few people at the bar. Most of the occupants of the room were seated at the small tables. She seated herself on a high stool. She ordered a dry Martini. She looked up in surprise when Kiernan said:

"Well . . . well . . . well . . . if it isn't little Antoinette Brown!"

She said: "Good heavens, Mr. Kiernan. How strange to meet you. I'm sorry I didn't see you, but you know my sight's not very good."

Almost imperceptibly the rumba band went into another tune—a slower form rumba. The trap-drummer, with one eye on the figure of Vincente Callao, who had already begun to move round the outer circle of tables, put his hand backwards, found the electric switch and brought the lights in the restaurant down to an even lower pitch. Now practically only the dance floor was illuminated, and the band platform.

This was the usual techniques. When ladies sent notes and asked for special numbers to be played, and Callao, after a preliminary inspection, decided to go and talk to them about it, the trap-drummer always checked the lights down. This enabled Callao to move about without being too obvious. Callao was nothing if not artistic.

When Aurora looked up, he was standing on the other side of her table.

He said in his attractive, hoarse voice: "Señorita, eet es ver' kind of you to ask me to play some special numbers for you. They are playing the second one now, I hope you like eet. I wonder if you would like me to sing eet for you?"

Aurora said softly: "Yes, I would. Is it an interesting song?"

Callao nodded. His face was strangely white in the near darkness. She could see his eyes shining.

He said: "Eet ees a ver' interesting song. Eet ees about a man who has loved many women and then, suddenly, he meets ones superb woman—like you, Señorita. And he realises that never before has he really loved. Would you like to hear that?"

Aurora said: "Please, Vincente. When you've sung it, come back. I'd like to thank you."

Callao smiled at her. He went back to the band platform. The violinist sat down. The tone and tempo of the music softened and Callao began to sing.

He put his heart into it. He sang in Spanish, and the rhythm of the language was accentuated by the attractiveness of his amorous voice. Aurora thought he was quite charming.

When the song was finished the band began to play another dance tune. The trap-drummer checked the lights down lower. Callao went back to Aurora's table.

He asked: "Did you like eet, Señorita?"

She said: "I thought it was lovely. I don't think I have ever heard any one sing anything as beautifully as you did."

He shrugged his shoulders. "Eet ees just a trick . . . jus' nothing. But, you see, mine ees not a very dignified or happy profession." He said these words with an air of the utmost sincerity. No one would have thought that they were an opening gambit he had been using for years.

She said: "I don't understand that. You're a great artist. You're very popular. You ought to be happy. Why should you be unhappy?"

Callao shrugged his shoulders again. His voice was very low. "The only reason I can think ees the song I was jus' singing."

Aurora got it. She didn't see why she should waste a lot of time.

She said: "You mean that I might be the person that made all the other women seem different?"

"Not different, Señorita," said Callao. "Jus' indifferent!" He went on: "Singing like this ees no good. I would like to sing to you somewhere where eet ees quiet; to sing to you with my own guitar; to sing you some even lovelier songs which are no good here because these people"—he waved one hand towards the dance floor—"do not appreciate really beautiful music."

She said: "I'd love that."

He asked suddenly: "What ees your name?"

She told him.

He said: "Señorita Aurora. . . ." He pronounced the word with difficulty, so that the way he said it made it sound very attractive. "Eet ees a mos' lovely name. When can I sing for you?"

"When you like," said Aurora.

He smiled at her. "To-night I am ver' lucky. A relief band is coming on in five minutes' time. That only happens once a week.

Eet ees a sort of half-holiday for us. Then I was going back to my apartment, which ees lonely, to play some music for myself. That ees the only way I get any pleasure out of life. If I dare ask you to come . . ."

Aurora said: "Why not?" She laughed softly. "I love listening to music, Vincente."

He asked: "Would you like to meet me in the back entrance in five minutes' time? I will be waiting for you."

"Yes. . . . I'll do that."

He said quietly: "Adios, Señorita. . . ."

He went away.

The lights in the restaurant began to go up. Aurora looked round for her waiter; asked for her bill.

Back on the band platform Callao winked at the trap-drummer. He said: "Call on the telephone to the manager. Tell him I don' feel well. Tell him I'm going home."

He grinned at the drummer; showed his white teeth.

The bar-tender brought the dry Martini which Antoinette had ordered. She took off her glasses; looked up at Kiernan. Her eyes were large, a little soulful, very admiring.

She said: "Mr. Kiernan, I've only recently found out what you were really doing during the war and in Nuremberg. I can't tell you how much I admire you . . . what terrible risks you ran . . . what chances you took." She sighed. "And to think that I was doing secretarial work for you for those few weeks in Germany and didn't know about you. Life's quite strange, isn't it?"

"Yes. . . ." Kiernan looked at her sideways. He thought that she wasn't a bad little piece; that she had possibilities. He thought if his mind weren't busy with other things he might even get around to Antoinette. But his mind was busy with others things.

He asked: "What are you doing here? Waiting for a boy friend?"

She shook her head; drank some of her Martini. Kiernan thought that the shape of her mouth was attractive.

"I don't have a boy friend. Actually, I've been dining with someone you know."

He smiled. "You couldn't mean Aurora Francis?"

She nodded. "I left her in the restaurant. We had dinner together. It was she who told me about you and what you did during the war. She's quite charming, isn't she? I like her a lot."

"Do you?" asked Kiernan. "Why?"

"She has the courage of her own convictions," said Antoinette. "She's quite a character. She has a very definite personality, and she's looking very beautiful to-night. I think she's a most attractive woman."

Kiernan said: "Yes?"

She went on: "I left her because I thought she had an appointment with somebody and I didn't want to play gooseberry." She looked archly at Kiernan. "On the way out I decided to buy myself just one little Martini. I don't know why; it's a thing I seldom do. So I came in here, and saw you."

He said: "It's rather extraordinary—we three meeting here, I mean—because I dropped in on the chance of seeing Aurora Francis. She told me she came here a lot when she was in London; and I knew she was due to arrive in England. But I hadn't a chance to go into the restaurant. I met an old friend here and we talked."

"This seems to be a sort of general meeting place, doesn't it?" said Antoinette. "Do tell me . . . was your friend somebody else from Nuremberg? That would be too funny, wouldn't it?"

Kiernan said: "No . . ." He thought: What the hell does it matter? "It was a man I knew in Romania—a fellow called Nielecki—one of those odd types. The sort of person who used to hang around the Court House at Nuremberg. You know?"

"I know." Antoinette made a mental note of the name.

He said diffidently: "Aurora's just the same, isn't she? Quite casual about people. She arranges to have dinner with you and then finds she has an appointment with somebody." He smiled at her. "Or perhaps she hadn't the appointment when she arrived here."

Antoinette said: "You know, its funny but you're right. I think Aurora is rather attracted by the leader of the rumba band here. He's a most fetching Spaniard called Vincente Callao. I rather thought she wanted to talk to him, so I made myself scarce!"

Kiernan grinned, but underneath the grin there was an odd spurt of anger. There was also an idea that he was going to do something about it, and he realised that he wasn't just being jealous of Aurora. There was something rather more important behind it.

"Well, girls will be girls, I suppose," he said easily, "especially if they're like Aurora. And as she was looking particularly beautiful to-night, maybe she felt she must try her allure on somebody."

Antoinette nodded. "She's wearing the most wonderful red frock." She sighed. "Sometimes I wish I were like her."

Kiernan grinned at her. "I shouldn't worry if I were you. You've got something, you know, Antoinette."

She looked at him with large, innocent eyes. "Do you think so, Mr. Kiernan? I never think that."

His grin broadened. "It doesn't matter very much what you think, does it? It's what some man is going to think one of these fine days."

Her face became prim. "I hope not, Mr. Kiernan." Her voice became a little sharp. "I don't think I like thinking about things like that." She finished her drink; slipped gracefully off the stool. He saw that her legs and ankles were really good.

She held out her hand. "I must be going. I hope we shall meet again. Are you still on service work now? It can't be very exciting these days—after what you did in the war, I mean."

Kiernan shook his head. "No, I've finished. They gave me a gratuity and that was that. I'm just going to have a good time for a bit—and then I may go abroad. London isn't what it used to be."

"No," said Antoinette. "Well, good night, Mr. Kiernan."

She went away. He watched her slim figure till it disappeared through the glass door.

Outside she walked quickly towards Green Park Station. Arrived there, she went into a telephone box. She'd learned Frewin's telephone numbers off by heart; tried three of them. She got him the third time.

She said: "Mr. Frewin, I left Aurora Francis about fifteen minutes ago in the restaurant at the Cockatoo. She was wanting to talk to the band leader Vincente Callao. As I was passing the cocktail bar I looked through the door and saw Mr. Kiernan. He was there because he thought there was a chance of meeting

Aurora Francis, but he hadn't seen her because he'd met somebody he knew in Roumania—a man called Nielecki. I'm talking to you from Green Park Station."

Frewin said: "I see. . . . You left Kiernan in the bar?"

"Yes. I think he'll go into the restaurant to find Miss Francis, that is if she's still there."

"What do you mean by that?" asked Frewin brusquely. "D'you mean there's a chance of her going off with the band leader?"

"I think it's very probable," said Antoinette.

"All right. Ring me up in the morning. Good night."

She said good night.

Frewin hung up the receiver; drummed with his fingers on the table top. He picked up the receiver of another telephone—a direct line. He asked for Colonel Goddard.

He said: "Goddard . . . Anthony Kiernan—slim, about six feet, blue eyes, dark brown hair, broad shoulders, clear complexion, good-looking—will be in the cocktail bar or the restaurant of the Cockatoo in about five minutes' time. Put a tail on him, will you? And don't lose him. I want to know what he does. Earlier in the evening he was talking to a man called Nielecki. I don't know what nationality, but he's probably a foreigner, so you should be able to check easily through the police. Find out who and where Nielecki is. Get his address so that I can pick him up in the morning if I want to. If necessary, put a tail on him. Have you got that?"

Goddard said he'd got it.

Frewin hung up; lighted a cigarette. He thought that, all things considered, it wasn't so bad for one night's work.

Kiernan wondered whether he would drink another Martini. He decided not. He ordered a whisky and soda. Liquor did little to him. It affected neither his physical nor mental outlook. Unlike those volatile people who became excited and temperamental after drink, Kiernan maintained an even mental equilibrium. His mind was as hard as his body. He drank because it amused him.

He began to think about Aurora Francis. Her technique, he thought, was the same as ever. She'd arrived in England, met Antoinette Brown, asked her to dinner at the Cockatoo, because she wanted a companion just in case the Vincente Callao thing didn't come off. And she wanted a companion whom she could easily get rid of if it did come off. And apparently it had come off.

Kiernan wondered what the set-up was going to be between Callao and Aurora. He grinned. This, he thought, was a case of Greek meets Greek. Both of them were tough; both of them were inclined to be cynically curious. Both had a mild streak of cruelty in their natures. Normally, thought Kiernan, it might be a lot of fun standing on the side lines and cheering, but in this case—because of this and that—it might not be such fun. Not having regard to what was in the back of his mind. He wondered what was going to happen.

Supposing, he thought, Aurora went off with Callao. She might easily do that. Well, in certain circumstances, that might be a good thing. It might be. He finished the whisky and soda; lit a cigarette; walked out of the cocktail bar into the restaurant.

He found the maître d'hôtel at his small desk under a shaded lamp. He said: "I'm looking for a Miss Francis. I think she engaged a table here to-night."

The maître d'hôtel smiled. "Yes, sir . . . she was here with a friend, but she's gone. She left a little while ago."

"I suppose she went off with Mr. Callao?" Kiernan's tone was so casual that the maître d'hôtel, who was usually a very tactful man, nodded.

Kiernan said: "Thank you."

He went out of the restaurant; got his hat from the cloakroom. He turned into Piccadilly; began to walk eastwards.

Now his mind was on Nielecki. Nielecki, thought Kiernan, was an interesting proposition. And he had brains. He thought it was a lucky stroke that Nielecki had come into the bar at the Cockatoo and seen him. He thought that the fifty pounds he'd given to the Pole was cheap.

And there was the matter of Kospovic. Kiernan thought that something ought to be done about Kospovic. He thought about Quayle. He wondered whether it would be in the picture for him to go and see Quayle and tell him about Kospovic. Quayle, he thought, would appreciate the gesture, because Quayle must be interested in Kospovic. He might do that—after he'd seen Kospovic. Or he might do something else. That depended on Kospovic's attitude of mind. Kiernan, who liked moving quickly, thought that the obvious thing for him to do was to go round to the garage, pick up his car and go to South Brent.

He looked at his watch. It was ten o'clock. By the time he'd got the car, returned to his room and done a few things that he wanted to do, it would be one o'clock. He could be at South Brent at eight o'clock in the morning—early enough to talk to Kospovic before he started another day.

That, thought Kiernan, might be a good idea; might be the obvious idea. But there was something else. There was the Aurora-Callao thing. It might be important for Kiernan to deal with that now. And now seemed the ideal time if Aurora had gone off with the rumba band leader. He threw his cigarette stub away; lit another. Then he walked across the road and down the Piccadilly tube.

He went into a telephone box; looked up the name Callao; found the address in Clarges Street. He came out of the station at a quarter-past ten. He thought he'd give them another half-hour. He smiled a little; went into the Brasserie on the corner; ordered a dry Martini. He drank it slowly.

He thought that, in any event, life was invariably amusing—to somebody.

The apartment was in one of the old houses in Clarges Street. It occupied the whole of the first floor and Callao, whose sense of the artistic was well developed, had spared neither pains nor expense to make it a fitting background for his life and the amatory situations which he liked so much.

It was "T" shaped, the entrance being at the bottom of the down-stroke of the letter. You looked up the long room; were intrigued; wondered what you would find in each of the wings at the top. In one, screened by Spanish latticework, was Callao's bedroom, with the low, wide, double bed. In the other wing, was the piano, an expensive grand—a present from a middle-aged woman, a collection of guitars and other string instruments; some good Spanish art and a superb collection of Mexican paintings, murals and eighteenth-century Indian work.

The place had an atmosphere that could be cut with a knife. It had an air that was a trifle decadent but extremely attractive. It possessed that indefinable something which certain places have; something that reaches out and affects every one who goes there. Men—when they came to Callao's apartment—found themselves a little perplexed and inclined to be irritated. They could not explain why. Women, on the other hand, liked the place even if they were a little afraid of it. But then Callao knew that women like being a little frightened, which is one of the reasons why, from time immemorial, men considered to be dangerous have always attracted "nice" women.

In the feminine breast there is an inborn desire to reform the erring male and the more sensitive and charming the feminine breast the more it desires to indulge in the reforming act. Callao knew this. All men who are inclined to be really wicked know it. Which is the reason, of course, why men of good character, of upright and truthful mentalities, of sterling and honest qualities where women are concerned, invariably froth at the mouth when they see some sweet, good and intensely desirable woman smiling up into the slightly sardonic eyes of some pestiferous type who, at that moment, is in the process of being reformed. And liking it.

Aurora stood just inside the closed door. She made a perfect picture against the background of the off-white wall. She watched Callao as he went to the top of the room and turned on some electric light switches. The concealed wall-lighting, two electric fires and some artistically shaded lamps, came to life and infused into the atmosphere a soft, very warm and almost moonlit effect.

Aurora thought it was very pleasing. She experienced a feeling of palpitating expectancy and anticipation. She thought it possible that to-night anything might happen and probably would—if she desired it. If, of course, she did not desire it it would not happen. By which it will be understood that Aurora considered herself to be in control of most of the situations which might happen in her life.

Callao took his hand away from the electric light switch and turned towards her. They stood looking at each other with the length of the long, narrow room between them. Aurora was smiling, her beautiful lips slightly parted. He could see the whiteness of her small teeth beneath them. He came towards her.

He said: "You know, Señorita Aurora, that never has this apartment been so lovely. That ees because you are here. I think I am the luckiest of men."

Aurora thought: If he tries anything now he'll be inartistic and I don't think he's that. She said: "I'm awfully glad to be here."

Callao moved a big arm-chair in front of the electric fire. "Sit down. . . . I will play you some music."

Aurora took off her coat; relaxed on the chair. She leaned her dark head against the back of the chair; closed her eyes and thought. She thought that life was a lot of fun.

Callao went into the right-hand extension of the room and came back with a guitar. He put the guitar down on a chair; went to a table on which stood a coffee service; lighted the flame under a glass percolator held in a Mexican silver stand.

He said: "There are two things I can do. I can play the guitar. I can make coffee."

"I like both things, Vincente. . . ."

He looked at her quickly when she said his name. He thought it sounded very attractive when she spoke it. He picked up the guitar. He began to play very softly. He played two or three old Spanish love songs and then sang an attractive rumba song. Whilst he was singing he seemed to take on a new and even more provocative personality, she thought. The idea occurred to her that it might easily be that Vincente's real life was in his music; that the rest of it was something that didn't matter a great deal. That, she thought, might be convenient. Men sometimes became too serious when things mattered too much to them.

The coffee in the percolator began to bubble. Callao stopped singing; poured it out. He brought her a cup. She tasted it. It was excellent coffee and she told him so. Now she was certain that life was amusing. She liked the appearance and personality of Callao. She liked the sharp taste of the coffee. She liked the rather unusual atmosphere of the apartment with its faint suggestion of some exotic perfume. Life, she thought, was definitely beginning to acquire a South American accent. She liked that too. . . .

Neither of them spoke. When she had finished her coffee Vincente took the cup; put it on the table. When he turned back towards her she was standing up in front of the fire.

She said: "I'm enjoying this immensely. I'm having a lovely time."

"You should always have lovely times," said Callao. "Because you yourself are so lovely."

Aurora took a step forward which brought her quite comfortably into Callao's arms, which closed about her. She put up her face. As his mouth descended on hers, she murmured: "Vincente . . . I shouldn't be doing this. . . ."

The kiss lasted a long time and, as kisses go, it was extremely satisfying. As her mouth left Vincente's, Aurora thought that now was the time for the talk which inevitably followed such kisses. She thought that Callao would now produce an example of his superb technique—because it would be superb. The technique of any man who could kiss as he kissed must be good.

He stood looking at her, his large brown eyes no longer soft. They were hard like diamonds. He said: "I theenk you are the mos' divine person."

She smiled at him. "I'm glad you think that. Now show me the rest of the apartment. Is it as interesting as this room is?"

"There ees not much," said Vincente. "You see at the top there are the two large alcoves to the left and right. The one on the right ees my music room."

He took her hand. They walked up the room together. At the top he switched on some more lights. The alcove to the right was another large, long room. On top of the grand piano were two or three guitars; piles of music. She looked casually round; then turned towards the other alcove. She moved away from him; pushed open the door in the Spanish iron lattice-work screen. She stood in the opening, looking into Callao's bedroom.

This room, even in the half-light that flooded through the lattice, was almost barbaric in the splendour of its colours Aurora caught her breath. The decor did something to her.

Callao said: "It ees interesting. Ees eet not?"

"Yes," said Aurora; "but, I should think, a little difficult to sleep in. Aren't there too many colours?"

He shook his head. "No . . . there cannot be too many colours. . . . And see, when the lights are up . . ." He switched on some lights, and she noted with approval that the soft tones of the light shades did, indeed, most artistically, blend the colours of the walls, hangings and bedspread.

She stepped into the room; began to examine the pictures. She felt him close beside her. At the last one she turned. He was waiting for her with open arms. Aurora sighed and surrendered herself to another of Callao's South American kisses.

Both of them moved and turned quickly at the voice.

In the lattice doorway stood Kiernan. He was smiling. Aurora could see the strength of his thin jaw, and his white teeth. He was swinging a bunch of keys in his right hand, holding them by the long peculiar shaped "spider" key with which he had opened the door.

"What a bastard you are, Callao!" He said it almost happily.

Aurora picked it up from there. She thought: Isn't this odd? This is what Antoinette suggested vaguely might happen and it has happened. This is going to be fearfully amusing. She moved away from Callao and sat down on the bed.

Callao looked unhappy. He frowned. His large eyes became soft again. He looked rather like a small boy who has been unjustly accused of stealing jam.

He said: "Señor, I don' understand. I don' understand what you are doing here. I don' understand how you came into my apartment."

Kiernan put the keys into his trouser pocket. He put his hand into his jacket pocket; produced a cigarette and lighter. He lit the cigarette. He was still smiling.

He said: "You don't understand, you Spanish son-of-a-bitch. . . ." There was a certain ebullience in the tone of his voice. "In a minute you'll tell me you don't know who I am. My name's Kiernan. Remember me? If you don't understand how I got into your apartment I'll tell you. I got in with a key. It's one of those things. It opens most locks."

Callao said: "I would like to know why you call me the son of a bitch. . . ."

"For the obvious reason . . . I think your mother must have been one." Kiernan said a word in Spanish—a word of two syllables which suggests most of the things that can be suggested about someone's mother.

Aurora clasped her hands. She thought: I wonder what he's playing at. He's trying to get Callao's temper roused. I wonder what the idea is. She still thought it was a lot of fun.

Callao said: "No man comes into my house and speaks like that to me."

"No?" said Kiernan cheerfully. He said two more words in Spanish—one of one syllable and one of two. They were even more all-embracing than the first.

"Aren't you being a little tough about something?" asked Aurora.

Kiernan turned towards her. It was the first time that he had looked at her. He gave her a cheerful grin. He said: "No, this is normal. Tell me something, Aurora. Do you know about this one? I should think he's the most complete and utter pimp that ever walked. . . . The Rumba King—Señor Vincente Callao."

"That's as maybe," said Aurora; "but he's very attractive, and it was rude of you to interrupt like that, Tony."

"I don't think so." Kiernan turned to Callao. "You've got a hell of a reputation with women. I've no doubt you are very successful with them, but I don't like you to make passes at my friends."

Callao said: "That ees a lie. I did not make a pass at your friend."

"Possibly not," said Kiernan. "It may be that she made one at you. You still don't have to play. Do you understand, bastard?"

Callao flushed; then he went white. Beneath the apparently placid exterior was a nasty temper.

He said: "You know . . . you go too far, Señor."

"You don't say!" said Kiernan. "Even you are going to do something about it, aren't you? You're going to get tough. Maybe you're going to throw me out. Why don't you do that?"

Callao said: "Perhaps I will."

Kiernan took two quick steps forward. He smacked Callao across the, face—once with his left hand, once with his right. Aurora thought the slaps made a queer staccato noise. Now she was definitely thrilled.

Callao brought up his knee in a vicious jerk. Kiernan, who knew that technique, side-stepped and slapped him across the face again. A thin stream of blood began to run down Callao's upper lip. Kiernan hit him in the face. The noise was just like a hammer on wood. Callao went down and came up again like a tiger. His teeth were set; his mouth working; his eyes blazing. He made peculiar movement towards Kiernan—an undecided movement; stopped suddenly; seized a heavy Mexican sconce from a table; threw it.

Kiernan ducked, but the end of the heavy sconce hit him in the neck. He fell against the wall, his hands over his face. Callao sprang towards him. When he was almost there, Aurora thrilled again as Kiernan took his hands away from his face. She saw he was laughing. His left foot shot out, caught Callao on the right shin-bone. She sighed tremulously. She knew what was coming.

Kiernan feinted quickly with the left hand; then he brought his right hand with a judo cut across Callao's face. Callao yelped— an exclamation of pain that was almost knocked out of him. He stepped back, his arm across his face.

Kiernan went to work. He went to work on Callao systematically. He stepped in and punched. Sometimes they were long, follow-through punches; sometimes staccato with drawn hand-clips. Sometimes he hit him with the flat of his hand; sometimes with the side. It took five minutes. At the end of that time Callao lay on the floor. He was sobbing. Aurora thought that the noise he made sounded like the child who had been unjustly accused—after he had had the cane.

In a corner on a table was a bottle of Spanish brandy and some glasses. Kiernan carefully stepped across the recumbent figure of Callao; poured himself out a drink. He said over his shoulder to Aurora: "Would you like a piece of this?"

She shook her head. She smiled at him. "You know, you're quite impossible, Tony."

He asked: "Why?" He drank the brandy. He came back, sat down beside her on the bed. "You're an awfully attractive but stupid bitch, aren't you? This man, believe it or not, can be dangerous with women."

She laughed. "I should think he'd be dangerous to you after this, Tony."

He shrugged his shoulders. "Well, it looks as if the fun's over. What are you going to do—stay behind and nurse your boy friend, or shall we go for a walk?"

Aurora looked at Callao. She thought he seemed particularly undignified. She thought that no matter how attractive a man may be he never gains much by getting a good hiding, even if he doesn't deserve one.

She said: "You know, this is all rather unfair. I wanted to come here."

Kiernan grinned. "That's all right. I wanted you to come too, but I didn't want you to stay—not too long, anyway. I allowed half an hour for the preliminaries. How many songs had he sung?"

She laughed. "I suppose the idea is that you want me yourself?"

"Maybe," said Kiernan. "Let's go for a walk and consider that, shall we?"

She got up. They went into the main room. Neither of them even looked at Callao. She picked up her coat; put it on. Outside, on the landing, Kiernan locked the door carefully.

As he put the keys back in his pocket, she said: "Talking about sons-of-bitches, Tony . . . I think you're one." She was smiling.

He grinned. "You're telling me!"

They walked down the stairs.

CHAPTER TWO
BEGUINE

SUNDAY

NIELECKI, who lived in the second-floor back room at King's Cross, heard the nearby church clock strike seven. He'd heard it strike most of the hours of the night. He wondered why it was that he never went to sleep like other people; why it was that so many hours were spent in a pointless reiteration of what might or might not have happened if something or other had been different.

The sharp knock at the door did not surprise him. Nothing surprised Nielecki. He said: "Come in . . ." put out his hand and switched on the unshaded light globe that hung over his bed.

His landlady—an unprepossessing female with tatty grey hair, a scant bosom and a vacant look, stood in the doorway. Behind her, disinterested and large, loomed the figure of the Special Branch man.

She said over her shoulder: "This is 'im." She threw an unpleasant look at Nielecki and went away.

The Special Branch man came into the room. He asked: "Are you Nielecki—Anton Valessi Nielecki?"

Nielecki nodded. His quick brain was already working. Either Kiernan had done something or said something about him or, alternatively, the police were interested for some other reason.

He yawned. Being awakened by the police early in the morning was nothing new to Nielecki. It had happened to him many times before—in Poland, in Germany; in many other places. He was used to it and here, in England, it was less unpleasant than anywhere else. Probably, thought Nielecki, that was what was the matter with the English. They did not know how to be really unpleasant—even in these days when half the world was plotting to upset the other half, when every subversive means was being used to carry on an underhand war with the potent weapons of lies, propaganda, secret kidnapping, rigged elections, intimidation and every sort of mayhem; even in these days the English, as far as was possible, tried to behave like gentlemen—as if behaving like gentlemen had got them anywhere against the Germans or the Japanese.

The English police could be stern, of course, and mildly unpleasant, but you knew where you were. They did not start work with a beating-up, or a week's slow starvation, or a fortnight on salt herrings with one half-cup of water a day. They did not indulge in these softening-up processes—all of which Nielecki had experienced.

The Special Branch man produced his Warrant Card. He showed it to the Pole. He said: "I'm an officer of the Special Branch. Get up and dress. Somebody wants to ask you some questions. Make it snappy."

He sat down in the dilapidated arm-chair and produced a cigarette. He smoked morosely whilst Nielecki dressed.

When he was nearly ready Nielecki said: "Please . . . what am I supposed to have done, I have committed no offence. I . . ."

The Special Branch man said casually: "Nobody said you had. I'm not charging you with anything, am I? Somebody wants to talk to you. Nice and quietly and not like they do it in your country where they'd probably use a rubber truncheon on you for an hour or two first. Get a ripple on."

They went down the stairs and got into the car that was waiting. Nielecki relaxed in the back seat. He rested his head against the side of the car and thought. He thought that when all was said and done the English authorities were extremely efficient. He did not believe now, not for a moment, that his being picked up was due to any action of Kiernan's part. Why should Kiernan want to do that? If he had wanted to do that he would never have parted with the fifty pounds. No . . . he had been picked up because of his association with Kospovic. Maybe, he thought, they had kept Kospovic under observation. Maybe they had known of his meeting with Nielecki at the Rambling House in Devonshire.

He gave up thinking. He considered the process was, at the moment, without value. He would soon know what it was all about.

The car stopped outside the house in South Kensington. The Special Branch man looked over his shoulder at Nielecki. He said, not unpleasantly: "You're going to see a Mr. Frewin. He's a very nice gentleman—if he gets what he wants. He can be good and tough if he doesn't. Even if he doesn't use a rubber truncheon. See?"

"I see. . . ." Nielecki got out of the car; followed the man up the steps to the front door. He thought that life could be extremely difficult sometimes.

Frewin was sitting in an arm-chair in front of an electric fire. There was a table with a tea service on it between him and the arm-chair which faced him directly from the other side of the fireplace. He was wearing pale-blue silk pyjamas under a black silk dressing-gown. His initials were embroidered on the pocket of the gown. He was smoking a cigarette and he looked tired and bored. Nielecki thought he was good-looking. He thought that he did not look like a Secret Service operative. Then he thought that English people who did that sort of work never looked like that.

The Special Branch man said: "Good morning, sir. This is Anton Nielecki."

Frewin said: "All right, Frayne. Got and get some sleep."

Frayne went away.

Frewin got up. He began to walk restlessly about the room. Then he said: "Sit down; take off your overcoat; give yourself some tea and eat some bread and butter and jam. There are cigarettes on the tray. Make yourself comfortable and relax."

"Thank you. . . ." Nielecki took off his overcoat and sat down in the arm-chair. He poured out some tea and sipped it. It was good, strong tea and he liked it. He lighted a cigarette.

Frewin sat down in the chair opposite and watched Nielecki. Then: "It's going to be very good for you to tell me the complete truth. And it's not going to do you any good to give me half-truths or to try to evade anything. If I'm satisfied with you you'll be all right. If I'm not you'll find yourself on your way back to Poland in no time. You wouldn't like that . . . would you?"

Nielecki, his cigarette in one hand, took a piece of bread and butter and jam, and began to eat it. "No," he said, with his mouth full. "I should not at all like that. Especially at this time. It would not be so good for me in my own country."

Frewin nodded. "During the war you worked for both sides. I understand that. You had to. If you hadn't done what the Gestapo asked you to do in Poland they'd have hanged you on a piece of telephone wire—if not worse. Afterwards, you worked for us. You hadn't much choice about that either. You either told us what you knew or we made things hot for you. Naturally, we have a complete dossier on you. I've read it. I think I understand you very well."

Nielecki said nothing. He continued to eat bread and jam.

Frewin went on: "In Germany, soon after we went in, you met one of our agents—a man named Kiernan. You gave him some very valuable information. You were well paid for it and, as a result of your services, you are here in this country now. I want to know about yesterday."

Nielecki said: "Yes—?"

"Yesterday," continued Frewin, "you had a conversation with Kiernan in the cocktail bar at the Cockatoo. You probably met him by accident. I'm not interested about that. I want to know what you talked about."

Nielecki slowly masticated the food in his mouth. When he had finished doing that he picked up a fresh cigarette and lighted it. He thought quickly.

He thought that this looked like serious business. The idea occurred to him that maybe they were more interested in Kiernan than in him. If Kiernan had intended to tell any one about their conversation he would not have given him the fifty pounds. Someone had seen them talking; someone who was interested and who was in touch with Frewin or some other member of a Secret Service detail. So they had picked him—Nielecki—up for questioning on the chance of finding something out.

He drew on the cigarette and looked at Frewin, who was watching him patiently.

They would know, thought Nielecki, about Kospovic. Kospovic was a foreigner and must report to the police. They would know that Kospovic was in Devonshire. They might know that he, Nielecki, had seen and talked to Kospovic.

It might even be that Kospovic had talked; that Kospovic had tricked him, Nielecki, by telling him that he did not intend to talk at the moment, so that he might make a deal without any interference from Nielecki.

He made up his mind. The situation, he thought, was not easy. It might become dangerous. It might become very dangerous for him. To be deported meant Poland and . . .

He said: "There is no reason why I should not tell you anything I know. I have always, as you know, told of everything I knew to the British. But always. Naturally, I was glad to see Captain Kiernan. I have always liked him. We talked about the old days and then I said that I had seen a man called Kospovic in Devonshire, at an hotel called the Rambling House, at a place called South Brent. I told him that. I told him that Kospovic had information about two lists of war criminals, which had disappeared or been stolen. He asked me why Kospovic had not given the information to one of the Service Intelligence departments. I told him that Kospovic had said that he was not inclined to do so at this time; that he did not wish to embroil himself in any trouble at the moment; that he intended to wait until he was in better health."

Frewin nodded. "And then?" he asked.

"Captain Kiernan gave me some money. I think he was a little sorry for me."

Frewin laughed cynically. "That must be a new sensation for Captain Kiernan—being sorry for someone. I seem to remember that you made an official complaint against him in 1945 for having burned your hand with a piece of hot telephone wire—when you wouldn't talk."

Nielecki shrugged his shoulders. "That was a long time ago. Things were perhaps different in those days. People were harder. They had to be. Perhaps now he is sorry."

"Perhaps," said Frewin. "In any event, you got some money out of it. How much?"

Nielecki told him.

Frewin got up. He walked over to the window and stood, his back to Nielecki, looking out into the quiet square.

"Kospovic made a telephone call last Friday afternoon," he said. "He telephoned to my chief and talked to him about the two stolen lists."

Nielecki sighed. He felt relieved. He was glad he had played it the right way.

Frewin came back to the fireplace. He stood opposite Nielecki, on the other side of the tea table, looking down at him.

"All right," he said. "You run off and bowl your hoop. Go on with the job you're doing and behave yourself. Mind your own business and you'll be all right. In any event, you've made fifty pounds out of this."

Nielecki got up. He picked up his overcoat. He smiled dimly at Frewin.

He asked: "I wondered why he gave me the fifty pounds. I could see no reason for it. I thought that he must be a little sorry for me."

Frewin grinned. "Don't tell damned lies, Nielecki. You know why he gave you the fifty pounds. He gave you the money because you told him the name of a person who knew something about those missing lists—Kospovic. If what you have told me is true I expect Captain Kiernan either to come to me with the information or, if he prefers to check it first, to go to South Brent and talk to Kospovic himself. I expect he will do that. If he does not go to see Kospovic, or if he does not tell us what you have told him, I shall conclude that you have been lying. That won't be so good for you."

Nielecki picked up his hat.

"I have not lied to you. I have told you the complete truth."

"No," said Frewin. "Not the complete truth. When you saw Kiernan you knew he would be interested. You knew he would give you some money."

He helped himself to a cigarette.

"I suppose," he continued, looking at Nielecki through the flame of his lighter, "you wouldn't know who stole those two lists?"

"No," said Nielecki, looking at the floor. "No . . . I don't know. How should I know?"

Frewin asked: "You don't like Kospovic, do you?"

Nielecki shrugged again. "I have no opinion one way or the other. But if he has told who stole the lists . . ."

"He hasn't," said Frewin coldly. "I said he telephoned and talked about it. He telephoned and said he knew who had stolen the lists; that maybe someone would give him some money for the information."

"I see. . . ." Nielecki continued to look at the floor.

"So you will realise," said Frewin, "that it will be to your advantage to continue to mind your own business. My advice to you is to confine yourself to your work and to forget everything else."

"Yes," said Nielecki. He was beginning to feel frightened. The net, he thought, is already beginning to tighten. "I shall do exactly as you say."

Frewin smiled suddenly. "Wise man," he said. He held the door open for Nielecki to go out.

He closed the door; went back to the window. He stood, his hands in his dressing-gown pockets, watching the figure of Nielecki as he crossed the square. Nielecki was walking slowly; almost ponderously, Frewin thought. He grinned. The Pole, he imagined, would have plenty to think about.

Frewin had no delusions about Nielecki, He understood him. He understood the implications of his existence. Nielecki, like many of his compatriots, had been pushed around to such an extent that he found himself time and time again forced by circumstances to play things his own way to his own advantage.

Frewin believed that Nielecki had told the truth, but he knew that he had not told the whole truth, Nielecki had said nothing about his reasons for going to the Rambling House at South Brent. He had not explained the extraordinary coincidence of his meeting with Kospovic there. He had not said a word about how he had met Kospovic in the first place, or why Kospovic should confide in him—Nielecki.

These points, thought Frewin, did not matter a great deal at the moment.

He went into the next room, which was furnished as an office, with several heavy, steel filing cabinets about the place. He went to the telephone; dialled a number.

He asked: "Goddard . . . is your man reporting on Kiernan?"

Goddard said: "Yes, he's coming through about every half-hour. Kiernan apparently is still sleeping off last night."

"If my guess is right," said Frewin, "he's going to South Brent in Devonshire. He used to have a very fast car. He's probably still got it. I want to know if he goes."

Goddard said: "I'll try and let you know."

Frewin hung up.

He went back into the other room; sat down in the arm-chair; looked into the electric fire. After a minute he poured himself out a cup of tea. It tasted strong and bitter. It had stood too long. He drank the tea; made a wry face; sat looking into the fire. He was wondering just what Quayle was playing at. From the first, the technique in this business had not been the technique that Quayle usually employed. For some unknown reason the picture of Antoinette Brown came into Frewin's mind. He grinned. She, he thought, was an intuitive piece. Maybe she'd have an idea of what Quayle was getting at. Sometimes a woman guessed. Sometimes she put her finger on some small point that had escaped the logical outlook of a man.

Frewin was not quite certain as to what Quayle intended him to do. Quayle himself could not have known what Frewin was to do, because on Friday nothing had happened. No circumstances had arisen which would led to any action. Quayle must have known that. Frewin shrugged his shoulders. He thought that time would show.

At eleven o'clock the hall porter of the Berkshire apartments in Lowndes Square rang through to No. 21 to tell Aurora Francis that Miss Antoinette Brown was downstairs and would like to see her. Aurora, who was in her bedroom, told him to bring Miss Brown up.

She powdered her nose; considered that the blue circles under her eyes, due to tiredness, did not detract greatly from her beauty.

She went into the tiled kitchen; watched the coffee percolator bubbling on the electric stove. The coffee tray stood ready on the table. She put the percolator on to the tray; carried it into the drawing-room.

Antoinette Brown arrived at that moment. She closed the door quietly behind her; stood looking at Aurora.

She said: "You look quite wonderful, Aurora. That green velvet house-coat suits you immensely. I wish I were as beautiful as you."

Aurora laughed softly. Her eyes swept over the slim figure standing just inside the doorway. She thought to herself that

Antoinette Brown was rather a fool; that she was really quite attractive but didn't know it. She thought that the blue wool frock which she wore under her fur coat made, with the beautifully matched blue felt hat, quite a charming picture. She concluded by thinking that if Antoinette didn't know that she was attractive she wasn't missing anything much.

Aurora said: "Have some coffee. Do I look very tired?"

"No," said Antoinette. She put down her handbag and gloves; sat down in an arm-chair; regarded her friend smilingly. "I believe you had an interesting evening." She laughed. "You look rather like the cat that swallowed the canary, Aurora. I believe you've been swallowing canaries again."

Aurora poured the coffee. She brought a cup over to Antoinette; gave it to her; stood, her back to the fireplace, a little smile playing about her mouth.

She said: "My dear . . . I had the hell of a night—just nobody's business—and very enjoyable." She looked sideways at Antoinette. "You know," she went on, "I think you're a very good prophet. You wondered what would happen if Kiernan appeared; if he found out about Vincente." She laughed. "Apparently he did find out about Vincente. He came to the Cockatoo last night. He found I'd gone off with Callao. He came round to Callao's flat."

"No!" said Antoinette. "Did he tell you that he saw me?"

Aurora shook her head. She raised her eyebrows.

Antoinette said quickly: "When I was going out I thought I'd have a cocktail. I felt a little depressed—I don't know why—so I went into the bar. He was there. We talked for a little while, and I told him I'd been dining with you. Of course I didn't say anything about Callao. I went away and left him there."

Aurora said: "Apparently after you left he discovered I'd gone off with Callao, so he looked up the address in the telephone book, and came round as I told you. I've never been so thrilled in my life. Kiernan called Callao everything he could lay his tongue to. Then he beat hell out of him."

"I wonder why he did that," said Antoinette.

Aurora shrugged her shoulders. "I don't know. It was all the more odd because Kiernan didn't seem to be awfully angry with

Callao. But he obviously knew him; knew a lot about him. The thought occurred to me that he behaved in that way because there'd been trouble between them some time before—trouble over a woman possibly."

Antoinette said: "I see. I shouldn't have thought Callao and Kiernan were the sort of people who'd find themselves rivals about a woman. They are two entirely different types." She looked at Aurora. "I can't see any woman preferring Callao to Kiernan."

"Neither can I." Aurora shrugged her shoulders again. "Maybe Kiernan was being a little theatrical. Maybe he thought that his treating Vincente roughly would have its effect on me. Anthony certainly gave him an awful beating."

Antoinette asked: "Did Callao like that?"

Aurora shook her head. "Not one little bit. He didn't like it at all. It was really rather thrilling. He threw a heavy silver sconce at Anthony. The thing hit him and Anthony pretended that he was finished. He leaned up against the wall holding his head, and when Vincente went over to finish him off Kiernan just grinned at him and gave him hell. We left him lying on the floor. He was crying."

Aurora turned; opened the silver cigarette box on the mantelpiece behind her; took a cigarette; lighted it. "Poor Vincente . . . he looked so undignified. Actually I was, and still am, very sorry for him. He's a most attractive man."

Antoinette sighed. "You have a most exciting time, don't you, Aurora . . . fearfully exciting?" There was admiration in her voice. "I suppose Kiernan did that because—well, he must be awfully keen on you."

Aurora nodded. "He is." She laughed. "He's definitely a type, my sweet. I said he was a man with a capital 'M,' and I assure you he is. Having disposed of Callao, I suppose he thought I was going to drop into his mouth like a ripe plum."

"And of course you didn't?" said Antoinette.

"Oh, no . . . we went off and he asked me if I'd like to go to his rooms and have a drink. He said he thought it was indicated. I asked him if he thought he was going to make love to me. He said, yes. I said then I wouldn't go. We had quite a little argument in Clarges Street, but eventually I made him realise that I meant what I said, so he promised."

Antoinette nodded. "And he kept his promise?"

"Well . . . nearly . . ." said Aurora. "But I stayed there talking to him for a long time. He has rooms in Charles Street—a nice place. I think he's the most fearfully interesting and romantic man I've ever met in my life. There's something about Kiernan . . ." She went to the tray and poured herself a cup of coffee. "Something on which I can't even put my finger, but which I find most interesting."

Antoinette said: "You know what I think, Aurora. I think you're in love with this man. I think that at last you've really fallen for somebody."

Aurora drew on her cigarette. She said slowly: "Ye-es . . . I think you're right. But I don't intend to let him know for quite a while."

"Why not?" asked Antoinette.

Aurora drank a little of the coffee from the cup; put it back on the tray; began to walk about the room. Antoinette thought that her movements were graceful and alluring.

After a while Aurora said: "Kiernan's had things pretty much his own way with women. He's the type of man who has that sort of personality. He gets what he wants. I think possibly he gets it too easily so he doesn't appreciate it. That's why I propose to see that he doesn't get me easily."

"Do you think he wants to marry you, Aurora?"

The other nodded. "Yes. He will . . . eventually."

There was a silence. Antoinette finished her coffee; put down the cup. She asked if she could have a cigarette; took one and lighted it.

She said: "You've got an awfully good technique with men, haven't you, Aurora? I wish I knew as much about them as you—about the way they talk and feel—their reactions; I'm so stupid about them. But even so, I can't help thinking that you may be playing with fire with Kiernan."

"I like playing with fire," said Aurora smilingly. "And I know what I'm doing. Kiernan's unsettled. You see, he's lived an awfully tough life for the last five years. Now he's finished with the Intelligence Services he's inclined to be bored—to seek excitement. He's going through a phase. But he'll get over that. Eventually he's going to settle down to do something. Perhaps it's time I settled down too. Perhaps when I know him better I shan't feel so keen on him. Perhaps I shall be even keener. He attracts me and I admire him, but that isn't enough, is it? You see, there are other things. I want to travel. I want to go to places like South America. I love colour. I'd want Tony to have a job—to do something which would take him to places like that. Then I think I could be happy. I think he's like that too. A boring existence wouldn't suit either of us."

Antoinette said: "No, I don't suppose it would." She got up. "I've got to run along, Aurora. I have a luncheon appointment and I've several things to do first. I'm staying at the Mordaunt Hotel. You'll find the number in the book. Do give me a ring. I want to see a lot of you." She smiled suddenly. "I'm fearfully interested in you, Aurora. I have a great admiration for you. I wish I were more like you. You have such a—well, almost sensational—existence, and I go placidly along with nothing ever happening."

Aurora looked at her. "Don't worry. Something's going to happen one of these fine days." She looked at her wrist-watch. "I must put some clothes on. I promised to go round after lunch and see Kiernan. I think he wasn't very pleased about last night really. He thought I was going to be more affected than I was by the little scene in Vincente's place. I think he was disappointed. I think I ought to go round and console him a little."

"Yes," said Antoinette. "And what about the unfortunate Mr. Callao? I suppose he's had his marching orders now?"

Aurora raised her eyebrows. "I'm not quite certain. Poor Vincente . . . he sings so beautifully. He has such an attractive voice. I feel very sorry for him. Sorry enough perhaps to—"

"To do what?" asked Antoinette.

"I'm not quite certain. Let's leave it at the fact that I feel a little sorry for him. But I shall certainly have to see him again. I shall have to hear what he thinks about Kiernan. I expect he'll evolve some quite wonderful story to explain why things happened as they did."

Antoinette said: "Yes. I feel a little sorry for him too. Captain Kiernan's quite an overwhelming person, isn't he?" She walked to the door. "Good-bye, Aurora."

Aurora smiled. "I'll telephone you. We'll meet quite soon. Perhaps I'll have some more to tell you."

"Please do," said Antoinette. "I adore listening to you." She went out.

At half-past twelve Miss Brown arrived at the house in South Kensington. When she was shown into the office Frewin was still in his pyjamas and dressing-gown. She thought he looked tired.

He said: "Good morning. Sit down. Would you like a cigarette?" She shook her head.

Frewin noticed she was not wearing her glasses. It seemed that she could do without them when she wanted to. He wondered vaguely if she only wore them for effect and if so, why. She arranged her skirts primly as she sat down.

She said: "I've just left Aurora Francis, Mr. Frewin. I had a talk with her."

He began to walk about the room. "Yes?" he said. "What goes on? After you telephoned last night I put a tail on Kiernan. He went to Piccadilly; went into a call box; checked a number. Then he went into the Brasserie for half an hour and afterwards went to an apartment house in Clarges Street—Callao's place. He was there for some time, and came out with Aurora Francis."

"She told me all about it," said Antoinette. "He went there because he'd heard she'd gone to Callao's apartment. Kiernan beat Callao up—a theatrical gesture, I think, intended for Aurora's benefit. It seems to have succeeded. She went back to his rooms in Charles Street. She stayed there talking for a long time. She seems very much interested in Captain Kiernan."

Frewin returned to the desk; sat down behind it. He said: "The man Nielecki whom you phoned about was one of the people we used after the war. He was one of Kiernan's contacts. Kiernan had quite a lot of information from him. Nielecki told Kiernan that a man called Kospovic, who is living at South Brent in Devonshire at the present moment, knew who had stolen the two lists that Mr. Quayle wants recovered. Mr. Quayle told you about those?"

She nodded.

"Kiernan gave Nielecki fifty pounds." Frewin smiled. "There might be several answers to that." He got up; began to walk about the room restlessly.

She wondered why he was telling her all this. She'd never known Frewin to talk quite so much. She thought he was worried. She was amazed to find herself a little concerned for him.

Frewin went on: "I'm telling you this because I'm in rather a spot."

She smiled suddenly. He thought that when she smiled like that she looked very attractive.

She said: "That's an admission from you, isn't it, Mr. Frewin? I never thought I'd hear you say that you were in a spot; that you were in some position that you couldn't handle."

"Nobody can handle some things," said Frewin. "I don't even know where I am. I'm not quite certain as to what Quayle wants me to do. He hands me a few odd facts on a plate, goes to Germany and expects me to take some action about it. At the present moment no action is indicated. All I can do is to wait and see what happens."

There was a silence; then she said suddenly: "Mr. Frewin, could I have a cigarette?"

He gave her the cigarette; lighted it. He went over to the window and stood watching her.

She said: "You know . . . Mr. Quayle never really tells anybody anything. Most of the time he's using everybody for some reason which he himself knows. I think something—"

Frewin interrupted: "What?"

"I think Mr. Quayle knows a great deal more about this business than either you or I know. I think we're just two stooges that he's using at the moment to create a situation. When I talked with him on Friday afternoon he asked me if there was any woman I knew in whom Kiernan had been interested in Germany. There was, and I told him so. I told him that Kiernan had been interested in Aurora Francis." She looked at Frewin and smiled. "I believe Mr. Quayle knew that. But he wanted to get the information from me. I believe he knew that Aurora Francis was going to arrive in London the next day, but he wasn't inclined to let me know he knew. He suggested to me that she might be used as a stooge in this business, and when I told him that I didn't think she'd be good for any confidential sort of work because she's too easily attracted by men he took not the slightest notice. I believe he knew that if Kiernan came to London he'd try and find Aurora."

"I see . . ." Frewin thought for a moment. "Quayle might have known that Kiernan was coming to London."

She nodded.

Frewin said: "Quayle told me that we might use Kiernan on this job; that we might use Kiernan to find out who'd stolen those lists; that we might re-employ him; put him back on the list of agents. And then"—Frewin smiled cynically—"look at the coincidences. They're almost too coincidental. You meet Aurora Francis. Aurora Francis asks you to dine with her at the Cockatoo. Kiernan turns up at the Cockatoo and would doubtless have gone into the restaurant and seen Aurora except for the fact that Nielecki had also arrived in the cocktail bar and told him about Kospovic—the man who knows who stole those lists. What a coincidence that Nielecki should go into the cocktail bar at the Cockatoo at that moment. It's almost too good to be true, isn't it?"

She smiled. "Or else Mr. Quayle's almost too good to be true. You know quite well, Mr. Frewin, that Mr. Quayle has always had a list of every foreigner registered with the police in this country, whether they ranked as friendly or enemy aliens during the war. At some time or other he must have known that there was a contact in Germany between Nielecki and Kiernan."

Frewin said: "I'm beginning to see. I wonder whether you're thinking what I'm thinking."

"I believe so," said Antoinette. "And if what we think is right, Mr. Frewin, there isn't any need for you to worry, because the situation that's been created by Nielecki, Kiernan, Aurora and myself is probably one that Mr. Quayle desired to create. There's only one thing that doesn't quite fit it."

"Precisely. One person doesn't quite lit in to the picture—the gentleman who was beaten up—Mr. Vincente Callao."

She nodded. "He comes into it somewhere, doesn't he? He came into it almost naturally."

Frewin sat down at the desk again. He lighted another cigarette. He looked at her through the smoke. He said: "Kiernan's no fool. I can't imagine Kiernan for no reason at all going to a man's apartment and beating him up—unless he knew he was safe in doing that."

"You mean unless he knew quite a lot about Callao—unless he knew that Callao had got to stand for what happened to him?"

"Exactly," said Frewin. "That is what I mean."

The telephone on his desk jangled. Frewin took off the receiver. He said: "Yes . . . I see . . . at twelve o'clock. Thank you, Goddard. . . . No, don't worry to send anybody down. Just leave it like that. He'll have to come back some time, and we'll know when he gets back. If I want you again I'll ring you." He hung up. He smiled at Antoinette.

"Goddard, who's got a tail on Kiernan, tells me that he picked up his car at his garage at twelve o'clock. He got a route for South Brent from the garage man. He's going to see Kospovic."

She got up. "It's quite exciting, isn't it, Mr. Frewin?"

Frewin said: "Yes. The situation is beginning to create itself, or rather"—he smiled sideways at her—"the situation that Quayle wanted is slowly developing."

He leaned back in the big office chair and looked at her. She could see that for the first time since she'd been in the room he was relaxed.

He said: "When Kospovic phoned Quayle on Friday afternoon, he told him that he knew who'd stolen those two lists, but he didn't say who. Quite obviously, he wanted to do a deal. Kospovic was either scared by the information he had and wanted protection, or he wanted money. It seems rather strange that Kospovic who, for some reason best known to himself, had not come to Quayle with this information before—and Kospovic knows and fears Quayle—it seems strange that Kospovic should have discussed this business with Nielecki."

She asked: "You know that?"

"I had Nielecki picked up this morning early. I've talked to him. What he said was, I believe, mainly the truth. He said he'd been down to this place in Devonshire and met Kospovic. It's rather peculiar, I think, that Nielecki should have had this meeting with Kospovic and then run into Kiernan and told him about it."

She said: "One would have thought, Mr. Frewin, that as Kiernan had been such a distinguished operative for Mr. Quayle and had done such good work, he would have passed that information on immediately."

Frewin nodded. "One would have thought so. But then he had other things on his mind, hadn't he, Antoinette?" He lingered a long time over the name. "He had Callao on his mind and Aurora Francis. He had to do something about those two first."

She said: "He hasn't got Aurora Francis so much on his mind to-day. She was going round to see him this afternoon. When she gets there he won't be there." She smiled. She showed her fine white teeth. "That might be very good for Aurora. I think she gets things much too much her own way."

Frewin said: "Kiernan's gone down to see Kospovic probably to check on the information that Nielecki gave him. When he comes back the thing for him to do would be to come to see me or Quayle; to find us and tell us what he knows."

There was a long silence.

She asked: "You think he'll do that, Mr. Frewin?"

"I don't know. But if he doesn't—"

They looked at each other.

The telephone bell rang.

Frewin picked up the receiver. He said: "Yes. . . . Yes . . . in three hours . . ."

He hung up the receiver. He looked at her. He said: "Can you guess who?"

She smiled at him; then she nodded her head.

Frewin thought that there was some indefinable quality about Antoinette Brown—a quality he could not quite place—something which eluded him. He looked at her for a long time.

She sat motionless and relaxed. Her face was placid and, from the angle from which he looked at her, Frewin could see the clean-cut line of her jaw and the sensitive outline of her nostrils. He thought that one of these fine days he must find out all about her. He thought that she was definitely interesting in a quiet, unobtrusive sort of way.

She said softly: "That was Mr. Quayle, wasn't it?"

He smiled at her. "Yes. I think your guess was right."

The house, set in the middle of a miniature wooded park, stood in the cleft of the hills. The afternoon sun reflected on the windows, threw into prominence the white walls and red roof. Away in the distance the quiet Somersetshire road, winding across the valley and over the hills, disappeared like a carelessly thrown white ribbon. Quayle paid off the hired car at the door; walked up the wide steps; opened the entrance door; crossed the hall. He put his suit-case and document case on a chair and whistled softly.

A door on the opposite side of the hall opened. Quayle smiled at the woman who stood in the doorway. She was of middle height, auburn haired, white skinned. She was smiling as she came towards him.

"Mr. Quayle, I believe," she said. "You're quite a stranger in these parts, aren't you? Remember me? I'm Laura Quayle. I married you quite a while ago."

"I know." Quayle smiled at her. "They told me about it."

She disengaged herself from his arms. "I suppose you want tea," she said. "Am I permitted to ask where you've been; where you are going to; if you propose to stay here or what? Or is it all too fearfully secret?"

He followed her across the hall into the drawing-room. She rang the bell; ordered tea.

Quayle said: "I've just got back from Germany. A quick trip. I got myself dropped at Exeter and hired a car. I shall be here for a few hours and there are some people coming to see me. Two people, to be precise—Frewin and Ernest Guelvada"

She looked at him quickly. "Guelvada?" she queried. "That looks as if something's afoot that isn't going to be awfully pleasant for somebody or other. And I had an idea that all that sort of business finished with the war."

"Had you?" said Quayle grimly. "That pre-supposes that you thought the war was finished. But haven't you forgotten what the Americans call the 'cold war?' That's still on, you know, and while it is on . . ."

"You've got to go on doing what you do, and taking chances, and worrying my few remaining auburn hairs into the grave. By the way, I found another grey hair this morning."

Quayle grinned. "I think grey is an awfully nice colour. Save it for me. When you've collected some more I can have it put in a locket and wear it round my neck."

The maid came in with the tea. Laura poured it; brought his cup over to him.

She asked: "What is it this time? . . . Are you still chasing those lists—that war criminals thing?"

He nodded.

"You never give up, do you?" She smiled at him. "It's awfully lucky for you that you've such an accommodating wife."

There was a knock at the door.

The maid came in.

"A Mr. Frewin to see you, sir."

Quayle got up. "Not even time for tea with you, Laura," he said. "I'll see him in the study. By the way, can you give us all dinner about seven-thirty?"

"Yes," she said. She flashed a smile at him. "You use this place merely as an hotel. When are you leaving?"

"To-morrow morning." Quayle went to the door. "I'll play you billiards after dinner."

"Thank you, sir," she said. She continued seriously: "Do you mind finishing this nasty business with which you are dealing as soon as possible? Then perhaps I could have a little peace of mind."

Quayle grinned at her. "When it's finished, something else will start. There are too many tough guys in the world trying to cause trouble. Somebody has to look after them. But I've often wondered why it has to be me."

He went out.

When Quayle went into the study Frewin was standing at the window looking out over the garden.

Quayle said: "Well, Michael . . . how's it going? Sit down. You'll find cigarettes on the table."

"Thanks. . . ." Frewin sat down; helped himself to a cigarette; lighted it. He said, with a wry smile: "You wouldn't know how things are going, would you? You don't know anything at all?"

Quayle asked: "What do you mean?" He lighted a cigarette; smiled at his assistant.

"I was talking to Antoinette Brown this morning," said Frewin, "just before you came through. She has a definite idea in her head that you've been using me as a stooge—merely someone to create a set of circumstances so that you can start work when you want to. Well, I hope we've created the circumstances. Incidentally," he went on, "supposing you hadn't come back from Germany—what did you expect me to do?"

Quayle began to walk up and down the room. "I didn't expect you to do anything. I knew I was coming back from Germany, but it wasn't any use telling you what I thought, and I knew that somehow or other you'd create a situation—get something started—so that we could move. Actually, what has happened?"

Frewin told him.

Quayle said: "Nice work. I think it's very satisfactory. In one way, if not in another."

Frewin asked: "Was this meeting between Kiernan and Aurora Francis an arranged thing? Was the fact that Nielecki turned up pure coincidence? Was the business with Callao the mere result of events? Or was there some definite plan behind all this—something emanating from someone's mind?"

"Whose mind?" asked Quayle. "Obviously not Callao's; obviously not the Francis woman's and obviously not Nielecki's."

Frewin said: "That leaves Kiernan."

"Quite . . . that leaves Kiernan." Quayle sat on the edge of the large oak desk. He drew on his cigarette; exhaled tobacco smoke; watched it as it disappeared into the air. "I went to Germany because I wanted to check up on one or two things. I've done it. I'm satisfied we're working on the right lines. I don't believe that the meeting of all these personalities at the Cockatoo was planned and I don't believe it was accidental. It was half-planned—half-accidental. When I first talked with Antoinette Brown I asked her if she knew of any woman in whom Kiernan had been interested in Germany. She mentioned Aurora Francis. Now, you probably know as much about Kiernan as I do. He's a forcible, forthright personality, but behind that façade; behind that good-tempered and determined nature, there is a very cunning, very clever mind. Look at his record. Look at the things he got into and out of in the war. He's as brave as a lion and as cunning as a monkey."

Frewin said: "You mean to say he does nothing that he doesn't plan."

"That's exactly what I do mean. Kiernan went about in Nuremberg with Aurora Francis. He took her all over the place; had drinks with her; took her to the army shows; went for walks with her. But didn't make love to her. Really, his friendship with her was the sort of casual warm comradeship that is liable to happen between English people working in a foreign country under conditions such as obtained then. Well, Kiernan doesn't do a thing like that for nothing. He had something in his mind."

"What could he have had in his mind?" asked Frewin.

Quayle shrugged his shoulders. "How do I know? But, knowing Kiernan's mentality, I would say he plans a long way ahead. He takes advantage of any little thing that's going to be of use to him. At that time Aurora Francis probably seemed just another little thing that might be useful in the future, and when we come to consider the one great asset which she possesses we might begin to understand the workings of his mind."

Frewin raised his eyebrows. "What's her great asset?"

"Her beauty," said Quayle. "She's damned beautiful and damned alluring. She's got 'it' with a capital 'I.' The woman's a mass of sex attraction. Which makes it all the more extraordinary that Kiernan didn't make a pass at her in Germany—and Kiernan always makes a pass at any woman in whom he's interested."

Frewin said: "So he didn't make a pass at her for some definite reason?"

"Precisely. . . . He knew that by not making a definite pass at her she'd be interested in him. He knew she was beautiful and he knew that Vincente Callao and his rumba band were in London at the Cockatoo."

"I've got it," said Frewin. "Kiernan knew what sort of man Callao was. He knew that Callao falls for any really beautiful woman; that if he saw Francis he'd have to try and do something about her. Which means—"

"Which means that Kiernan already had something on ice for Callao," said Quayle. "See how it adds up. Really there's only one thing that comes into the picture by accident, but we'll forget that for a moment. Consider the position. Kiernan becomes good friends with Aurora Francis in Nuremberg. He impresses his personality on her. She's keen to meet him again. They agree that they'll meet in London at the Cockatoo. Kiernan believes that when Francis goes to the Cockatoo she'll be attracted by Callao and he by her. This means that he's studied both those personalities very definitely. I don't believe it's a coincidence that Kiernan arrived in London just after Aurora Francis got there. He'd kept tabs on her. The probability is that he'd mentioned Vincente Callao to her; that he'd told her what an awfully attractive fellow this man was; that he'd already stirred the curiosity in her mind—and Kiernan knew she was passionately interested in men. So he came over immediately after her. It's my guess that if she hadn't already made a contact with Callao, Kiernan would have introduced them."

Frewin. said: "In other words he's been using her as a stooge from the start."

"Right," said Quayle. "She's one of those intelligent, rather clever women, who think they are so damned clever that they never know when they're being made use of. She thought she was stalling Kiernan, but the boot was on the other foot. So Antoinette Brown meets Aurora Francis and goes to the Cockatoo with her, which was lucky for us. Kiernan arrives soon after. Then the thing which wasn't planned happens—at least we imagine it wasn't planned."

"My God!" said Frewin. "You don't mean to say that somebody planned that too. You're referring of course to Nielecki?"

"Of course I'm referring to Nielecki. It might have been a coincidence that Nielecki came into the cocktail bar when Kiernan was there. It might have been, or it might have been planned."

Frewin said: "It couldn't have been planned by Kiernan."

"I'm not suggesting it was planned by Kiernan. I'm suggesting it was planned by Kospovic."

Frewin whistled. "I'm beginning to see daylight."

"Work it out for yourself," said Quayle. "First of all let us consider Kospovic, which by the way, isn't his name. I know all about Kospovic. I knew that he was at South Brent. I knew how he got into this country. In fact, I've been interested in him for some time."

Frewin nodded.

"At some time or other—probably during the war," Quayle continued, "Kospovic must have met Nielecki. But Kospovic and Nielecki didn't like each other. That's another thing I've found out in Germany.

"The next move in the game is that Nielecki goes down to South Brent to meet Kospovic. These two, in spite of the fact that they don't like each other, are joining forces in order to secure the one thing they want; or the two things they want—money and security. Kospovic tells Nielecki that he knows who stole those two missing lists. He asks Nielecki what's the best thing to do about it. Nielecki tells him to do nothing; that the thing to do is to wait; that eventually a situation will arise that they can make use of.

"Nielecki comes back to London. He must have friends in Germany. He knows people in every country in the world. And he knew when Kiernan was coming over here. The probability is that he followed Kiernan; saw him going into the front entrance of the Cockatoo; slipped in by the side door and was in the cocktail bar before Kiernan arrived. That is what he would do, because from the cocktail bar he could get to any part of the restaurant. He could arrange an accidental meeting in any event. But he didn't have to because Kiernan came into the cocktail bar. And then Nielecki tells him about Kospovic and Kiernan gives him fifty pounds for doing him a good turn."

Frewin said: "I wonder was it a good turn?"

Quayle shrugged his shoulders. "It might have been or it might have been blackmail. It depends on what we think about Kiernan."

Frewin said: "I see. . . ."

"Kospovic," Quayle continued, "does not know that Nielecki has seen Kiernan. He does not know that Kiernan has given Nielecki some money, but after Nielecki had left South Brent and come back to London Kospovic got a little scared. He got scared because he knows me. He knows I'd fix him if he held out on me. So he tries to cover himself, but he doesn't want to give anything away. He rings me at my office and tells me that he knows who has those lists. He says he'd like to talk to me about it some time. And then he hangs up before I can say very much about it. That was rather extraordinary behaviour on his part, wasn't it?"

Frewin said: "I wonder he had the nerve."

"Exactly. Why should he have the nerve? There's one very good reason. The reason is that the secret he held—the name of the person who'd stolen those lists—was so important that he thought even I would have to handle it gently. Well, having made this telephone call he feels safe for a bit. He feels that I shall sit down and wait for him to come up to London and tell me what he knows; that I shall offer him some money or British nationality—which he wants—or both, to get him to talk. And he doesn't know that Nielecki has seen Kiernan."

Frewin asked: "What about Kiernan? He's the principal actor in this drama-comedy. What's he playing at?"

"Precisely," said Quayle. "What is he playing at? He can be doing one of three things. I'll give you three guesses." He grinned at Frewin.

Frewin said: "I'll try the three guesses. I think I'll be right. One, Kiernan stole the lists himself. He would easily be able to do that. He had access to all documents at that time. He was one of your principal agents. That's my first guess. The second guess is he knows who has those documents and he's playing some game of his own—probably money. Kiernan's fond of power and if you're fond of power you have to have money."

"Those two guesses aren't so bad," said Quayle. "What's the third one?"

"The third one might be that Kiernan wants to make a come-back. He stopped working for you a year ago. He's a man who loves excitement and danger. The work he was doing in the war suited him down to the ground. It gave him a certain power—a certain authority. When it was over he felt deflated. Maybe when Nielecki told him about Kospovic knowing who had those lists, Kiernan saw himself able to make a come-back in a big way. My idea was that he might go down to see Kospovic to try and get what he could out of him and then come back and see you, and confront you with a fait accompli. The return of Anthony Kiernan—the world's finest international agent! Maybe he wants a job. Maybe he wants something that you could give him. That's the third guess."

Quayle nodded. "What we have to do is to find out which of those three guesses is right."

There was a knock at the door.

Quayle said: "Come in."

The maid entered. "Mr. Guelvada . . ." she said.

Quayle grinned at Frewin. "Show him in."

Ernest Guelvada came into the room. He stood in the doorway looking from Quayle to Frewin, smiling. His personality was such that it is worth a few words.

He was of middle height, a little inclined to plumpness, with a pleasant and amiable expression. But there was something about him which was definitely disquieting. When he came into a room he brought with him a sense of vague discomfort. You always felt the presence of Ernie Guelvada. Not that there was anything antagonistic about him. On the contrary, his attitude towards life and people was invariably pleasant. Only the people who had worked with him in the war knew about the worm that lived in Mr. Guelvada's guts.

They called him the Free Belgium. He'd been born in a bakery in Ellezelles. He had been intended for the church, but the world war of 1914 which occurred when he was a boy put an end to those dreams. It also finished the career of his father who was shot by the Germans for cutting the throat of a corporal of German sappers. His mother had already quitted this life. She had been killed by the corporal of sappers for putting out one of his eyes with her thumb while he was trying to rape her.

From that time the hatred of certain types of people had lived in the insides of Ernest Guelvada. He had spent the second world war working for Quayle; working with Michael Kane and other top agents in Lisbon and all over the world; engaged in his one hobby—killing Germans.

Beyond this his amusements were looking at beautiful women and listening to music, both of which he liked very much. He spoke several languages, including a peculiar and pedantic English which he interlarded with American expressions.

Quayle said: "Come in, Ernie. Sit down and have a cigarette."

Guelvada came into the room. "I'm very glad to see you both," he said. "It's a hell of a time since I saw either of you. Life's been very interesting."

Quayle asked: "What are you supposed to be doing, Ernest?"

Guelvada smiled. He showed his neat white teeth. "I'm a courier. I take old ladies about the Continent. It's most amusing . . . the old ladies, I mean. But not very exciting. I was very glad to get your message." He helped himself to a cigarette; sat down on a chair. He was entirely relaxed. His eyes were quiet and roved about the room as if they took an interest in the different objects of furniture.

Quayle said: "I don't quite know what you're going to do, Ernest. But I have a vague idea. Michael here will give you the set-up." He turned to Frewin. "Quite obviously, our friend Vincente Callao is intended to have some part in whatever business Kiernan has in mind. I know a little about Vincente. During the war he worked for the Nazis. He was able to do that. He had a Spanish passport and he was a neutral. Also he had a band. A rumba band is an international thing and nobody worries if it moves about from place to place. Part of the time Callao had a band in Lisbon. You remember that Kiernan was there just about the time that Kane and Guelvada were working out there. The possibility is that Kiernan got to know Callao—or at least got to know something about him—whilst he was there. He intends to use Callao for something, I imagine. Somebody's got to find out what that is.

"Well, it seems to me we shouldn't have great difficulty in finding out everything because, from what you tell me, Aurora

Francis likes talking to Antoinette Brown. She uses her as a sort of safety valve. If Kiernan's going to suck her into something; if he's going to push her into some situation for his own purposes, the probability is that then she'll get scared. She'll talk to Brown. So we may know that end. The other end—the end that I think Ernest could take care of"—he smiled at Guelvada—"is Vincente Callao." His smile became a little cynical. "I should think that Callao would be just about Ernest's meat."

Guelvada said softly: "Vincente Callao. . . . If I remember rightly the full name is Vincente Marie Jesu Callao. . . . I think I remember . . ."

"He's a band leader," said Frewin. "He runs a rumba band. He's very good-looking. He likes women and they like him."

Guelvada said very softly: "Ah . . ." He continued smoking.

Quayle stubbed out his cigarette; lighted a fresh one. "I think we'll go and drink a cocktail with my wife. Otherwise she may be a little peeved. I believe she thinks she doesn't see enough of me. She doesn't realise that the war is not yet really over." He sighed. "There are a lot of people like that. So we'll drink a cocktail and then we'll talk. After dinner you. Michael, will take Guelvada back to town; watch circumstances and see how they develop; lay on what you think best. I'll be back myself to-morrow. I think events during the next two or three days may be amusing."

Frewin said cynically: "I think we're going to have a lot of fun. What do you think the next move is going to be?"

Quayle said: "You think that Kiernan's gone down to South Brent to see Kospovic. Whatever they talk about one of them has got to do something. One of them *must*. Because Kospovic will realise that Nielecki has sold him out. So he may decide to come and talk to me quickly to save his own skin before I put the Special Branch on to him. Or, alternatively, Kiernan will persuade Kospovic to keep his mouth shut, and come back and talk to me himself. Even Kiernan isn't sufficiently brave to think that he can get away with this sort of business in this country without letting me know something about it. One of those two things must happen. We'll wait for that."

Frewin nodded. "Really, by and large, things have worked out the way you wanted them to."

Quayle said: "I don't think we're doing so badly. Let's go and drink that Martini. . . ."

It was just after four o'clock when Kiernan pulled his car in to the side of the road at South Brent. Round the curve behind him lay the public house, the garage, the few straggling cottages. A hundred yards in front of him, approached by a narrow drive, was the place to which he had been directed—the Rambling House.

Kiernan lighted a cigarette and considered the matter of Kospovic. He found himself intrigued. He had never imagined that Kospovic would have the nerve to try and fight back in his present circumstances. He wondered what his explanation was going to be. Kiernan shrugged his shoulders.

He started up the car; reversed; made a "U" turn. He drove back past the little village to the cross-roads where he'd seen the telephone box. He went in; looked in the directory; called the Rambling House.

A voice with a Devonshire accent answered.

Kiernan said: "Good afternoon. My name's Grant. Is Mr. Kospovic in?"

The voice said: "No, Mr. Grant. He's out. He always goes for a walk in the afternoon."

"I see," said Kiernan. "I suppose you don't know what time he'll be back."

The voice said it didn't know. It went on: "But I can tell you where you will find him. He always walks along the path that leads from our back garden across the meadows and into the wood about a mile away. If you're anywhere near the main road and you keep straight on you'll come to the wood. It's not very large. He usually walks about there in the afternoon for an hour. He says it does his chest good."

Kiernan said: "Thank you." He hung up the receiver.

That suited him very well. He thought it would be much better to say what he had to say to Kospovic in private.

He went back to the car. He drove on, re-passed the village, passed the Rambling House. A mile ahead, the road narrowed; then divided. The right fork Kiernan could see led through a small wood. He stopped at the edge of the trees; parked the car on a grass verge; selected a path; began to walk. Inside the wood it was cold. A breeze had sprung up.

He began to think about Nielecki. He thought it was an odd coincidence—a lucky one—that Nielecki had been in the Cockatoo at the crucial moment. Kiernan thought that if his conversation with Kospovic was satisfactory, it might easily happen that he would find himself in a position to go and see Quayle or Frewin or somebody else in the organisation and say what he knew. There were moments, thought Kiernan with a grin, when candour and complete honesty were the only things that mattered—at least that's what the official mind thought.

Now the leafless trees were thicker. The path on which Kiernan was walking divided again. That which ran to the left was narrow, overgrown with bushes. The right fork looked more inviting. He took it; walked for a few minutes.

The path led into a small clearing. On the right of it, leaning against a bank, his head lolling to one side, was Kospovic.

The thin body of a long-legged man was leaning against the bank with the head in a grotesque position hanging over to the right. There was a great deal of blood on the face and coat. A couple of feet away Kiernan could see the Mauser pistol. Vaguely, he recognised it as the type used by German infantry officers in the '14-'18 war.

He went over and stood looking at the body. It was probably suicide, he thought, by the position of the body. The pistol—which had apparently fallen from the hand of the dead man—had been projected with a reflex action of the hand after death a few feet from the body. Everything looked like suicide.

Kiernan bent down and looked at the wound. There were no powder marks about it, but there seldom were powder marks from a Mauser pistol—not unless the barrel of the gun had been held right against the head.

Kiernan thought there was just a chance that it might have been murder. He wondered who would want to kill Kospovic or, for that matter, why Kospovic should want to kill himself.

He began to look closely at the body. The man was wearing a ready-made brown wool suit with a peculiar and rather glaring tie of the type often worn by foreigners. His hat was on the top of the bank. Probably he had placed it there. Kiernan leant over and looked at what remained of the good side of the face.

It was still recognisable as that of Szlemy. International agent provocateur, spy, trickster, thief. Kiernan thought that he was rather sorry that Szlemy, or Kospovic as he was calling himself, was dead. If Szlemy had been alive, Kiernan could have handled the situation very easily. He would have had the dead man where he wanted him. He remembered with a grin some of the things he knew about Szlemy—enough to bet an immediate deportation order, if not worse. And deportation to Szlemy would mean death. There were many people who would give a great deal to get their hands on him; many people who would be very pleased to know that he was dead.

Kiernan felt in the pocket of his leather driving jacket; produced a pair of gloves. He put them on. He opened the coat of the dead man; felt in the breast pocket. There was an old leather wallet in the pocket. He took it out; went through it. There were twelve one-pound notes, a list of addresses, a passport, a temporary identity card of the type issued to friendly aliens. The card showed that Kurt Kospovic was resident at 14 St. George's Mansions, Clerkenwell, and attached to it was a permit indicating that he had permission to live at the Rambling House, South Brent, in Devonshire.

Kiernan looked at the passport. That too, was in the name of Kurt Kospovic. Kiernan replaced the documents in the wallet; put it back into Kospovic's pocket. So Kospovic—or Szlemy—was dead. Kiernan wondered whether he liked that or not. He was not quite certain.

He stood for a few minutes looking at the dead man. Then he lighted a cigarette. Then he went back to the car. He drove on to the deserted main road; sped through the village. He was rather pleased that he had telephoned the Rambling House; glad that he had not been there; not allowed himself to be seen. That, in the circumstances, might be useful.

He drove rapidly towards London. The situation he thought, so far as he was concerned, was practically unchanged; if anything it was more favourable. Kospovic, thought Kiernan, had found himself in a spot, and one of two things happened. Kospovic knew that he'd have to talk to somebody; that when he talked they'd find out about him. He was scared of something, so he killed himself. Because he was sick; because he was fed up; because life held very little for him.

Alternatively, someone else had known about Kospovic—someone else who thought he might talk—someone who wanted to stop him talking. Kiernan thought there might be quite a lot of people who would feel like that. His mind switched to Nielecki. It might even have been Nielecki. The idea sounded far-fetched, but you never knew. Definitely, thought Kiernan, in these days you never knew.

At six o'clock Aurora Francis, looking very neat and attractive, turned into Charles Street. She thought that Kiernan would probably have spent most of the day in bed. He had told her he liked to be lazy. Now he would be up, probably having a cocktail. He would be glad to see her. Even if he did not particularly show his gladness. She thought, with a little smile, that she and Kiernan were both playing exactly the same game.

She rang the door bell.

When the housekeeper opened the door, she said immediately: "Are you Miss Francis? Mr. Kiernan thought you might call. He left a note for you."

A peculiar sense of disappointment overcame Aurora. She had believed that Kiernan would be there. He was not there. Not only was he not there, but he had known she would call. She smiled a little wryly. Sometimes Kiernan knew too much. Perhaps he had a little of that woman's intuition at which he laughed so much.

The woman gave her the note. Aurora thanked her and turned away. She walked down Charles Street; picked up a taxi-cab at the bottom of the street; told the driver to take her to Lowndes Square. In the cab she opened the note. It said:

"My sweety,

"If I know anything about you you will spend the morning in a dressing-gown waiting for me to ring. I shan't do that because I don't think you ought to get your own way in everything, and also because I have a job to do.

"If I'm right and you call, if you're not doing anything important this evening, and like to stay in your apartment, perhaps I'll call through—if I can.

"Yours,

"Tony."

Aurora tore the note into little pieces; threw them out of the window. She relaxed in the corner of the seat; took a cigarette from her handbag; lighted it. She wondered what Kiernan was doing. He would ring up, she thought, and ask her out to dinner.

When she arrived in Lowndes Square, she paid off the cab; went up to her apartment. She took off her clothes; got into a robe; lay down on her bed. She began to think about Kiernan. She wondered when he would telephone. She found that she was impatient; restless.

But she waited a long time. It was eleven o'clock before the telephone rang.

On the other side of Salisbury Frewin let in the supercharger. Guelvada, who liked speed, settled down in the passenger seat; watched the speedometer go up to eighty-five. The headlights cut the dark road for a hundred and fifty yards ahead. Guelvada took out his cigarette case; lighted two cigarettes; passed one to Frewin.

He said: "I'm very, very interested in this thing. I think it's going to be amusing! I think we're going to have a hell of a time. I like it."

Frewin grinned. Guelvada always gave him a certain amount of amusement. He liked Guelvada's attitude to life. They had worked together for so many years that both these men knew the intricacies of each other's natures, and beneath their respective façades they liked and trusted each other. In their sort of business you have to trust people, and it is a good thing to be able to like them too.

Frewin asked: "Why, Ernie?"

Guelvada shrugged his shoulders. "I'm interested in this Vincente Maria Jesu Callao. Jeez . . . that's a hell of a name, don't you think? A man with a name like that has to be something, or"— he grinned wryly—"he has to think he was meant to be something. Actually, Vincente isn't anything—not a goddam thing! No, sir! . . ."

Frewin said: "So you met Callao?"

"Yes," said Guelvada. "In Lisbon during the war when I was working with Michael Kane, we had an amusing time killing German agents." Guelvada sighed. "They were happy days."

Frewin asked: "Was Callao a German agent?"

"Not on your life. Do you think that that punk has enough guts to be an agent for anybody? He was a postman—on the safe side. Callao was one of those people who like to pretend that they are very brave and strong and secret persons doing difficult work. Actually, he never took any chances or any risks. He was a contact man between enemy agents in Spain and enemy agents in London, so he worked over neutral territory. He never took chances at all. And, you see, he always had a good excuse for being anywhere. He was a band leader. It gave him a secret and mysterious background. It gave him an air, and women like a man to have an air. And that was important to Vincente, because, you see, he has only one hobby—women."

Frewin said: "I see. . . ."

"This Aurora . . ." Guelvada continued. "By what Quayle has said, and by what you have told me Miss Brown has told you, this Aurora is quite a piece. Some baby, hey? She sounds beautiful to me. It's a pity that she's playing such an important part in this affair; otherwise I know somebody who might like to be interested in Aurora."

Frewin grinned. "You mean our little Ernie?"

"Precisely," said Guelvada. "To me she seems the sort of lady who was made for Ernie. But," he continued, "never do I put pleasure before business—well, not so that you'd notice it. But I can understand this Callao being attracted to her. Probably Callao is now more or less financially secure. He has this band playing in London. He is probably earning good money. For once in his life he can permit himself to feel a little altruistic about women." He looked at Frewin sideways. "You know," he went on, "usually he takes women for everything they have. He's got something—that one. Women have sold their jewelry for him before now. He has a good line, hey . . . goddam him. I don't think I like Callao very much."

Frewin asked: "What's in the back of your mind? You've got something hotting up."

"Search me," said Guelvada. "At the moment I don't know, but I have this idea. It might be useful. Callao is a man who can be frightened very easily. Perhaps when Quayle comes back to London to-morrow, and we've had another talk about all this; perhaps when things develop a little more, our esteemed chief will let me frighten Callao a little. I'd like that. It's a long time since I frightened anybody."

Frewin said: "I see. You're getting restive."

"Why not?" said Guelvada. "What the hell! Look, in the war it was good; there was excitement; there was danger. One did a little killing, for instance, in Lisbon, or alternatively, one was oneself killed. Now everything is so quiet. Now everything has to be done with kid gloves. Now nobody must do anything at all without the risk of causing some international situation—as if international situations mattered." He laughed. "There's been an international situation going on to my knowledge for the last twenty-five or thirty years. They go on because nobody does anything definite about them; because everybody's scared. I like people to be definite."

Frewin smiled. "What you really mean is you like to use that funny little Swedish knife of yours on somebody in a dark alley— preferably in a neutral country."

"Yes," said Guelvada. "I don't mind that. What you mean is I like to kill him before he kills me. In any event, anything—even an affair like this—is better than rusticating, even if nobody is going to get very hurt, hey?"

Frewin's headlights picked up the rear light of a car in front. He accelerated to pass it. Now the speedometer showed ninety.

Guelvada said: "A nice fast car this."

"About people getting hurt," said Frewin. "I wouldn't like to bet that nobody is going to get hurt over this job. If things go one way, it's not a question of whether anybody wants to hurt somebody; it just means that somebody has got to be hurt."

"Precisely," said Guelvada. "I suppose you're thinking of the same thing as I am."

"Yes . . . I believe I am. . . ."

Guelvada asked: "Do you think it's like that?"

"How do I know?" said Frewin. "We shall see. . . ."

The speedometer moved up to ninety-two.

Guelvada said: "I find this is lovely. This is a nice road for driving."

"You're not going any faster," said Frewin. "We'll be at Stockbridge before we know where we are. Relax. Take it easy."

Guelvada smiled in the darkness. "My friend . . . I have always been relaxed. And, as you know, I take anything easily."

At eleven o'clock the telephone rang. Aurora got up from the bed; crossed the room. She was feeling a little bad-tempered. She was feeling bad-tempered because she had wanted the phone bell to ring; because she was impatient to hear from Kiernan.

He said: "Hallo, sweet. I've just got back to London. Did you get my note?"

She said shortly: "Yes. How did you know I should come round?"

He laughed. "You knew I'd know you'd come round. I didn't think you'd be able to keep away. I thought our meeting last night was—a little unsatisfactory, shall we say, to both parties?"

She said: "It wasn't unsatisfactory to me, Tony . . . just because I made you behave yourself for once."

He laughed again. She liked the low tone of his laugh. It did something to her.

He said: "And you liked that, didn't you? You liked my behaving myself."

She asked: "Is that what you rang me up for—to tell me that?"

"No. . . . Would you like to come round and see me? I want to talk to you about something that's rather urgent and important—something that might make a difference to us."

There was a pause; then he said: "Don't bother if you're disinclined."

"I didn't say I was disinclined. . . . I was thinking."

"All right. Have a good think, my sweet. But aren't you being rather bad-tempered and rather foolish?"

She asked: "Exactly what do you mean by that?"

"Use your common-sense, my girl. Quite obviously, our lives are going to run together, for a little while in any event; maybe longer, if we like it. You know damned well that if I tell you that something's urgent as far as we are concerned you are interested. But if you're not and you don't want to come round, just say so, and that's that."

She said: "If it wasn't me I expect it'd be some other woman." She imagined him grinning.

"Of course," said Kiernan. "But as it's you, why worry about some other woman at the moment. Or do you like doing that?"

"I'll put a frock on. I'll be round in twenty minutes," said Aurora. "I've been waiting in the whole evening. I expected you to telephone."

Kiernan said: "I'll be seeing you. It's the woman's business to wait sometimes, and it's not nice when the woman is as impatient as you are."

She heard the receiver click as he hung up.

When she arrived Kiernan opened the door. He led the way along the passage to his suite at the far end. It was a large, comfortably-furnished suite. Kiernan, who could bear discomfort as well as any man, preferred luxury when he could get it.

He pushed forward an arm-chair. He said: "Take off your coat and have a drink. I'll mix you a Martini."

She said: "So I'm not even to be kissed?"

Kiernan, on his way to the sideboard, stopped. He grinned at her. "I thought you were so keen on my behaving myself. But if it's like that . . . Come here, baby. . . ."

She went to him.

When he had mixed the drinks he stood in front of the coal fire, the Martini in his hand, looking down at her.

She thought: I wonder what's coming. I wonder what he's going to tell me. I wonder how it concerns me. She felt very curious.

Kiernan said: "I don't very often talk to people about things that matter, especially not to women, because I don't usually trust women—not because I think they're untrustworthy but because sometimes it's good for them not to know too much. This time is one of those exceptions that prove the rule."

She sipped her Martini. "I see. . . . But why am I an exception? Why do I come into this?"

"I'm stuck on you, Aurora," said Kiernan. "And I think you feel the same way about me. You and I are odd kinds of people. We're neither of us particularly weak, and we both of us know what we want. I certainly do. Incidentally, I think I know what you want."

"Do you?" she asked. "You're awfully certain of yourself, aren't you, Tony?"

He grinned. "You wouldn't like me very much if I weren't, would you? That's one of the things you like about me. You know that I know what I want and that I usually have some sort of definite scheme for getting it."

She asked: "What is it you want now?"

"Two things," he said. "The first one is you. But I also want some money and some prospects. I am in a bit of a spot and I don't quite know how to play it—at least, I do know how to play it, but shall we say I need a little assistance?"

"What is it you want me to do?"

Kiernan said: "You'd better hear some of the story. You didn't think, by any chance, that I came round to Callao's place last night and beat him up just because I felt like that?"

"I haven't thought much about it. I would put you above any sort of crazy thing. I thought you just didn't like him."

"I don't awfully," said Kiernan. "I think Callao's a son of a bitch, but at the moment he's important to me."

She asked: "Why?"

"Listen to me . . ." said Kiernan. "During the war, as you probably know, I had a pretty tough time, but a very interesting time. I like taking chances. It's the salt of the earth to me. I like excitement. Well, I took a hell of a lot of chances and I got a lot of excitement. I had other things too. I had a certain amount of power; quite a lot of money at my disposal." He lighted a cigarette. "I suppose," he went on, "that I was one of the most efficient secret agents employed by the British Government. Quayle always thought I was his best operative. I certainly did more work for him behind the German lines than anybody I have known. And not only there. I have worked everywhere for Quayle; taken every sort of chance for him."

She said: "Quayle? Is he important?"

Kiernan nodded. "He runs an extremely important section of British Intelligence—probably the most important section." He blew a smoke ring; watched it sail across the room. "You can imagine," he continued, "I wasn't fearfully pleased when my job finished. They gave me a gratuity and that was that. And there it was. I ceased to be important and I began to be an individual floating about the Continent, trying to delude myself that I was having a good time, but all the time I knew I wanted to get back."

Aurora moved a little in her chair. She finished her cocktail; put the glass on the floor beside her. She said: "Tell me something, Tony . . . if you were so good, why did you finish? Surely there's a good deal of work still to be done—work that you could do?"

He nodded. He walked over to the chair; bent down; picked up the glass. He kissed her casually on the mouth; went to the sideboard; poured another cocktail; brought it back to her.

He said: "There is a good answer to that one. You know, in wartime a certain type of soldier is very successful—a man who is quick, cunning, reliant, forceful and who is prepared to take a hell of a chance if necessary. My sort of man. But in peace time he's not always fearfully popular. He's the wrong sort of soldier for peace time. See what I mean? Think of all the good generals in the last war. Go through the list and see how many of them were really popular in peace time, because the unfortunate thing about these intervals of peace that we have these days between

wars is that everybody seems scared of action. They just sit around
and let situations develop until it's too late to do anything very
much about them.

"Well, people like myself don't like that. They want to do
something. So we're not popular. Now do you understand?"

She nodded.

Kiernan went on: "I walked into a situation. I found out
something by accident and I am trying to make the best use of
it. If I do I can get myself back with Quayle. I made up my mind
that I was going to play this thing in a nice, quiet, easy way that
Quayle would like, so that he would realise that be could still use
me. But something went wrong."

She said: "Tell me." She was extremely interested.

Kiernan refilled his own glass; went back to the fireplace.

He said: "Last night, before I came round to Callao's place, I
was in the cocktail bar at the Cockatoo. There was a fellow there
whom I knew—a man called Nielecki. Nielecki had been an agent
during the war. He'd worked for all sorts of people. He was one
of those unfortunate people who get pushed around and have to
do what they're told. Nielecki told me that he'd been talking to
a man in Devonshire—a man of his own type—another ex-agent
named Kospovic; that Kospovic knew the man who had stolen two
lists of enemy war criminals and agents that Quayle wants badly.
I knew about those lists. I was working for Quayle in Nuremberg
at the time they were stolen.

"I had a talk with Nielecki; gave him some money because I
thought that was a clever thing to do and because he knew damned
well that he'd given me some good information. And to-day I went
out to talk to Kospovic. I got down to the place where he lived.
I telephoned; found that he was out; that he'd gone for a walk.
But they told me where I might find him. I found him in a little
wood. He was dead. He'd either shot himself or somebody had
killed him. I think he shot himself."

She said: "Have you any idea why he should do that?"

He nodded. "He wasn't Kospovic. He was a man I knew called
Szlemy—a rat. He would have been run out of here in five minutes
if the authorities had got wise to him. When I found that he was

dead I wondered about Nielecki. I wondered why Nielecki had told me that Kospovic had this information. Because Nielecki would guess that I'd want to see Kospovic. I wondered if Nielecki had telephoned Kospovic and told him that I was probably coming down to see him." He smiled. "That would account for his killing himself, because Kospovic would know that with me after him he wouldn't stand a chance. And he was one of those tired, sick and unhappy people who are weary of life. He probably thought the easiest way out of more trouble was to kill himself."

She nodded. "But you didn't get your information? He wasn't able to tell you who had those lists."

Kiernan grinned. "I didn't say I particularly wanted the information from him. I wanted to talk to him. I wanted to know why he had decided to withhold this information from the authorities. I wanted to know all about Kospovic, but I didn't want the information."

She said: "I see. . . . But wasn't that information important to you, if you were trying to make a come-back with this man Quayle?"

"The information wasn't important to me because I know who stole the lists. I know who's got them." Kiernan grinned at her. "I want to hand those lists back to Quayle on a plate. I want Quayle to feel sorry that he was ever able to let me go. I want to make a big come-back with Quayle. I've got a lot of ideas at the back of my head and great deal of experience. I could be very useful to him, and if I could get back with Quayle in the way I want I think life might be amusing for us both, my dear."

She smiled for the first time during the evening. "So you think I come in on this too?"

He said: "Don't be a damn fool, Aurora. Of course you come in on it. You come in on it as Mrs. Kiernan, I hope. Do you think you'd like that?"

"I don't know . . ." said Aurora.

"Yes, you do. But you don't feel like admitting it right away. Anyway, we can come back to that point later."

She said: "Give me a cigarette, Tony."

He gave her a cigarette; lighted it.

She said: "Does it matter to you that the man Kospovic, or whatever his name was. is dead? It doesn't matter if you know who's got those lists. All you have to do is to get them."

Kiernan said: "It's not as easy as that. Those two lists are dynamite. The person who's got them knows what they're worth. He also knows this: That they're worth money to Quayle; but they're worth a damn sight more money to the people who originally had them stolen. Do you think he's just going to hand them over because I ask for them? Do you think he's going to admit he's got them? Do you think he's going to do anything at all except tell me I'm talking rubbish?"

"I see," said Aurora. "So it's difficult. But you must think there's some way of getting the lists; otherwise you'd consider the thing to be entirely hopeless."

"Quite," said Kiernan. "I want to get them, but I want to get them my way. I want to do something that Quayle can't do. When I've done that I'll be in a very strong position. And I think I can do it if you help."

She raised her eyebrows. "So it's like that, Tony! You're really asking me to help you in this. I like that."

"Do you?" He looked at her. She thought she liked the cut of his thin jaw, his white, even teeth, the curve of his mouth. He said: "Come here. . . ."

She went to him. He took her in his arms. He said: "Are you going to play ball, baby? Are you going to do what I tell you? There won't be any danger for you—well, very little . . . and it might be a lot of fun."

Her eyes gleamed. "I'd love it, Tony. And you're perfectly right . . . I am crazy about you. I know that our lives must go together whatever happens."

He said: "Now you're beginning to talk sense. Go back to your chair; sit down and relax."

She went back to the chair. She sat there looking at him.

Kiernan lighted a cigarette. He said: "This girl Antoinette Brown . . . she's rather a friend of yours, isn't she? You like her?"

Aurora shrugged her shoulders. "She's a nice little thing. I like her very much. I think she's rather afraid of life. Awfully efficient, but not too deep. I don't think she thinks a great deal of men."

Kiernan grinned. "An efficient bachelor girl, eh?" he asked.

She nodded.

Kiernan said: "You might be right about her and you might be wrong. All I know is that when Antoinette Brown worked for me in Nuremberg she came to me from Quayle's office. I'm taking no chances about that girl. Maybe she's what she seems to be, but Quayle's damned clever. So we'll use her."

She said: "Yes? How?"

"Listen," said Kiernan. "She's your friend and she's in your confidence. Next time you see her take her word of honour that she won't repeat what you tell her. Then tell her about you and me; that we're in love with each other; that I'm playing this thing about the lists on my own because I want to make a come-back with Quayle; I want to start working for him again."

Aurora said: "I see. You think this is a good idea, Tony?"

"I don't think . . . I know. If Antoinette Brown is what you think she is, and she keeps her word to you and says nothing about it, or if on the other hand she goes to him and tells him what you've told her, I'm covered whatever I do. Quayle will believe I'm doing it to try and get back with him. So that's what you do, honey."

She said: "That'll be quite simple. She loves talking to me. I'll see her; tell her what you say. Tony, I want another drink."

He mixed her a fresh cocktail; brought it to her.

She said: "Tell me something. Who is it has these lists—somebody interesting?"

"It depends on what you call interesting. The man who's got those lists somewhere or other is your late boy friend—Vincente Maria Jesu Callao. And now, my sweet, I'll tell you what we're going to do. . . ." He began to talk.

Laura Quayle lay in the darkness looking at the ceiling. She listened to Quayle's regular breathing. She thought about many things. Especially, she wondered where this new adventure would lead him.

She had spent years of her life worrying about Quayle and telling him little of her worries, maintaining the light-hearted air which he liked, because it was the easiest thing to do. And she had thought that the days of worrying would end with the war. It seemed that she had been wrong.

The telephone by the bedside jangled. She reached out for the receiver.

It was Frewin. He said: "Hello . . . is that you, Laura? Is the Chief anywhere about?"

She said: "At the present moment he's sleeping, with his mouth half-open. I'll wake him up."

Quayle was already awake. He asked: "Who is it—Michael?"

"Yes. . . ." She switched on the bedside light.

Quayle got out of bed. She thought that in scarlet silk pyjamas he looked positively intimidating. He walked round; sat on the edge of the bed; took the receiver from her.

He said: "Hallo, Michael. What is it?"

"Kospovic . . ." said Frewin. "Somebody found his body in a little wood at South Brent this evening. They went and told the local police about it. He's dead."

Quayle said: "Interesting, but not very surprising. Was he killed?"

"I don't know. The Divisional Police Surgeon says it looks like suicide."

Quayle said: "It could be that too. Anything else?"

"Yes . . . it seems that soon after four o'clock this afternoon somebody, who said his name was Grant, telephoned to the Rambling House where Kospovic was living and said he wanted to see Kospovic. They told him that Kospovic had gone for a walk. They told him where Kospovic usually went for a walk. They told him how to get there."

"Exactly," said Quayle. "That would be Kiernan. You say that was soon after four?"

"Definitely it was between four and five," answered Frewin.

Quayle asked: "At what time does the Divisional Police Surgeon think Kospovic died, or was killed?"

"He doesn't seem to be certain. But believes he had been dead for some time when they found him—maybe three or four hours."

"If it was as long as that it would let Kiernan out," said Quayle.

Frewin said: "But you don't think—"

"Why shouldn't I? I can think anything I like, can't I? It's a free country, Michael." There was a pause; then he went on: "I wonder why Kospovic should have wanted to kill himself—if he did kill himself. Because he was scared perhaps. He'd rung me up and told me he was going to talk to me and then something turned up that made him change his mind. I can guess what that was."

Frewin said: "Can you?"

"Look," said Quayle, "pick up Nielecki. Find out if Nielecki telephoned through to Kospovic that he'd told Kiernan that Kospovic knew who'd stolen those lists. If he'd done that Kospovic would know that Kiernan would come down. He would also know that Kiernan would immediately recognise him as Szlemy and Kiernan knew a lot about Szlemy, as I did. In the ordinary way he wouldn't have been allowed to stay in this country for five minutes. But it suited my book to let him stay."

Frewin said: "I see. You think that Kospovic or Szlemy, or whatever his name was, knew that Kiernan was coming down and got the breeze up. He was so scared that he took the easiest way out."

Quayle said: "That's what I think. But put the heat on Nielecki and find out if he did call through. Anything else?"

"That's all. Isn't it enough?"

"It's enough for to-night," said Quayle. "I wonder why it is I never get any uninterrupted sleep. I don't mind it, but Laura gets awfully peeved." He smiled at her. "So long, Michael." He hung up.

He walked across to a chair; picked up his dressing-gown; put it on. "I'm going down to the library. I'll switch the 'phone through there in case anything else turns up. I want to do a little thinking."

She said: "I see. That means you'd like some tea."

"Yes, I would. But don't you worry. You go to sleep. I'll make it."

"Like hell you will. . . ." She got out of bed.

*

Kiernan and Aurora stood in front of the fireplace. Her arms were about his neck; their mouths pressed close together. After a minute she disengaged herself; stood away from him. She took two cigarettes from the box on the mantelpiece; lighted them; put one in his mouth.

She said: "You know, Mr. Kiernan, you've got a hell of a nerve." She smiled at him.

"Maybe I have," he said. "But the scheme's pretty good, isn't it? One way or another it's going to come off."

"You know, this Mr. Quayle ought to be very grateful to you, oughtn't he?" she asked. "You're doing quite a lot for him, after he laid you off."

Kiernan said: "Don't get Quayle wrong. I explained to you about that. He had to lay me off. Lots of other people were laid off too. But if I pull this thing off I make a big come-back and things should be pretty good for me, especially as I'm no actually working for Quayle."

"Meaning what?" she asked.

"Work it out for yourself. Even if they take me back, what I've done for them has been done at a time when I was a free and independent citizen just trying to pull my weight for my country. So they'll give me something, won't they? Those lists are worth a hell of a lot of money. You'd be surprised if you knew what the other people would pay for them once they were got out of this country. And," he went on, "Quayle doesn't know where they are and I do, and even if he did he'd be in a spot to get them, whereas, as I think you'll agree, if this thing's played properly my scheme's watertight."

"Yes. . . ." She smiled. "Even if you have to sacrifice me; even if you have to hand me back to the wicked Vincente Callao." They both laughed.

He said: "I should worry. You're a good actress, Aurora, and you don't have to give anything away that belongs to me. You better hadn't."

"Don't worry," said Aurora. "I won't."

"All right, baby," said Kiernan. "Now run back to that apartment of yours and get some sleep." He took her in his arms again and kissed her.

She said seriously: "This is for keeps, Tony, isn't it? You meant what you said about our getting married?"

He looked at her. "What do you think? Do I look like the sort of person who'd string you along? Do you think I'm stringing you along? Don't you think too much depends on this for me to play games with you in any event?"

She said: "Yes. I do think that."

"Besides which," said Kiernan, "you may not know it, young woman, but I'm nuts about you."

She put her arms round his neck. She said: "That's what I thought and hoped."

He helped her on with her coat.

CHAPTER THREE
RUMBA

MONDAY

A WINTRY and undecided sun percolated through the net curtains of Quayle's office windows, forming odd shadows on the carpet. The shadows reminded Quayle of a jig-saw puzzle—something akin to the one in which he found himself engrossed.

He began to think about Kospovic. He concluded that the Kospovic business might be fairly obvious. Kospovic had committed suicide because he was frightened. He was sufficiently frightened of something or somebody to desire to have done with this world and its works. He was without hope, and death seemed to him the easiest way out.

The reasons for his lack of hope were apparent. He was an alien, with a bad record, in a strange country—the only country in the world that could shelter him from the effects of his past; sick, despondent and with no line of retreat; something had happened to Kospovic after his telephone call to Quayle that had proved to him that death was preferable to a dangerous uncertainty.

The telephone call, thought Quayle, had been a last effort to protect himself from the results of the circumstances in which he found himself involved. He had hoped that Quayle would eventually do something about him. Then, after the call, the balloon had gone up. Something else had happened, and Kospovic had taken himself for his last walk and blown out his rather peculiar brains which, quick and opportunist in the past, could not help him in his present dilemma.

Frewin came into the room. He was, as usual, immaculately dressed, and the inevitable cigarette hung from the corner of his mouth. Quayle thought he looked tired.

He asked: "Well? . . ."

Frewin avoided the question. Instead he said: "You know, that girl Brown has brains. Possibly I've underestimated her. Possibly she's cleverer than I thought."

Quayle smiled. "I've always had a considerable opinion of Antoinette. But what made you change your opinion. Or is merely that you're finding her a little more fascinating." He looked sideways at Frewin. "She is fascinating, you know—or haven't you noticed?"

Frewin shrugged his shoulders. "I was talking about her mind."

"Yes?" said Quayle. He got up; walked over to the window; looked out. "What about Nielecki?" he asked.

"I talked to him early this morning," Frewin answered. "I sweated him considerably. Eventually he gave me the whole story. He's scared stiff. He thinks there's a good chance that you may have him deported."

Quayle went back to his seat. "He's perfectly right. I've already arranged for that. What did he have to say?"

"He'd heard that Kospovic was at South Brent," said Frewin. "So he went down to see him. He was curious about Kospovic. Nielecki knew all about him. He knew that if Kospovic was lying low it wasn't only because of his chest. He says that Kospovic was scared and very worried; that he had to talk to somebody. So Nielecki got to work on him, and eventually Kospovic told him that he knew who had stolen the lists. Then Nielecki was intrigued. All the more intrigued because he knew that those lists were dynamite and that the knowledge that Kospovic had was dangerous. He asked Kospovic what he was going to do about it; told him that if he kept such information to himself it would do him no good; that he would get up against the authorities here and that he might easily be deported. Nielecki worked on him, hoping that Kospovic would be inclined to tell him more. But Kospovic wasn't playing. He said that he would do nothing for the moment; that he would think things over. So Nielecki came back to London."

Quayle nodded. "Did he know that Kiernan was coming over?"

"Yes," said Frewin. "He knew that because of his work on the Refugee Commission. They have an International hook-up and Nielecki was able to keep in touch with his friends abroad. They put him wise to the fact that Kiernan was coming to London. He got some time off, picked Kiernan up at the airport and followed him to his rooms in Charles Street. He'd made up his mind to get what he could out of the information he'd had from Kospovic. He believed that Kiernan was still working for you and that even if he didn't get any money out of it he'd be able to do himself some good by talking to Kiernan. He said that he saw Kiernan going into the Cockatoo and went in after him."

"And then he got into touch with Kospovic, whom he dislikes, and told him what he'd done?" said Quayle.

"Yes. . . . Nielecki said he did that because he thought he ought to tell Kospovic that he'd told Kiernan. He says that Kospovic had no right to withhold any information which he had, and that he, Nielecki, was merely doing his duty."

Quayle grinned. "Like hell he was. He was looking after himself."

He got up; began to walk about the room. "Now we know why Kospovic killed himself," he said. "He knew that Kiernan would be after him immediately he got the information from Nielecki. He was scared of Kiernan so he took the easiest way out."

Frewin asked: "Why was Kospovic so scared of Kiernan? Why did he have to kill himself because Kiernan knew that he had some information about the missing lists?"

Quayle shrugged his shoulders. "Your guess is as good as mine. But we'll know soon. Kiernan has to do something about it, hasn't he. He must come and tell me about it or do something else."

There was a knock at the door. Quayle's secretary came into the room. "Mr. Guelvada is here, Mr. Quayle."

Ernest Guelvada came into the room. He stood aside, an odd little smile on his round face, to allow the secretary to go out. He watched the door close behind her.

He said: "You know . . . that girl is not unattractive. My God, no! She's not bad. I'm telling you! Angular maybe; thin possibly; short-sighted, yes . . . but she still has something. Even if I don't know what it is . . . hey? To see her again intrigues me."

Quayle smiled at him. "Why, Ernest?"

Guelvada shrugged his shoulders.

"During the war when I was working for you in Belgium, one evening I found myself at a place called Miselles. The Germans were going to build an air-strip there. I was to report on the work for you. So . . . one evening I found myself in an estaminet. I was extremely bored because the Gestapo were very active in that sector and also because I desired feminine company. Then a girl arrived. I did not consider her to be beautiful—not by a long chalk. No . . . but she was a girl. I knew about her. Her name was Alphonsine Garroux and she worked at a nearby farm. Do I interest you?"

Quayle nodded. "Of course, Ernest." He grinned at Frewin.

"So," continued Guelvada, "I thought to myself that I would make some approach to her. You will realise that I am not unattractive to women. . . . No, sir! So I went over to her and I said, 'Excuse me, Mademoiselle, but I consider that you have eyes like stars and that your figure is both superb and alluring. Perhaps you can find it in your heart to drink a glass of wine with me, after which we would walk for a little and I would make love to you in the most exquisite manner.' "

"Charming!" There was sarcasm in Frewin's voice. "And what did she say?"

Guelvada shrugged his shoulders. He made a wry face. "She said to me very quietly: 'Please don't embarrass me, Mr. Guelvada,' and she walked out of the place."

Guelvada sighed. "Consider . . . it was the girl who is now your secretary, who was also working for you in that area, and I had not even recognised her." He sighed again. "Such are the penalties of love. . . . You're telling me!"

Quayle said: "Too bad. Now give yourself a cigarette, Ernest, and sit down. I take it you didn't come here to tell me about your past amatory designs on my secretary."

Guelvada took a cigarette from the silver box on Quayle's table; lighted it. He sat down, hitched up his well-creased trousers and regarded his polished shoes and silk socks with equanimity.

He said: "No. My mind is concerned with more important things. I have been thinking about the man Callao. I have been remembering all sorts of things about him."

Quayle nodded. "He acted as messenger between Spain, Lisbon and Germany during the war. He was never regarded as being any one of importance. We have a dossier on him. It is not particularly interesting."

"Quite," said Guelvada. "That is my point. This man Callao . . . what is he? I think the man is a push-over, hey? He bores me. Therefore I ask myself what is he doing in this galère. Here you have people of personality; people who are at least definite. You have Kiernan, who is a considerable man. He was a distinguished agent—a thorn in the flesh of the enemy. You have the woman Aurora Francis, who is apparently beautiful and not dumb. You have the man Nielecki who, whilst he is an indifferent sort of person, knows his way about and has a brain. And, lastly, you have the man about whom Frewin here told me this morning—the man Kospovic, who seems to have decided that he would be happier in heaven, or wherever it is that dead agent provocateurs go. All these people," said Guelvada with an airy wave of the hand, "are personalities in their own line. And then we come back to the man Callao. . . ."

Guelvada inhaled cigarette smoke; exhaled it delicately; watched the smoke cloud pass through the air.

He went on: "Callao has two things only. He is a good musician and he has a flair for women. He has that peculiar quality which attracts even nice women; which makes them make fools of themselves for reasons which they eventually discover were merely ridiculous. But even with women he is stupid. I consider the man to be a big bum. . . . You understand?"

Quayle said patiently: "I understand, Ernest. What is the point?"

"The point is," said Guelvada, "that I don't understand what Callao is doing in this thing. I have an idea in my head that somebody is making use of him. I ask myself," he continued, putting his head on one side and smiling at Quayle and Frewin, "in what way could it be possible to make use of Callao? The answer is in two ways, first because of his connection with some woman, and second because he is a man who is easily scared."

Quayle said: "Ernest might be right, Michael."

"I am invariably right," said Guelvada airily. "I think somebody has got something on ice for this man Callao; that in a moment he is going to be used for something."

Quayle said: "Possibly. I have no doubt that in due course all things will be made plain. In the meantime you might do a little work yourself, Ernest. You might keep a fatherly eye on Kiernan, Aurora Francis and Callao. Do what you think best. But keep it quiet."

Guelvada asked: "Have you ever known me to make a great deal of noise about anything? Always I have been distinguished for subtlety and quietness. . . ."

The telephone jangled. Frewin picked up the instrument. He listened for some minutes; then hung up the receiver. He said to Quayle: "This is rather interesting. Aurora Francis telephoned through to Antoinette Brown this morning. She wanted to see her. They lunched together at the Mordaunt Hotel. Aurora Francis was extremely confidential. She told Antoinette quite a lot about herself."

Quayle said: "Yes? Such as?"

"First of all," said Frewin, "she is going to marry Kiernan."

"Very interesting!" said Quayle. "When is this happy event to take place?"

"When Kiernan gets back on your staff." Frewin smiled at Quayle. "It looks as if my third guess was right."

Quayle said: "Your third guess . . . that was that Kiernan had interested himself in what Nielecki had to say, gave him that fifty pounds and then went down to see Kospovic, because he wanted to make a come-back with me. How does marriage to Aurora Francis prove that?"

"It doesn't," said Frewin. "But she also told Antoinette in the strictest confidence that Kiernan had made up his mind to find where the missing lists are; that he has an idea where they are; that he is going out after them. And that when he's finished the job he's going to bring them to you on a plate and see what you propose to do about it."

Quayle said: "I see. . . . Well, we couldn't have a better man working for us than Kiernan even if we're not supposed to know it."

Guelvada yawned. He looked extremely bored. Quayle looked at him quickly. He asked: "What's on your mind, Ernest?"

"Nothing," Guelvada answered. "Nothing at all . . . I was just thinking." He stubbed out his cigarette; picked up another from the silver box with slim, well-kept fingers.

Quayle said: "Don't be mysterious. What were you thinking?"

Guelvada shrugged his shoulders nonchalantly. "Consider Kiernan. Here is a man who is contained, self-reliant and strong. But definitely a man! We know his record. We know what he did in the war. As an agent he was quite superb. So this man meets Nielecki, who gives him some information, for which Kiernan gives him fifty pounds. Not a great deal of money, but still fifty pounds! After which he takes the trouble to go to see this Kospovic, who has so successfully killed himself. He then decides that, by reason of some special information which he has, he can possibly secure the two missing lists for you.

"And then what does he do? He tells a woman! Figure to yourself . . . he tells a woman. . . . Is that like him? Is that like Kiernan?"

Frewin said: "Remember that the woman he told was the woman whom he proposes to marry."

"I'm remembering that," said Guelvada. "But I don't like it. As the Americans say, it stinks, hey?"

Quayle said: "You might be right—or wrong! Kiernan might be doing what he says he's doing. Personally, I shouldn't be surprised if that were so. In any event, he wasn't to know that Aurora Francis would run off and tell Antoinette Brown."

Guelvada got up. "These are merely ideas of mine. They probably mean nothing, although," he continued, with a smile, "I am considered to have an extremely good brain. Actually, I never understand why I have not been approached by the Brain Trust. The reason is probably jealousy!"

He went to the door. With his hand on the door knob he turned. "I will, as you suggest, keep a fatherly eye on our friends Kiernan, Aurora and Vincente Callao. Michael here tells me that Aurora is beautiful. That appeals to me very much. I like to keep an eye on beautiful woman. Does that meet with your approval?"

Quayle nodded. "Yes, Ernest. If you are as tactful and discreet as usual they won't even know what's happening. But don't take any definite step outside observation without letting me know all about it."

Guelvada flicked an invisible speck of dust from the lapel of his coat. "Of course. . . . It may be that I may need some assistance. If so—?"

"Goddard will give you any one on his staff whom you may need. If you want help, call him. I'll give him instructions."

"Thank you," said Guelvada. "There is one other little thing. The girl Antoinette Brown. I remember her. A most seductive and pleasant person. One might almost say that she is at times quite fascinating. I think that I might desire also to use her services."

Frewin said quickly: "Brown's working with me. I'm using her as a contact with Aurora Francis."

Guelvada smiled politely. He looked at Frewin. "I consider that her use as a contact with the beautiful Francis is almost concluded. If you ask me why I shall not tell you. On this matter, at the moment, I propose to keep my trap very well and truly shut. It is essential, I think, that I have the use of Brown."

Quayle said: "If you want to use Brown, Ernie, do so. Michael here will tell her. She's staying at the Mordaunt Hotel. You can get her there."

"Excellent," said Guelvada. "I remember this Antoinette in Nuremberg. I consider that she has possibilities both as a co-operator in my work, and, possibly, as a woman. I think she will be very pleased to work with me."

He regarded Frewin with self-satisfaction.

Frewin said sarcastically: "You hate yourself, Ernest, don't you?"

Guelvada shrugged. "No. . . . But I am of extremely good value. Especially with women who adore me. And why not? I am a man of personality. Also I make love with the most effective and charming technique. Me . . . I am a wolf in wolf's clothing! You're telling me. . . ."

He smiled at them both; went out.

Frewin said: "I wonder what he's got in his head. And I hope he's not going to upset Brown at the wrong moment."

Quayle looked at him sideways. "Guelvada's got an idea all right. And I've discovered that his hunches are usually correct. As for Brown—well, you remember you said that she was inclined to be a little bit of a hypocrite. Perhaps Ernest might be good for her. Still . . . I'm glad to see that you take such an interest in her. . . . I like my staff to be happy about each other!"

He grinned wickedly at Frewin.

Frewin said: "I don't give a damn one way or the other."

He went out of the room.

Quayle sighed happily. He lighted a cigarette; leaned back in his chair.

He began to think about Kiernan.

At seven o'clock Guelvada stepped into Antoinette Brown's sitting-room at the Mordaunt Hotel. He was immaculate in a dinner suit. He carried his black soft hat and silk-lined evening overcoat. Antoinette wondered how, in these days, Guelvada managed to be so well dressed. She qualified the query with the thought that Guelvada was the sort of man who usually did what he wanted to do.

This evening she looked very attractive, he thought. She wore a well-cut, red, dinner frock. Her hair was done in a new style. There was an orchid in her corsage. She had omitted to put on her glasses.

An expression of supreme admiration came over Guelvada's lace. He said: "Miss Brown, I am extremely honoured that you are assisting me in my work. Mr. Quayle told me that I could rely on your best co-operation. But, first of all I must tell you that I consider you are a most beautiful woman. When I came into the room and saw you, for a moment my heart stood still."

She said: "Really, Mr. Guelvada!"

He came a few steps into the room; put up his hand. "Please don't be unduly concerned. Consider, Miss Brown . . . or perhaps it would be better if I called you Antoinette . . . consider that I have seen alluring, attractive and beautiful women all over the world, but that I had to come to the Mordaunt Hotel in England to see the most superb of them all."

Antoinette laughed. "You say the most ridiculous things, Mr. Guelvada. But you say them as if you meant them. One might almost think that you actually believed what you were saying."

He raised his eyebrows. "Always," he said pleasantly, "I tell the truth. Always I believe what I am saying at any given moment. It is much more convenient. For myself, I never tell lies . . . much."

She asked: "Would you like a cocktail or a cigarette?"

"I would like both. . . . Because, having told you of my personal feelings for you, I think the time has come when we should talk a little business. Hey, baby?" He put his overcoat and hat on an arm-chair.

She went to the sideboard; poured out the cocktails from the shaker; brought one to Guelvada. He went over to the fireplace; stood, his cocktail glass in his hand, looking at her.

He said: "Sit down, Antoinette."

She sat down. She thought Guelvada was an interesting personality. She liked quite a lot about him. His immaculate clothes, the manner he assumed, the almost childish delight he took in his own personality. But Antoinette had heard of the real Guelvada underneath—the quick brain, the utter ruthlessness. A good friend; a dangerous enemy.

She asked: "What do you want me to do?"

Guelvada shrugged his shoulders. "I am not quite sure, because if you know anything about all this business, you will realise that at the moment everything is merely a matter of personalities. Nobody quite knows what anybody else is doing." He smiled. "I have some vague ideas. Perhaps you may help me to decide whether they are right or wrong."

"Of course," she said. "I wonder what your ideas are?"

Guelvada said: "I'm interested in Kiernan, in your friend Aurora Francis, and especially in Vincente Callao. Consider to yourself. . . . Kiernan is a man who is strong, intelligent, very clever. He is a man who has always been interested in women, but who never stays with one. Then we have Aurora Francis, who is beautiful and alluring and clever, but tough, I am told. Lastly, we have Vincente, who has a flair for music and women and beyond that nothing at all. These three people are concerned together in something. It is obvious that Kiernan is out for what he wants, hey. He will get it at any cost. Francis, your lovely friend, believes that she is going to marry Kiernan." Guelvada shrugged his shoulders again. "It may be that I am wrong," he continued; "but I cannot see Kiernan tying himself to any woman. These two have something in common that concerns Callao. That is what I believe."

Guelvada spread his hands. "It may be that Kiernan believes that Callao knows who has the missing lists; that he may know where they are. For myself I desire only to find something from which I may start working. This is how you can help me. First of all, tell me what you think about Kiernan."

She said: "I know now about his record in the war. But my own personal knowledge of him is merely that of a secretary. I did some clerical work for him at Nuremberg."

Guelvada asked: "Did he make a pass at you?"

She shook her head. "Not actually. He's too clever to do that. Not with someone who was working on his staff, but"—she hesitated—"I think he was a little interested."

Guelvada nodded. "You must understand, Antoinette, that we must handle this thing with hooks. It would be very unwise if we allowed Kiernan to think that we were too much occupied by him. My idea is this: I understand from my good Michael that this morning Aurora Francis came to you here and said that she was going to marry Kiernan at some time or other. Then she told you in confidence that Kiernan had an idea where these missing lists are; that he proposed to do his best to find them so that he may once again be appointed to Quayle's staff.

"Now,"—he wagged a well-groomed finger at her—"supposing for the sake of argument, Antoinette, that you were very much in love with Anthony Kiernan; that you had fallen in love with him when you worked for him in Nuremberg but, being a shy, modest person, you had kept your feelings to yourself. But now you are angry. You are angry because Aurora Francis has told you that she is going to marry him. Supposing," said Guelvada, with a wicked smile, "she had also told you that she did not love him, but that she was marrying him because she thought it was a good thing to do. You understand, hey?"

She said: "Yes, I understand. Well, supposing that—"

"What then would be the normal thing for you to do?" asked Guelvada.

"If I felt strongly enough about it I might even go and talk to him." She smiled. "Women get very jealous of each other."

Guelvada nodded. "Precisely! . . . Now, figure to yourself that I have wasted no time. I have discovered all about the layout of the apartment in Charles Street where Kiernan is living. It is an old-fashioned house. The front door is locked, but I have a key that will open it. Sometimes when the housekeeper goes out for a few minutes she leaves the door on the latch. The door of Kiernan's rooms, which are on the ground floor, is not locked. So we select a time when he goes out. You let yourself into the house. You go quietly to his apartment and you search. If Kiernan should return you tell him that you had his address from Aurora; that you were passing and found the front door open; that you could not resist the temptation to come in and tell him that this woman whom he proposes to marry is not in love with him. If he asks you why you've taken this trouble you tell him it is because you have always cared for him."

Antoinette sighed. She said: "Oh, dear. . . ."

Guelvada went on: "Every man is easily flattered by a woman who tells him that she loves him. Kiernan would be so amazed at this admission coming from such a delightful, modest person as yourself, that he would not be inclined to think too much of your waiting for him in his rooms."

She said: "Don't you think it might be a little dangerous for me, Mr. Guelvada?"

"Of course," said Guelvada. "Everything is dangerous, Antoinette. Even I am very dangerous. But the worst that could happen to you would be that he might kiss you a little."

She said: "I see. . . . And what am I searching for in his rooms?"

Guelvada spread his hands. "I don't know. But consider to yourself . . . there is always some small and innocent thing—the sort of thing that a man forgets to hide because he thinks it doesn't matter—which gives you a clue. I remember once . . ." He shrugged his shoulders and stopped. "That is an old story and does not matter. The thing for you to do is to search through his rooms; to look for anything—any document, letter or paper—which you think may have any bearing whatsoever on this business in which we are engaged. I will try and arrange your visit so that you have some time at your disposal."

"Supposing I am discovered by someone in the house?" asked Antoinette.

"That is simple," said Guelvada. "You will say that he gave you the key and asked you to wait for him. Is all this understood?"

She nodded. "I understand. When do you think that you'll want me to do this?"

"I don't know," said Guelvada. "The sooner the better. There may be an opportunity to-night. In the meantime I suggest that you remain here and wait for a telephone call. I hope," he went on earnestly, "that you had not an important engagement for this evening. With some boy friend. I notice that you are supremely dressed."

"Mr. Frewin had asked me to have dinner with him," she said. "I'll telephone him."

Guelvada looked a picture of misery. "But how terrible," he said. "I am so sorry. But duty calls and the unfortunate Frewin, who is so very much attracted to you, will have to wait."

"You're quite wrong," said Antoinette. "Mr. Frewin really dislikes me. He thinks I'm a good operative, but that is all."

"Like hell," said Guelvada. "The man Frewin goes for you in a big way. He was angry because I wished you to work with me. A spot of jealousy . . . the green-eyed goddess . . . hey? But never mind. There will be another time."

She said: "Of course, Mr. Guelvada."

He picked up his overcoat and hat. Then he went over to Antoinette; took her hand; kissed her fingers gracefully.

He said: "Antoinette, I think you are quite divine. I would go further than that . . . you're some baby, hey? I'll be seeing you!"

He went out.

At nine o'clock Frewin stopped his car in a side street in Chelsea. He locked it; crossed the road. He went through the gateway of a small detached house; took out his keyring; let himself in. He closed the door; switched on the light; walked through the long passage that led towards the back of the house. He knocked at a door at the end of the passage; entered the room.

The walls of the room were lined with steel filing cabinets, and a battery of telephones stood on the mantelpiece. In one corner were two tele-type machines.

Quayle sat at the big table at the far end of the room. He said: "Good evening, Michael. Is anything wrong?"

"I think so," said Frewin. "I know you don't like being disturbed when you're working here in this holy of holies, but I'm worried."

Quayle asked: "About the Kiernan business?"

Frewin nodded. He sat down in a chair opposite Quayle's table; lighted a cigarette. He said: "I know that you don't tell people more than you have to tell them and I know that sometimes it suits your book to appear to be vague. I don't profess to know what's going on in your mind over this Kiernan business except of course what you've indicated." Frewin smiled suddenly. "And you very often say something and mean something else. But I don't understand what Guelvada's doing."

"What is he doing?" asked Quayle. "I told him to do nothing, except keep Francis, Kiernan and Callao under observation."

"He tried to see you," said Frewin. "But you couldn't be found, so he got in touch with me. I said I'd talk to you about it. There's still time to stop what he proposes to do."

Quayle exhaled tobacco smoke. "Exactly what does he propose to do?"

Frewin shrugged his shoulders. "It seems that Guelvada discovered that Kiernan's leaving London to-night. He had his car oiled and fuelled. He told the garage he was taking it out at eleven-thirty to-night and wouldn't be back until some time in the morning. On the strength of this information Guelvada has a stupid idea about Brown searching Kiernan's rooms. He proposes to send her there to-night."

Quayle asked: "To find what?"

"Precisely," said Frewin. "To find what? Guelvada has an idea that there may be something in Kiernan's room which will give him a pointer. I asked him what would happen if Kiernan returned suddenly and found Brown there. And he explained to me that he'd give her some sort of story about being jealous of Francis marrying Kiernan; that she herself was keen on him; that she'd come round and waited for him to tell him that Aurora Francis wasn't really in love with him. It sounded rather phoney to me."

Quayle said: "All the true things in life sound phoney. I remember noticing when Antoinette Brown was acting as Kiernan's secretary in Nuremberg that he took more than a passing interest in her. Brown, as you know, is not an ordinary type. It could easily be that she was keen on Kiernan and that, Francis having told her all about this marriage business, she would be a little jealous. Women do all sorts of strange things. I don't think the story's too bad."

"I thought the whole idea stupid," said Frewin. "Kiernan might get very tough with Antoinette if he came back and found her there."

"How could he?" asked Quayle. "I think he's much too clever." He got up, exhaling clouds of tobacco smoke. He began to walk about the room. "I don't think the idea's stupid. Even the cleverest person is inclined to slip up sometimes. It might be that Antoinette will find something there which will give us an indication."

Frewin said: "All right. An indication of what?"

"I don't know," said Quayle.

Frewin stubbed out his cigarette in the ash-tray on the desk. "I wonder what's going on in your mind. You pretended to accept the theory that what Kiernan told Aurora Francis was true; that he had an idea that he might find those lists; that if he found them and returned them to you he'd do himself a lot of good. He'd get back on your staff. If you believed that why have his rooms searched?"

Quayle stopped walking. He looked at Frewin. "I didn't say I believed it. I never believe anything until I know."

Frewin said: "I see. So there's a possibility that you don't believe Kiernan's story?"

"Of course," said Quayle. "There are all sorts of possibilities in life."

"And yet," said Frewin, "you said that it wouldn't be a bad thing to have a first-class man like Kiernan working for us."

Quayle smiled. "I think Kiernan is working for us. I didn't say he knew he was. Is that all, Michael?"

Frewin got up. "That's all. If you approve of this thing I'll telephone through to Guelvada and tell him that it's all right."

Quayle said: "I do approve. I don't see that any harm can come of it and it might do a lot of good. Get in touch with me at the other office some time to-morrow, Michael."

"Very well," said Frewin. "Good night."

He went out. Quayle thought that he looked very unhappy.

He went back to the desk; sat down in the big arm-chair; relaxed. He sat there, the cigar stuck between his teeth, looking at the ceiling. After a while he got up. He went to the mantelpiece; picked up a telephone; began to dial a number.

*

Aurora Francis stood in front of the cheval-glass in her bedroom. She was amused with life. She liked the subdued lighting of the room, the pinkish-white colour of the walls, the quiet tones of the rugs and furniture. But more than this she liked the picture of herself in the mirror.

She wore a black evening frock of heavy silk. Over it a long, clinging, velvet cloak caught with a jewelled clasp. Her dark hair framed the attractive whiteness of her face. She thought that life was beginning to be really exciting. She thought that you never knew what was waiting round the corner.

Kiernan, she thought, was amusing; magnetic. There was something about him that was very attractive—so attractive that it was sometimes difficult to realise the extreme toughness that lay beneath the pleasant exterior. Yet, Aurora considered, most women would fall for him. He possessed that peculiar, indefinable something that women of all types and classes like in a man.

Actually, thought Aurora, Kiernan was not unlike Callao. He was a tougher, more cynical, brainier specimen. Yet, basically, the two men, strange as it might seem, were not unlike.

Kiernan was a little fear-producing; that was all. He had something that would frighten most women; and, in being frightened, they would be the more attracted.

She wondered if she were afraid of Kiernan. The thought made her smile and shrug her shoulders.

She began to think about Callao. Callao was amusing, but infinitely more amusing now that he had taken his place in the scheme which Kiernan and she had concocted for him. She felt a certain pity for Vincente Callao. As she looked at her wrist-watch, saw that it was midnight, the telephone rang. She went over to the instrument; took off the receiver. She heard Kiernan's voice.

He said: "He's gone home. Get cracking, Aurora. Good luck and don't pull your punches."

She said softly: "Darling, I won't. Good night, my sweet."

She hung up; waited a moment; dialled Callao's number. After a moment his voice came on the telephone. She spoke softly but urgently.

She said quickly: "Vincente, this is Aurora. I called you because I had to tell you how utterly sorry I was for what happened on Saturday night. I can't tell you how I detest that man; how I admire you for your restraint."

"What could I do?" said Callao. "I was very unhappy. Never in my life has such a thing happened to me."

She said: "I realised that the only thing to do was to get him away from your apartment. I had a great deal of trouble with him. Yet for some reason I attract him." She laughed. "Not that that matters. I was very rude to him. But, Vincente . . . I am afraid . . ."

"Yes? . . . Of what are you afraid, Aurora?" he asked.

She said: "A little for myself, but more for you." Her voice softened. "Vincente, I'm very fond of you. You must know that."

"I theenk you are a very lovely person," said Callao. "I never had an opportunity to tell you—not in the way I wanted. But tell me, why are you afraid for me?"

"I can't tell you on the telephone. I must see you, Vincente. I must talk to you. I think he's going to be away for a few days. I want to talk to you before he comes back. Can I come round now?"

He said: "But of course. . . ."

She noticed a certain relief in his voice. She thought he was happier with Kiernan away from London.

He went on: "Come round at once, my sweet. I will make you some of that coffee which you like. Then you can talk to me. Then I will play you some music."

She said: "Dear-dear Vincente. I'm coming now."

She hung up the receiver.

Ten minutes afterward she paid off the cab at the end of Clarges Street; walked towards Callao's apartment. He was standing just inside the doorway.

He said: "Come in, Aurora. You don't know how glad I am to see you. I am a leetle worried about you. Come upstairs. I weel give you some coffee."

Upstairs, he busied himself at the coffee percolator. She took off her mink coat; threw it across a chair.

She said: "Aren't you going to kiss me, Vincente? You're not too worried to do that, are you?"

He turned; looked at her. He said: "You know, you are the mos' lovely thing." He took her in his arms.

After a minute she said: "That's enough. Now, give me the coffee. I've got to talk to you, Vincente. You and I might easily be in trouble, possibly in danger—you for one reason and I because I'm fond enough of you to come here and warn you."

He gave her the coffee cup. He said: "Sit down. Tell me . . ."

He sat in the chair opposite her. She thought that he looked a little scared.

She asked: "Are you frightened, Vincente?"

He shrugged his shoulders. "I think that life ees a ver' frightening theeng . . . and for me—a foreigner in a strange country. . . . I don' want to get into any trouble. Why don' you tell me what it ees about?"

She said: "Vincente, I wondered why Kiernan came here the other night. Do you know anything about him?"

"Not much. . . . I met him once in Lisbon in the war. He was mixed up with some commercial business. You know the English were buying lots of things at that time from the Portuguese. I was told he had something to do with some Purchasing Commission."

She said: "That was a lie. Kiernan's a secret service agent."

He raised his eyebrows. "So! And why because he ees a secret service agent does he have to come round to my flat and attack me?"

"I think he did that because he wanted to frighten you."

He nodded. "All right. So let us imagine that he succeeded a leetle. Let us imagine that I am a leetle frightened. So what then?"

She said: "Now he does something else. It seems, Vincente, that there were two lists—important lists of war criminals which had been compiled and sealed by the Allied Crime Commission. These lists were stolen. Apparently the British Secret Service have been looking for them ever since."

Callao said: "All right." He drank some coffee. "I still don' see what this has to do with me."

She asked: "Don't you? Is that really true, Vincente?"

"Of course it ees true. Why should I bother to tell a lie about such a thing?"

She said: "Kiernan says that you have those lists; that he's going to get them from you. He's serious about it and you know, Vincente, he's a very dangerous man."

He said: "I don' know anything about thees. I don' know anything about any leest."

"Vincente, you don't have to lie to me," said Aurora gravely. "You don't have to pretend about anything. The greatest proof of my affection for you is that I am here to warn you. The easiest thing for you to do, if you have those lists, would be to hand them over to Kiernan. He said you were leaving the country shortly. He said you had a contract to play with your band somewhere in Spain. He said you would be taking the lists out with you."

Callao sat back in his chair. She could see the little beads of sweat on his forehead. She thought that he scared very easily.

He said: "I tell you I don' know anything about these leest. I don' even know what Kiernan ees playing at." He looked at her. "Maybe he ees trying to, what they call, frame me, hey? Maybe he ees going to pretend that I have them because he cannot find them. Thees clever secret service agent . . . he ees going to make a monkey out of me and say that I have them."

She said: "Why should he do a thing like that, Vincente? Why don't you be sensible? The best thing for you to do would be to talk to Kiernan. If you have those lists or if you have any idea where they are, why don't you tell him? It would be the easiest thing in the long run; otherwise I think he might make things very difficult for you."

He asked: "What could he do?"

"I don't know. . . . But he could do a lot of things. Possibly the authorities would stop you leaving the country. Perhaps they'd put you in prison. They could do all sorts of things."

"Even if I told them that I did not know anything about these cursed theengs?" Callao was almost angry.

She said: "That would be the very obvious thing for you to say, wouldn't it, Vincente? But it doesn't mean that they'd believe you." She leaned back in her chair. "And Kiernan's a very clever man. I can't see him making an accusation against you unless he'd got some evidence behind it."

Callao said: "I'm so unhappy. I just don' understand anything at all about thees. I don't know anything about it. Always I am unhappy through a woman. Because I am attracted to you this man comes to my flat and knocks me about. Now I am to be accused of having stolen secret leest about which I know nothing. Ees there no end to my misery?"

She thought that Callao was a little boring. Some men lacked spirit when they were frightened. And Callao was certainly frightened.

She said: "I mustn't stay here too long, Vincente. But remember what I have said. If you know anything about those lists be advised by me and tell him—or tell me." She paused; then: "Could you give me a cigarette?"

He got up and went to the table; brought back a box of cigarettes. He lighted one for her.

She went on: "Listen, Vincente. Kiernan told me that those lists were worth an awful lot of money. He said that there were people in Europe who would pay a great deal for them. If you've got them or if you know where they are, why don't you do the obvious thing?"

He said: "I tell you I don' know anything about them. But supposing I did, what ees the obvious thing?"

She leaned forward. "Vincente, I'm very much attracted to you. I'd like to be with you. Why don't we get those lists out of the country and sell them? If they suspect you, they won't suspect me. Give them to me. When you leave they'll be interested in you but not in me. Because Kiernan thinks I'm fond of him. I had to pretend I was. That's how I got all this out of him—simply so that I could come here and tell you. Why don't we do that?"

"Eet ees ver' nice of you," said Callao. "I theenk you are sweet to theenk about such a thing. But eet ees not possible because I don' know anything about those leest. I don' want to. All I want to do ees to play my music. If I do anything else something always happens to me."

She got up. "I must go, Vincente." Her voice changed. "I don't think you're being very sensible about this. Here's my address and telephone number. If you change your mind, telephone me."

He helped her on with her coat.

He said: "How can I change my mind? I have told you the trut'. I know nothing about thees."

She went close to him. "Vincente, I think you're a fool, and not a very brave fool either. And men who are fools and not very brave are clever when they're cautious. Be advised by me. Do what Kiernan says. You'll be safer. Good night, Vincente."

She kissed him lightly on the chin and went out of the room. He heard her high heels tapping down the stairs. The front door closed behind her.

He sat down in the chair. His hands hung immobile over his knees. Tears came into his eyes.

He felt very sorry for himself.

Antoinette Brown walked quickly out of Berkeley Square towards Charles Street. It was a cold, moonlit night. She thought the shadows on the pavements caused by the high houses were attractive and somehow romantic.

She turned into Charles Street. Only then did she bring her mind to bear on the business in hand. To her the search in Kiernan's rooms meant little. It was "one of those things." Often before, especially during the war years, Antoinette, because of her diffidence, her placid appearance, her air of innocence, had been selected to do such work. But in those days it was possibly easier. Life was different. The services which Quayles controlled had more power and authority than in these so-called days of peace.

Antoinette, who liked completing a job quietly and effectively without vexing ramifications, hoped that Kiernan would not return. She wondered what would happen if he did. She mentally shrugged her shoulders. Already she had rehearsed in her mind her version of the story that Guelvada had suggested to her. She smiled a little cynically. Whether Kiernan would believe such a story or not was another matter, but that, she thought, depended on her abilities as an actress which, as she knew well, were not inconsiderable.

The street was deserted. She reached the house; took the key which Guelvada had given her from her handbag; opened the front door; closed it and left it unlatched. The electric light was on in the hall. She moved swiftly and very quietly towards the door at the end of the passage which ran from the front to the back of the house, which she knew was the door of Kiernan's sitting-room. There was no sound in the house. The housekeeper, she thought, would be asleep and any one in the rooms upstairs would be too far away to be disturbed.

She closed the door of Kiernan's sitting-room behind her; found the light switch; snapped it on. She noted with relief that the curtains were drawn. She looked around the sitting-room; went into the bedroom, into the bathroom, back into the sitting-room. She stood in the middle of the floor, considered the situation. She thought it was rather amusing to be searching for something— something which one would probably not recognise even if one found it. But at the back of her mind was the idea that Ernest Guelvada was right in suggesting that she should look for an incongruity—something which was out of place. Even the most skilled operators—people with mentalities as quick and able as Kiernan's—would often leave some small indication.

She looked around the room. It was orderly, and the writing-table in the corner was bare except for the blotter, the ink-stand and rack for notepaper and envelopes.

Antoinette took off her coat; put it on a chair. She kept on her gloves from force of habit, because fingerprints might in any event be inconvenient, and went to work. She heard a neighboring clock strike two before she had finished with the sitting-room, in which she had found nothing at all. Kiernan, as she had imagined, was meticulously tidy. Such papers as were in the drawer of the writing-table were innocent and neatly put away. She admitted to herself that he was the sort of man who made a search an easy process.

She went into the bedroom. She was there half an hour. She found nothing. Guelvada, she thought, had possibly underestimated his man. Then, as a final gesture, she went into the bathroom; snapped on a light. On the glass shelf before the shaving mirror, Kiernan's toilet articles were arranged in orderly fashion. At one end was the razor stand with a safety razor, a brush and soap. Something caught her eye.

She walked over to the shelf; picked up the printed account form which rested against the mirror behind the razor stand. It was obvious that Kiernan had propped the account against the mirror to examine it whilst he was shaving. Antoinette thought that it could be important. It was an account for £27 14s. 6d. for repairs done, and the heading indicated that it had been sent by a firm of marine motor engineers with an address at Rye in Sussex. Antoinette made a mental note of the account; replaced the sheet of paper; took a final look around the bathroom; snapped off the light, went through the bedroom into the sitting-room. She stopped on the threshold.

Aurora Francis stood in the middle of the room looking at her. She said, not unpleasantly: "Good evening, Antoinette. It's nice seeing you."

Antoinette thought: This is it! I wonder if I can get away with this. She thought here was something which even the quick brain of Guelvada had not foreseen—the possibility of Aurora coming to Kiernan's rooms. Antoinette's face was almost severe as she looked at her friend.

She said: "Good evening. I suppose you wonder what I'm doing here?"

Aurora shrugged her shoulders. "Naturally. Have you been here long? I see you left your fur coat on the chair here. What have you been doing, my dear—taking a little look around? I wonder if you'd like to tell me what all this is in aid of." Her smile was cynical.

She turned her back on Antoinette; walked to the sideboard. She took up the cocktail shaker; began to mix a cocktail.

Antoinette said: "It's going to be rather difficult to explain to you why I am here. I doubt if you'll believe what I have to say."

Aurora went on with her cocktail mixing. She did not even turn her head. She said: "I find anything difficult to believe, my dear, especially where another woman is concerned."

Antionette thought to herself: "Good. Perhaps she's already got the idea in her head. Perhaps Guelvada wasn't such a fool.

"That's rather a funny remark, isn't it, Aurora?" She came into the room; picked up her fur coat; put it on. She said with a smile: "You're not actually considering me as a rival for Anthony Kiernan, are you?"

Aurora turned around. She stood leaning against the sideboard, jiggling the shaker in her hand. She looked at Antoinette. It was a long, embracing look. She poured out the cocktail; drank a little of it.

She said: "My experience has taught me never to trust anybody who doesn't wear trousers, and you don't. The possibility occurred to me that you were a two-faced little bitch; that this air of innocence of yours was a very definite disguise and a possible protection." Her eyes gleamed. "You were Tony's secretary in Nuremberg. Don't tell me that he didn't make the usual pass at you that he makes at most women who aren't actually repulsive."

Antoinette said: "If Anthony made a pass at me in Nuremberg he never got anywhere with it. But that doesn't mean that I couldn't be fond of him."

Aurora shrugged her shoulders. "Of course. He's the sort of man you would be fond of, probably because he wouldn't take very much notice of you—not unless he was extremely bored. Now I can understand why you joined him in the cocktail bar after you left me at the Cockatoo the night we had dinner. I suppose you wanted to see just what he was thinking about you nowadays; whether you still had a chance."

Antoinette thought: It's all right. You're getting away with it, my girl. Take it easy. Let her do most of the talking.

She said: "Supposing I did? Why shouldn't I?" Her voice sounded a little bitter.

"You don't really consider, my dear, that you've a chance with Kiernan, do you?" asked Aurora. "Do you think he'd be bothered with a person like you, who could best be described as mouse-like, with occasional flashes of something that might possibly be attractive? He'd be bored stiff with you in three months." She laughed. "Even if you are fool enough to come round to his rooms hoping that you'll find him here. Or did you consider that the lateness of the hour, and the fact that Kiernan usually drinks a little in the evening, might have influenced him to a more favourable frame of mind towards you?"

She finished her cocktail; put the glass down on the sideboard. She helped herself to a cigarette from the box on the mantelpiece; lighted it; stood regarding Antoinette coolly.

Antoinette said: "I suppose it never occurred to you that I might have come here for some other purpose than to persuade Anthony Kiernan to make love to me?"

"No," said Aurora. "I wonder what the excuse is going to be. Tell me . . . I should like to hear it."

Antoinette said in a hard voice: "The excuse is you. You've always treated me in a rather patronising way, Aurora. I know you consider that I'm not nearly as attractive as you are; that I haven't your allure, your beauty, your sense of power. To you, I'm just a rather small and insignificant person—somebody who can be made a confidante of; treated rather disdainfully if you feel like it. I suppose you feel towards me, Aurora, as you would towards a superior sort of secretary or something like that. I suppose it never occurred to you that I might have some feelings—decent feelings. But of course you wouldn't know anything about decent feelings."

"No?" Aurora's voice was dangerous. "So I don't know anything about decent feelings, and you are an authority on the subject. Exactly what do you mean by that?"

Antoinette shrugged her shoulders. "You're just an experimenter with men. When you arrived in London you were interested in Callao. When you found Kiernan had arrived you were interested in him. You're interested in any man. You play men as an angler plays fishes. All you want to do is to satisfy your curiosity, then take yourself off to some other man. You're not fit to associate with a man as good as Kiernan. This man is a strong, brave man who has run grave risks for his country. He deserves something better than a person like you."

Aurora sneered. "I see. . . . So it's just jealousy."

"Why not?" said Antoinette. "Why shouldn't I be jealous? I'm jealous of the fact that Anthony believes in you sufficiently to want you to marry him. I think he's worth something more."

Aurora said: "Now I understand. So you came round to tell him that."

Antoinette gave an inward sigh of relief. She realised that her line of dialogue had been successful.

"You don't think I came round for anything else, do you?" she asked. "I'm not that sort of person. I don't haunt men's rooms at half-past two in the morning. I leave that to people like you."

Aurora said: "I see. . . ."

"I'm glad you do. I came round here to tell Kiernan what I thought about you; what I knew about you. If it weren't Anthony, it would be Callao or if not Callao someone else. What do you care?"

Aurora laughed. "I am amused by this idea of yours that Kiernan, who loves me and whom I love, should be protected against me by you."

Antoinette said: "He may be fond of you, but you don't care for him. You're just using him. He'll find out, but I think somebody ought to warn him."

Aurora moved away from the fireplace. "And you've taken it upon yourself to do it. Well, I suggest there are other and better times for the process. You might have telephoned him; come round and seen him in the morning. I'm sure he would have been very glad to see you. It would have given him a big laugh for the day—something that he could have told me about."

Antoinette said with a modest air: "I was wrong to come at this time. I never intended to come round here. When I came out to-night I went for a walk because I was unhappy. I came past this place because I wanted to see where he lives; because, believe it or not, I can be fond of a man in a way that you can't even imagine. When I got here I thought I'd ring the bell on the chance of finding him up. The front door was open; so I came in."

"All right," said Aurora. "Having said your piece you'd better get out. I don't think when Kiernan returns he'll be very interested in what you have to say, but if it'll give you any satisfaction I'll tell him myself. I'll get him to telephone you if you like and tell you what he thinks about it."

Antoinette said: "That's what you say now. But I know that, in addition to your other attributes, you can be a liar, Aurora. You won't tell him that because you're hoping that I won't try to see him again."

"So I'm a liar, am I?" Aurora took two quick steps towards Antoinette. She smacked her across the face. "And now you get out, you poor little fool, and do what you like. Do you think I care? But be advised by me and keep out of my way. I don't like you. I don't like your mouse-like air of innocence; your maidenly charm. I think, inside, you're very different. You make me feel rather sick. Get out. . . ."

Antoinette sighed. She said in a meek voice: "I never thought you'd strike me, Aurora. But apparently I'm one of those people whose motives are always misunderstood. Good night." She went out.

Aurora waited till she heard the front door close. She mixed herself another cocktail. She went into the bedroom; took off her fur coat; threw it across the bed. She went back into the sitting-room; drank the cocktail; lighted a cigarette. She turned on the electric fire; pushed the big arm-chair in front of it.

She sat down. She waited for Kiernan.

Callao opened his eyes; switched on the bedside light; decided that that was not enough illumination for his frame of mind; switched on more lights. The colouring from the walls and furniture of the room came back at him; made his eyes tired. He turned the lights off, except the one by the bedside.

He was scared and his head was aching. Callao, like most of his type, indulged in intense fits of self-pity when things were not going his way and, he thought, they were certainly not going his way. He wished that he had never seen Aurora Francis.

He was afraid. More than afraid because he did not know what was frightening him. Uncertainty, he thought, was the worst thing of all, and he could understand nothing. He began to think of what Aurora Francis had said to him a few hours before. Behind everything she said was a threat and behind the threats was the ominous figure of Kiernan. Callao began to think about Kiernan. He remembered hearing about him in Lisbon during the war—tough, ruthless, cynical and bitter. That was Kiernan! Disguising a steel mentality behind a face of smiling bonhomie. A dangerous man.

Many people had told Callao that, but he had never visualised the time when he would find himself up against this personality. What, he thought, could be in Kiernan's mind? What was all this business about lists, of which Callao knew nothing? All this was part of some scheme; some deep and subtle scheme which Kiernan was playing for his own ends. His own ends or those of the British Secret Service. In any event, whatever it was, it did not matter. The results would probably be the same.

Callao tossed about from one side of the bed to the other. His pillows were hot. He was wretched; unhappy.

Also, he thought, he was unlucky. In a few days he was to leave England—this cold, desolate and rather grim country—to go back to his own beloved Spain, where the sun shone. Why had he not gone earlier? Why had he waited for this? Callao, who was superstitious, saw some grim hand of fate behind his meeting with Aurora Francis.

He stiffened. He heard a sound in the flat. There was the sound of a door shutting quietly. Beads of sweat stood out on his forehead. He sat up in bed. He heard steps in the long sitting-room outside—quiet steps. Then the door in the iron lattice between the end of the sitting-room and his bedroom opened.

Kiernan stood in the doorway. He wore a short leather jacket with a dark fur collar. A tweed cap was pulled over one eye. A cigarette hung out of the corner of his mouth. He was smiling.

He said: "Good morning, Vincente. How are you?"

"What ees it you want with me?" asked Callao. "What goes on? All the time you haunt me like some ghost. What ees it you want wit me? I have never done anything to you. I am a quiet man. I don' want trouble. What does all this mean?"

"I've come here to tell you," said Kiernan. "It's quite interesting. Suppose you get up and put on a dressing-gown—probably a very beautiful one, carefully chosen for your lady friends. Then you can come outside and make some of that coffee for which you are so famed. I want to talk to you."

Callao said: "Very well."

He got out of bed. Against the cream silk of his pyjamas his face seemed more swarthy than ever. The sweat glistened on his forehead. His hands were trembling.

Kiernan turned away; went into the sitting-room. When Callao arrived he was lounging back in one of the large arm-chairs. The room lights and the electric fire were switched on.

Kiernan said: "Make the coffee."

Callao went to the percolator. Kiernan watched him. A grim smile played about his mouth. He thought Callao was a push-over. He threw his cigarette stub into the grate; gave himself a fresh one.

He said: "Catch this. It'll do you good to smoke a cigarette. It might steady those nerves of yours. I've never known anybody so easily scared as you, you Spanish bastard."

Callao tried to catch the cigarette; missed it; picked it up from the floor; lighted it from the flame of the percolator.

"Sit down," said Kiernan.

Callao went to the chair opposite Kiernan. He sat down, his arms resting on the arms of the chair. He looked straight before him unblinkingly.

Kiernan said: "You listen to me, Vincente, and you listen carefully. If you do what I tell you, you're going to be all right. If you don't, it's going to be tough. Did you receive a visit from my girl friend to-night—Aurora?"

Vincente nodded. "Yes . . . she came here. She told me that you . . . she told me—"

Kiernan interrupted. "I know what she told you. She told you exactly what I told her to say." He laughed. "She told you what she believes. She came here and she told you that I was a secret service agent; that I knew that you had two missing lists of wanted war criminals—the original lists sealed by the War Crimes Commission—two lists which constitute the charge and the evidence against the people whose names are in them. She told you that you had them. Right?"

Callao nodded.

"She also told you," Kiernan went on, "that you'd never get those lists out of this country; that the best thing for you to do was to be a good boy, hand them over to me, and then everything would be all right. You told her of course that you didn't know what she was talking about. You told her that you'd never seen or heard of any lists; that she must be mad. Well, she expected you to say that. Probably she told you that it wouldn't help you to deny the fact; that the clever tiling for you to do would be to hand them over; that if you didn't you'd never get out of this country and that you'd probably find yourself in a prison cell for a few years. Right?"

Callao nodded. "Yes . . . that ees what she said. Of course none of it ees true. You know—"

Kiernan said: "I know it's not true. You don't have to tell me." He drew on his cigarette. "You listen carefully to me," he went on. "I'm going to tell you the truth. When I've told you the truth you'll know exactly where you are. But you've got to understand that Aurora Francis believes that what she said to you was true. She believes you've got those lists. I wanted to put it into her head that you had them. I was covering myself, you see."

"What do you mean?" asked Callao. "You were covering yourself? You mean—"

Kiernan said: "I mean I've got the lists." He smiled at Callao. "They're very valuable. They're worth a great deal of money—so much money that it almost makes me gasp. I intend to have it, and if you're very good you may get a little of it. I might even be generous enough to make it worth your while. If you're not good, God help you!"

Callao said nothing. He sat looking at Kiernan; then he ran his hands over his damp face.

He said: "I know you. You are a wicked man. I have heard about you. It ees not easy to fight with you. What ees it you want me to do?"

"Listen to me, Vincente, and I'll tell you. I'm up against a very clever man—a brilliant man. He's almost as clever as I am." Kiernan smiled at his thoughts. "A certain Mr. Quayle, who runs one of the secret service departments in this country. Quayle knew I was in Nuremberg when those lists disappeared. Quayle is a man who suspects everybody. He'd suspect his own mother if he thought it was his duty to do so. So I must come within the orbit of his suspicions. I finished working as an agent for this country after Nuremberg. I had those lists and they were much too dangerous for me to carry about with me. I had to get them over here." He grinned.

"That wasn't difficult," he went on. "They were sending over two or three European cheap-jacks that they wanted on ice in England. One of them was a man called Szlemy. I had a lot on Szlemy and he knew it, so I thought he was the person to bring the lists over here. It was all the more funny because I was in charge of the process of sending these people over. So I changed Szlemy's name and papers to Kospovic and when I'd got him safely on the boat, I gave him the lists. I knew there'd be no examination at the other end." He shrugged his shoulders.

"Kospovic got over here," he said, "and went down to the country where I told him to go. Before I came to London I went down there one night and got the lists from him. He wasn't very happy about that. He thought he was going to get something. He thought he was going to get some money and possibly British nationality." He grinned again. "You see, Callao, he thought I was still a British Secret Service agent. When he found he wasn't going to get anything; that the best I could promise him was that if he behaved himself he'd be all right, he must have got a little angry. So he did something very foolish. He talked. He told a man called Nielecki about the lists; that he knew who had them."

Kiernan's grin became more expansive. "I think that Nielecki didn't like Kospovic very much. He'd probably tried to make some sort of deal with him himself and Kospovic wasn't playing. So Nielecki told me."

Kiernan exhaled cigarette smoke. There was silence for a moment, except for the sound of the forgotten coffee percolator bubbling.

Then he went on: "My reason tells me that the conversation between Kospovic and Nielecki might have been interesting. If Kospovic was prepared to tell Nielecki that he knew who had the lists, he was certain to tell somebody else. Nielecki couldn't do anything for Kospovic. Kospovic would want to talk to somebody who could do something for him. My bet is that he probably talked to Quayle."

Callao said: "So . . . what has all this—"

"Shut up," said Kiernan. "You'll see in a minute." He threw his cigarette stub into the fireplace. "I suppose Nielecki must have told Kospovic that he'd told me. Kospovic got scared. He was right to be scared too. He knew what I'd do to him if I got after him. So he did a very convenient thing for me. He killed himself. That's excellent, isn't it? The man who brought the lists over for me—about the only person who could really have said anything definite against me—is dead. You understand?"

Callao nodded.

"Now," Kiernan continued, "my business is to get those lists out of this country. Not a very easy process for a man who may be suspected—not strongly but still suspected possibly a little— by the enterprising Mr. Quayle. So I have to be clever. There is where you come into it.

"Quayle knows that I've been getting around with Aurora Francis. The story is that I'm going to marry her. If I know anything of Quayle he'll believe that I'm using her as a stooge. Do you know what he'll believe, Callao? He'll believe that I'm going to use her to get the lists out of the country, because I wouldn't take a chance of them being found on me. That's why I told her that little story about you having the lists. Because she thinks she's going to marry me, she's going to do what I tell her. I've got that lady where I want her. So you're going to have the lists. I'm going to give them to you just to support my story to her that you had them all the time.

"And you're going to support my story even more by handing them over to her. Except that they're not going to be the real lists. They're going to be just some fake papers in a heavily sealed parchment envelope. I've got an idea that sooner or later Quayle is going to get to work on Aurora Francis when she tries to leave this country, which she'll do within the next day or two carrying those fake lists. He's not going to worry about me because I'm not supposed to be going to leave the country. But he's going to worry about her. They're going to let her get so far and they're going to pounce. They're going to open the parchment envelope and they're going to find some pieces of paper. Then they're going to look for me, but by that time you and I will be a long way away, my friend."

Callao said in a thick voice: "What do you mean? What are you going to do with me?"

"I'm not going to do anything," said Kiernan. "I'm just going to assist you on your journey. Some time ago, when I evolved this little scheme, because I knew how you go for women, and I knew you'd fall for Aurora Francis, I laid myself on a rather nice cabin cruiser. I was merely an agent acting for somebody—at least the vendors thought that. Do you know whom I bought it for? I bought it for Señor Vincente Jesu Maria Callao. How do you like that, Vincente? It's a nice boat. I've just had it serviced.

"On the day that Aurora Francis makes her preparations to leave this country, when everybody's attention is concentrated on her, you and I are going to take a little journey to the coast. We're going to do a night trip to France. Nobody's going to see us leave. Nobody's going to see us arrive. Once I'm there with those lists, I'm safe. There's a lot of money waiting for me. I've got rid of Aurora Francis, who's amusing but would bore me after a few months, and life will lie before me, in South America or somewhere like that, like one long dream. If you're good, as I told you, there'll be a little money for you. In any event your band will be in Barcelona and you can easily get there from France. I'm only going to interrupt your journey by a few hours."

Callao said: "But what do you want me for? Why do I have to go? If you're going to give me those leest to give to Aurora; if you want me to do that, all right. I'll do eet. I've got to do eet. But why do I have to go with you?"

"Use your brain, Vincente. Whatever happens to anybody else I'm going to be innocent. See? Supposing for the sake of argument that something turns up; that Quayle should get you and me before we get away from the coast. Accidents will happen, and I like to think of everything. Well, I've still got a story, haven't I? I'm after you because I discovered that the motor boat was yours. You'll have the lists and I'll be doing what Mr. Quayles thinks I'm doing—trying to get them back and sticking to the man who's got 'em. It's a good story, isn't it?"

Callao said nothing.

"Make up your mind, Callao. You're going to do one of two things. Either you're going to be framed with having those stolen lists and brought them into this country; I'm going to turn them over to Quayle and say that I found them here in your rooms; that I knew that they were here because I'd put Aurora Francis on to find out, and remember she's going to support that story; in which case things won't be so good for you. Or else you're going to do what I want. You're finishing at the Cockatoo; I know that. See your band off to Barcelona; hand over the fake documents I'm going to give you to Aurora Francis and wait to leave this country with me, in which case you'll be safe. Maybe there'll be a few million francs for you on the other side. But try any funny business with me and you know what'll happen to you."

Callao said: "I don' want to try any funny business. Eet looks as if I'm in a spot. All right. I'll do what you say."

"Fine," said Kiernan. "Now we're getting some place." He opened his leather coat; took from the inside breast pocket a thick parchment envelope. The ends of it were sewn with red tape. It was heavily sealed. "Some time to-morrow evening Aurora Francis is coming round for those lists. She's coming round because you're going to telephone her and say that you've decided to hand them over to her. Just give her this package. You don't have to talk. I think the night after, you and I will be leaving. The day after that you'll find yourself in France with some money, and your band waiting in Barcelona. That's fair enough, isn't it?"

He got up.

Callao said: "I don' like eet, but I've got to do eet."

"Wise man," said Kiernan. "I'll be seeing you."

He put on his cap. He walked to the door. He turned. He said to Callao: "The trouble with you is you scare too easily. Why don' you grow up? Good night."

Callao heard him go down the stairs.

*

As Kiernan turned the key in the doorway of his apartment house in Charles Street he looked at the illuminated dial of the wrist-watch on his left wrist. It was half-past three. He was tired, but satisfied with his day's work.

He walked along the passage, his mind busy with the day and the implications of the day. He thought of Callao. He smiled. That part of the business, he thought, would be perfectly all right.

He saw the light under the bottom of his sitting-room door; paused for a moment, then opened the door. He closed it softly behind him. He stood, his back to the door, smiling at the sleeping figure of Aurora. Kiernan thought she was a very pretty woman—not only pretty, but attractive. And with that strange allure which is somehow independent of beauty—a peculiar quality of sex that some women possess. He thought that she was not only beautiful but useful, which was not often the case where women are concerned.

He took off his leather coat and cap; threw them on the other arm-chair. He knelt down beside her; put his arms about her. She awoke with a little start. Her eyes were wide. Then she recognised him.

She said: "Tony, I'm glad you're back."

He kissed her. He got up; moved away from her; stood in front of the electric fire looking at her. She stretched sleepily.

"What goes on?" asked Kiernan. "What is this—attempted seduction or what?"

She sat up. "Not actually," she said. "I'm rather glad I came round here, Tony. Some odd things have been happening."

He lighted a cigarette. "Well, you can tell me about it in a minute. I've a spirit stove in my bedroom. I'm going to make you some tea."

He picked up her fur coat; put it over her knees; went into the bedroom. She thought Kiernan was pretty good. Most men would have been curious as to why she was there; as to what had been going on. But curiosity, like everything else in Kiernan's nature, was controlled. He could always afford to wait. Mainly, she supposed, because he was always used to dominating situations as he seemed to be dominating this one.

She got up; gave herself a cigarette. She went back to the chair; rearranged the fur coat about her. In spite of the electric fire, the room was a little cold.

He came back in a little while with the tea. He handed her a cup; poured one for himself; stood in his usual position in front of the fire, his feet planted firmly on the ground, looking down at her.

He said smilingly: "Well—?"

"I decided I'd like to see you to-night," said Aurora. "I wanted to tell you about Callao's reaction; how he took what I said to him. I didn't think it was very satisfactory. I thought I'd come here and tell you about it. When I arrived the front door was unlocked. I thought that was a little odd at that time in the morning. I came in here. The electric lights were on. I was wondering what to do when somebody came out of the bedroom. Who do you think it was?"

"I wouldn't know," said Kiernan, grinning. "Don't tell me it was Santa Claus?"

She looked at him. "It wasn't Santa Claus. It was Antoinette Brown." She watched his face. "You're not even surprised?"

He shook his head. "Nothing ever surprises me, and in this case I'm certainly not surprised. I suppose you asked her what she came here for?"

"Yes," said Aurora. "I asked her what she came here for, and she told me. So I smacked her face and sent her home."

Kiernan grinned again. "This is becoming quite exciting. It sounds almost like a scene in an old Lyceum play. Why did you have to smack her face after she'd told you what she wanted?"

Aurora said: "I've never realised what a fearful little bitch that girl is. She told me that she'd been out walking because she was worrying about you. What she really meant, I suppose, was that she was worrying about herself."

"Why was she worrying about me?" asked Kiernan. "That's rather extraordinary, isn't it?"

"Not according to her," Aurora answered. "It seems that she fell for you while she was working for you in Nuremberg." She smiled at him. "You probably encouraged her in some way, or made a pass at her, or something. But she considers herself to be in love with you. Of course she hasn't been able to say anything to you about it before because she's so charming and modest and diffident; so Victorian, one might almost say, in her outlook. But when she was out walking to-night and thinking about you, she came to the conclusion that you ought to be warned about me. She came to the conclusion that I was a bad, designing woman and not a particularly nice woman," said Aurora almost whimsically. "A woman who's too interested in men. In other words she thought I was stringing you along—two-timing you. So she came here to tell you." She shrugged her shoulders. "I suppose she thought she might even win something for herself on the rebound."

Kiernan said: "So you lost your temper and smacked her face?"

She nodded. "I loved doing it. Just at the moment she struck me as being so damned self-satisfied I could have killed her."

Kiernan put down his teacup. He lighted a fresh cigarette. He used the time it took to light the cigarette in thinking. He thought that the situation was quite good. He liked it. He thought that sometimes circumstances were rather lucky.

After a while Aurora said: "Well, do you think I did wrong? I suppose you don't approve of my hitting her."

"What do I care?" said Kiernan. "Any time you two want to have a stand-up fight I'll hold your coats for you. I don't mind who gets smacked. The thing that interests me is that quite obviously you believe what she said."

"My God!" said Aurora. "Do you mean that it was just a story; that she made it up—"

"Because she had to have an excuse for being here, my sweet," said Kiernan. "I think she's pretty good."

There was a pause. She said: "I see. . . . Tony, what do you think she was doing here?"

"Searching the place." Kiernan stood smiling at her.

"But why?" asked Aurora.

He shrugged his shoulders. "Use your common-sense, my sweet. But how could you know? You don't know Mr. Quayle. You remember what I told you before when I was talking to you about this Antoinette Brown. She came to me in Nuremberg from Quayle. She was supposed to be a secretary. My own guess always was that she was one of Quayle's operatives, and a damned good one too. That's the sort of woman he likes to have working for him—a woman who looks demure and innocent and shy—who looks like the sort of person who'd faint if someone tried to kiss her. That's why I told you to tell her in the strictest confidence that I was trying to get those lists so that I could hand them back to Quayle. I would have bet ten to one that she would have gone straight back and told him. Well, she's done so. Quayle pulled a fast one. Somebody evidently saw me drive off to-night." He grinned. "Not that they would have known where I was going because I drove all round London before I went to my real destination. But somebody saw me go off, so they put Antoinette in to have a look round. She was probably all ready with her story in case she was surprised. If I'd come in she'd have told me the same tale."

"I see . . ." said Aurora grimly. "And supposing she had, what would you have done—made love to her?"

"Why not?" said Kiernan. "I might have." He watched her face darken. "If it hadn't been for you. You forget, my sweet, I'm not interested in any one else but you. But she was all ready with her story. I didn't arrive but you did. So you fell for it."

She asked: "Tony, what was she looking for? Surely this Quayle didn't think that the lists were here."

"Why not? He might have thought that. You've got to realise that Quayle is a very clever man. He usually knows what the other fellow is thinking, except in this case. Remember I worked for Quayle for years, and so"—he smiled sideways at her—"I also have made a habit of working out what the other man is thinking. That's the story as I see it. Antoinette Brown went back to Quayle and told him I was after those lists; that I was going to hand them back to him on a plate when I got them. Quayle knew immediately that that wasn't quite true. I've told you, my sweet, that those lists are very valuable. Quayle knew that before I gave those lists to him I'd want to know where I was. I'd either want my old appointment on his staff back—and probably a much better one—or else I'd want a lot of money. I think he pulled a fast one. I think he thought he'd see if the lists were here. He might easily think that I'd already got them."

She asked: "Why should he think that?"

He looked at her. His expression was almost one of grief. "My darling, why don't you use your brains? Quayle knows me. He knows I don't talk to people. Yet I tell you something of very great importance and you tell Antoinette Brown in the strictest confidence. Quayle probably thought that I'd even laid that on so as to prepare him for the fact that I was going to turn up in two or three days' time and bargain. So he thought he'd try to get the lists first, because you will realise that if they'd been found here I couldn't have done anything about it."

"Why not?" she asked.

"Realise, my sweet, that those lists are the property of this country. I should have no right to have them in my possession from the legal angle. It would have been my duty as a man who knew their value, and as a British citizen, immediately to hand them over, although if I had them and wasn't prepared to disclose where they were what could they do about it? All they want is the lists."

She said: "I understand. And you're not perturbed?"

"Not in the remotest degree. It doesn't make any difference at all. Now tell me about your interview with Callao. You say he didn't react well?"

She shook her head. "No . . . he said he didn't know anything about any lists. He said you were trying to frame him. He became piteous and childlike."

He nodded. "I understand. What did you tell him then?"

"What you told me," she said. "I said it would be better for him to hand those lists over to me, so that he and I might get out of the country and make some money out of them. I told him I loved him. I told him all the stuff we arranged. He still said he hadn't got them; that he knew nothing about them."

"Did you give him your telephone number?" asked Kiernan.

"Yes . . . do you think he'll do anything about it?"

"I know he will," said Kiernan. "I know my Callao. Always his first idea is to deny everything and protect himself. Then he'll do a little thinking. Then he'll come to the conclusion that he'd better play it the safe way. He'll ring you up and he'll give you those lists."

"If he does," she asked, "what then?"

"Then we have to be very clever. I'll tell you why. I'm very glad that you came here to-night and discovered Antoinette Brown. It shows me that Quayle is quite definite in his mind about me having those lists. When I've got them, if I go to him and tell him I have them he might be a little tough. You never know with Mr. Quayle. And he could be tough."

"How?" asked Aurora.

"I'm a British citizen," said Kiernan. "I'm in possession of documents which rightly belong to a department of the State. Quayle might be quite agreeable. In order to get them quickly he might agree to do what I want, or he might not. He might prefer to play it the tough way. He could get me, under about five different acts of Parliament—two or three of them very old acts. They could even call it treason, and there's still a death sentence for that." He looked at her whimsically.

"I see. . . ." Her voice was a little frightened. "So what are you going to do?"

"What do you think? I'm going to put myself outside the jurisdiction of the Court. I'm going to do my bargaining from the other side of the Channel."

She smiled. "You're very clever, aren't you, Tony? I think you're quite good enough for this Mr. Quayle."

He nodded. He said gravely: "I think so too. Now, listen, sweet. The time has come when we have to get a move on. I believe that some time to-morrow, after he has had time to think this thing over, Vincente Callao will telephone you and will arrange to hand you those lists. If my information is correct they should be in a heavily sealed parchment envelope about fifteen inches by six inches, with the ends sewn with red tape and sealed so that it would be impossible for any one to open them without disclosing the fact. After you leave here to-night I don't want you to come near me again. But what you do is this:

"On Wednesday morning—that is to-morrow because it's Tuesday now—if you have the lists you go to the International Charter Company and charter a private plane to take you to Le Bourget. You've got your passport. You simply fly over the Channel go to Paris; go to the Plaza Athénée in the Avenue Montagne and wait for your future husband."

She said: "You're going over too?"

He nodded. "But not with you. You see, it's quite on the cards that Quayle might be rather interested in me, but he'll know one thing. He'll know I'd never let those lists go out of my possession once I've got them. He'd know I'd never trust anybody—not a single soul—with them. That's where he'll be wrong. I trust you because I love you."

She got up. She said: "Well, it all depends on Callao, doesn't it? You think he'll hand these things over to me?"

"Work it out for yourself," he said. "He's got to. He's due to leave for Spain in a couple of days. He believes I'm still a secret service agent. He knows perfectly well after your interview with him that he'd never be allowed to get out of this country with those lists; that he'd never be allowed to go unless he's done what I have suggested to him. He's so scared there's only one thing he'll do. He'll want to get rid of those lists and he'll want me to have them. So he won't even take a chance on me. My bet is that he'll give you the lists and he'll then get in touch with me and tell me that he's done so. Then he's free of all responsibility. He's passed the buck to you. Now," he continued, "it's time for little girls to go to bed."

She came into his arms. She said: "I'd do anything—go-anywhere—for you, Tony. I hope that everything happens the way you want it."

Kiernan said: "If Callao telephones you to-morrow and makes an appointment to hand those documents over to you, don't come near me. Don't even telephone me. Meet Callao; take the documents." He paused for a moment. "Which floor are you on in Lowndes Square?"

"On the third floor," said Aurora.

"Any windows facing the Square?" asked Kiernan.

She nodded. "My sitting-room is the end one. It's the end of the block. Two windows look out on to the Square."

"Good," said Kiernan. "If Callao gives you those documents to-morrow open the tops of your two windows—the one on the left about eight inches; the one on the right about twelve inches. I'll take a walk through the Square at four o'clock to-morrow afternoon. If your windows are open as I've described I'll know you have the lists. I'll know that the next morning, Thursday, you'll be leaving for Paris with them. I'll know that on Thursday evening you and I will be together in Paris, after which"—his face broke into a smile—"we'll do a little long-distance bargaining with Mr. Quayle."

She said: "I'll love that. I think he gave you a pretty bad deal, Tony. I think you're coming out right on top of this job."

He kissed her again. He said: "The funny thing is, so do I. Now go home, sweet. I'll see you on Thursday evening."

He helped her on with her coat; took her to the door; watched her as she walked down the deserted street. He closed the door; went back to his sitting-room; sat looking at the electric fire. He lighted a cigarette.

He went into his bedroom; paused for a moment; then went into the bathroom. He stood in front of the mirror looking at the account from the motor marine repairers standing behind the razor stand in the place where he had left it for Mr. Quayle's operative to see it.

TUESDAY

Antoinette Brown came out of the bedroom. She stood in the doorway looking at Guelvada who was leaning against the mantelpiece. His eyes rested on her for a moment.

He said: "So something happened? You found something, hey? A bit of luck, my beautiful Antoinette."

She came into the room. "How do you know, Mr. Guelvada?"

He shrugged his shoulders; spread his hands. "Guelvada knows everything. I have only to look at you. There is something in your eyes and I observe a fight, hey? Where did you get that scratch on your cheek?"

She put her hand to her face. "That was Aurora. She came back and found me in Kiernan's rooms. She smacked my face. Her ring scratched my cheek."

Guelvada whistled. "Sit down and relax. You're a little tired. Maybe a spot of reaction." He produced a gold cigarette case; gave her a cigarette; took one himself; lighted them.

He said: "So Aurora came back—not Kiernan. Not so good. I didn't think of that one. What happened?"

"I adapted the story you gave me in case he should come back," said Antoinette, "for her. I told her that I was very fond of Kiernan; that I resented her attitude towards men; that I had been out walking and found the front door open."

"Good," said Guelvada. "You know, I wish to tell you, Antoinette, that under that quiet exterior of yours there is a very excellent brain. Not only have you a superb figure, a graceful walk and charm—you have also a brain."

"Thank you very much, Mr. Guelvada."

There was a silence; then he asked: "What did you find?"

"I went through all the rooms. I found nothing at all. Then I went into the bathroom. I don't know whether it means anything but, propped against the mirror on a glass shelf, was an account. It was an invoice from James Fording & Sons, marine engineers. The address was at Rye in Sussex, and the invoice was for repair work done amounting to £27 14s. 6d."

Guelvada said: "Ha! ha! So now I begin to see something." He began to walk about the room. "Always the very careful person— the person like Kiernan—forgets something. Always because a thing is innocent to him, he thinks it will be innocent to everybody else. So I suppose he doesn't worry about the invoice."

She asked: "Does it mean anything?"

He shrugged his shoulders. "We shall see. . . . For me, I think it may mean a great deal. Maybe this Kiernan is not so clever. Maybe he's a fool, hey? Time will show. . . ."

"Would you like something, Mr. Guelvada—a cocktail?"

He shook his head. "I never drink cocktails after lunch. Always after lunch my brain is at its best. In the afternoons invariably I think." He drew on his cigarette. "Antoinette, I think you have done very well. I think that your work with me is finished. This afternoon, if I were you, I should rest. This evening—a scented bath; a charming frock. And then keep the appointment from which I took you last night, which by the way, is on to-night."

Guelvada smiled. "I have a message from Mr. Frewin. He asks that you will call for him to-night at his rooms in Kensington at seven-thirty." He looked at her mischievously. "Shall I tell you something about Michael Frewin, my little Antoinette?"

"Do," she said demurely. She looked out of the window.

"Our good Michael is in love with you," said Guelvada. "But in love. Figure yourself that when I asked for you he doesn't like it. He thinks that I am one of those people who will send you into some danger. As if that mattered to you. He's worried about you. So to-day he says to me that whatever happens you should dine with him to-night. He asks me to give you the message."

She said: "Thank you very much."

"You will keep the appointment?" asked Guelvada.

"Why not? If my work is finished I'd better report back to him."

"Excellent," said Guelvada. "I think you are a delightful pair. I think also"—his smile was mischievous—"you are extremely attracted to Michael. But of course you wouldn't say so. You are much too modest, aren't you, my Antoinette?"

"Mr. Guelvada, I don't know what you're talking about."

He picked up his hat. He said: "You don't. But you will. Au 'voir, Antoinette."

He went out.

Guelvada got a cab outside the Mordaunt Hotel. He sat back in the corner, chain-smoking cigarettes and thinking. He believed he had the solution. He believed it was impossible that he was wrong.

Guelvada was one of those people with a sublime faith in their own mentality. He was a great believer in the instinct of Guelvada, and he thought that this time it had worked.

When he went into Quayle's office he was sure he was right. He walked up and down. He was thinking about Kiernan; the mentality of Kiernan; how Kiernan would think about any given situation. He was so engrossed with his thoughts that Quayle came into the room from the inner office unobserved.

He said: "Good evening, Ernest. You look as if you're pleased about something."

"Please sit down and listen to me," said Guelvada. "I think I have arrived at the solution. Yesterday I sent you a message that I was sending Antoinette Brown to search Kiernan's rooms. Why did I do this? At the time I did not know. I thought that her quick eyes might light on something that mattered. Unfortunately, she was discovered there. Aurora Francis came in whilst Antoinette was searching. She had probably dropped in to see Kiernan who, I imagine, is her lover. There were words, Francis struck Antoinette."

Quayle said casually: "That doesn't matter. That's perfectly all right. Did she find anything?"

Guelvada nodded. "In the bathroom, on the glass shaving shelf, was an invoice from James Fording & Sons, of Rye in Sussex. The invoice is for repair work done by a firm of marine engineers. Figure to yourself what this means. Rye is very close to the coast of France. It means that Kiernan has a motor boat there. It means that Kiernan is prepared at any moment to make a getaway."

Quayle lighted a cigarette. "That could be."

Guelvada sat down. He edged his chair forward; put his elbows on Quayle's desk and leaned towards Quayle.

He said: "Listen. . . . From the first I have told you that I have been concerned with this set-up of Kiernan, Aurora Francis and Callao. I have said that this set-up stinks in my nostrils because I cannot understand it. None of these people matches up—certainly not as a trio. One understands Kiernan and Aurora. Here is a strong, brave man and a beautiful woman. But when you add to this a weak man with a passion for women the situation becomes obscure. But not to Guelvada.

"It is my belief," Guelvada continued, "that Callao, who acted as a messenger between Spain and the Nazis during the war, is the person who carried those lists. He has them here in England. Kiernan knows that. So what does he do? He arranges for Aurora Francis to meet him at the Cockatoo, because he knows that she will be attracted to Callao and Callao to her. Then what happens? She goes to see Callao in his rooms. Kiernan appears and thrashes Callao. But why does he do this? The answer is obvious. He's throwing a scare into Callao, hey? He's softening him up for what is going to happen afterwards. Realise that the last time that Callao met Kiernan was in Lisbon where Kiernan was an agent of the British Secret Service. Don't you see what's in my mind. Hey?"

Quayle said: "Yes. . . . You mean that Callao thinks that Kiernan is still an agent?"

"Precisely. . . . He believes that Kiernan is still an agent. So Kiernan, having thrashed, now threatens him. He says unless he hands over the lists he, Kiernan, will do this, that and the other. So Callao is now petrified with fear. So he hands over the lists."

Quayle nodded. He repeated: "That could be. But he could have done all that without Aurora Francis."

"Never," said Guelvada. "Because he must have a red herring. Look, Kiernan is no fool. He knows you; he knows your methods; he knows you suspect everybody. He knows that if necessary you will suspect him. So he must have a red herring, and this is what he does. Aurora Francis is to be the red herring. Aurora Francis is the person whom we are to watch because Kiernan will think that you will never believe that he will let those lists go out of his possession.

"So what does he do? First of all he makes love to this woman; then he promises her marriage. You say she's going to marry him. She won't let him down. So she acts as the stooge."

Guelvada sat back with an air of triumph. He lighted another cigarette. "What will happen?" he went on. "You will find that within a day or two the beautiful Aurora Francis will make arrangements to leave this country. So she will be watched. We shall watch her like a cat watches a mouse, but we shall not watch Kiernan because he will make no arrangements to leave." He spread his hands. "He doesn't have to. Nobody, he thinks, knows that he has already made preparations to leave in his own boat."

"It might easily be," said Quayle. "But you'd better get somebody on to that; to check if he has got a boat at Rye."

Guelvada said: "Listen. . . . I've worked for you for a long time. You know me. Leave this to me. I'm going to bring those lists back to you. I—Ernest Guelvada—within two or three days. This is what I propose to do. I shall get in touch with Goddard. I shall send one or two good men down to Rye. I shall check up on this firm of marine engineers. I shall find out if there's a boat there. They will find that there's a boat—of that I'm certain. And they will find it belongs to Kiernan. So they report to me. At the same time I put a tail on Aurora Francis. I'll bet every penny which I have in the world that within the next day or two this Aurora Francis will go and book herself an air or a boat passage to France or somewhere like that. She will do it because Kiernan will know that we have a tail on her.

"So suspicion is removed from him and we follow her. Possibly we arrest her. I don't think it matters. We could let her go because she will have nothing. The lists will be with Kiernan who will leave by the boat."

Quayle said: "You might be right, Ernest. What do you propose to do about it—supposing I allow you to handle it?"

"If I have carte blanche," said Guelvada, "when I have discovered that the boat really exists at Rye, I will go down there too. I will have a meeting with our friend Kiernan. I will bring back the lists."

"What about Kiernan?" asked Quayle.

Guelvada got up. "There are moments when I prefer not to answer questions. But there have been accidents before. Possibly you will remember that I am very good at accidents."

"I see," said Quayle. "Very well. And the woman?"

Guelvada said: "Let her go. Realise that Kiernan will not try to leave until he knows the woman has got away. It would be useless for us to arrest her on a railway station or at an airport and find that she has some fake documents. Then Kiernan would do nothing. He will not move until he knows she has safely gone."

"I think that's right" Quayle got up. "All right, Ernest, play it your way. I'm relying on you to bring me back those lists. I'll telephone Goddard and tell him you're to have anything you want; any assistance. Keep it nice and quiet, won't you?"

"You mean about Kiernan?" asked Guelvada. "But of course. I've always been very, very quiet, Mr. Quayle."

He put on his hat; smiled at Quayle; went out of the room.

*

At seven-thirty, Antoinette Brown arrived at Frewin's rooms in Kensington. She wore a black lace evening frock. Her hair was carefully dressed. She used a new and, she thought, subtle perfume.

Frewin's manservant showed her into his sitting-room. Frewin came in a moment later. He wore a lounge suit.

She said: "Oh, I'm sorry, Mr. Frewin, but I thought you'd dress."

Frewin asked: "What for, Antoinette?"

She looked at him. "But the message—the message you sent by Mr. Guelvada because we missed our dinner last night. He said that you'd asked me to dine with you to-night; that I was to be here at seven-thirty. That was in order because I'd finished my work for him, he said."

Frewin asked: "What else did he say?"

She looked at the floor. "It's not really important, Mr. Frewin."

"What happened last night, Antoinette? Sit down. I'll give you a drink."

She sat down in the arm-chair by the fire. She told him what had happened the night before.

Frewin said: "It's a damned shame. Guelvada's quite ruthless about the way he uses people. I wonder why he couldn't have done the job himself. If Kiernan had come back instead of Aurora Francis it might not have been so good for you."

"Possibly not," said Antoinette. "But I might have talked my way out of it, Mr. Frewin."

"Yes, you might have." Frewin looked at her. "Guelvada's a funny cuss. I wonder why he gave you that fake message from me about your coming here to-night at seven-thirty for dinner. I wonder what was in his mind."

She said: "I don't know, I'm sure, Mr. Frewin."

He looked at her for a long time. "You know," he said, "there are moments when I believe that Ernest has a certain amount of intelligence. Give me fifteen minutes to change. Actually," he went on, "I wanted you to dine to-night, but I thought you might still be working."

She said: "If you've anything better to do, Mr. Frewin, it's quite all right with me."

He smiled at her over his shoulder. "I can't think of anything better to do. Besides, I want to talk to you, Antoinette."

CHAPTER FOUR
SAMBA

WEDNESDAY

CALLAO opened his eyes; looked wearily about his bedroom; threw off the bedclothes; slung his legs on to the floor. He sat, his face buried in his hands, considering the miseries of life.

He thought that he would be very glad to get away from England—a country which was damp, which depressed him; where always, even at the best of times, he was oppressed by strange misgivings. Even the English people, he thought, were difficult. They were obsessed by austerity, cold, disagreeable.

He got up from the bed; went into the other room; began to make coffee. He looked in the wall mirror and discovered his face was haggard. He was not even surprised.

When he had made the coffee he sat down and considered his situation. He thought he could do nothing except what Kiernan wished him to do. For a moment Callao desired some of Kiernan's cunning, resourcefulness and strength. He wished he possessed the toughness of this man who had called him, Callao, a "pushover." He shrugged his shoulders. He supposed he was like that. He began to feel very sorry for himself. He thought that the only people who had ever understood him were women, and even they became more difficult as the years rolled by.

He realised he was in a grim position. A position from which there was no escape. He realised also that any previous difficult situations in his life had been concerned with women. He had been able to deal with these situations because, he thought, he had a flair for dealing with women. But he was not used to men like Kiernan. He did not know what to do about such men and, even if he had known, he would have been unable to do it.

This morning his band would leave London for Barcelona. He wished he was with them. For one moment the idea occurred to him of throwing discretion to the winds and joining them. Then a picture of Kiernan came into his mind. Then, immediately, he thought that he could only do what he was told; that this would be the only safe way. Otherwise he would run into grievous trouble.

And once out of England he would be safe. Once he had done what Kiernan wanted he could go back to his beloved Spain, where it was warm and people smiled.

He put down the untasted cup of coffee. He got up; walked across the room to the telephone. From under the telephone pad he took the piece of paper on which Aurora Francis had written her telephone number. He dialled the number.

Just for a moment, as he waited, a feeling of rebellion came over him. He thought he hated all these people who forced him into a corner like a rat, relying on the fact that he had not even the final bitter courage of a rat.

Aurora's voice came on the line. Callao said wearily; "Good morning, Señorita Aurora. Thees ees Callao. I have thought about what you said to me. I have thought that what you said was right. I shall do what you say."

"I'm glad, Vincente," said Aurora. "I knew you'd be wise about this—wise and cautious."

"There ees nothing else for me to do but to be cautious. I weel bring the package round to you in half an hour if you would like that."

"No, don't do that. I'll meet you in the vestibule of the Hyde Park Hotel in half an hour's time. It is better that you should not come here."

He said: "Very well." He hung up the receiver.

He thought he hated the woman Aurora. This woman whom he had thought so attractive. He grinned bitterly as the thought came to him that she too was a tool for Kiernan; that Kiernan had deluded her, was using her, just as he, Callao, was being used. Always the man Kiernan got his own way. Always people had to do what he wanted. One day, he supposed, the woman would know the truth; would know that she had been fooled and tricked from the start. He shrugged his shoulders. Even the thought of Aurora's eventual misery was not comforting.

He went into the bathroom. Whilst he was shaving he cut himself—one of those objectionable little nicks which bleed so profusely. Tears came into his eyes. Life, he thought, was quite impossible. Nothing went right—not even shaving.

When he was dressed he unlocked the bottom drawer of his wardrobe; took out the bulky sealed package which Kiernan had given him. He looked round his apartment regretfully, rather as if he had an idea that he would not see much more of it. He went down the stairs slowly.

At twelve o'clock Kiernan told his taxi-driver to drive through Lowndes Square. He sat back relaxed, looking out of the window. As he identified the two windows at the end of the block—the windows of Aurora Francis' sitting-room—he grinned to himself. One window was open about twelve inches; the other eight inches. So that was that!

He sat back in the corner of the cab; lighted a cigarette. He stopped the cab at the Ritz; went into the Palm Court; ordered a double Martini. He began to check up on himself, his mind working quietly and consistently as it always had done, picking up all the points, thinking of all the personalities who were concerned in his scheme.

First of all there was Aurora. Women, thought Kiernan, were easy to deal with if you allowed for the small feminine foibles of their minds. Most women would forgive everything except not being made love to if they loved a man. He was certain that Aurora loved him. He thought, when it came to the show-down; when she found that things were not to be exactly as he had promised, there might be a little scene. He smiled to himself. There had been scenes in his life before but usually, one way or the other, he had managed to come out on top.

He finished his drink; ordered another. Now he thought about Quayle. The idea of looking into Quayle's mind amused him. During the years that he had worked with and under Quayle he had learned every move in the game—every part of Quayle's extraordinary technique.

To think of what the other man is going to do. Even to allow for his thinking that you knew what he was going to do and then, deliberately, to allow for his doing the opposite. The double double-cross used a million times in the war by "double-agents"—those supreme beings who worked on two sides but gave loyalty only to one side. Quayle knew all about the double double-cross. Kiernan had seen it at work on a dozen occasions in a dozen different sets of circumstances. But this time it could not possibly fail. He thought that he need not be concerned greatly with Quayle. Not enough to worry about.

He thought about Antoinette Brown. He smiled at the thought of her. The idea of Aurora discovering her in the act of searching his rooms intrigued him, because Antoinette Brown had found what he had intended her to find. Unwittingly, Quayle had been a great help to him.

From the first, he thought, Quayle had used the girl Brown against him. Because she was a friend of Aurora's; because Quayle thought that Aurora might give Brown her confidence. Kiernan grinned. Quayle would never know—not until it was too late—that Kiernan had even used Brown as an unwitting ally.

He began to think about life. It would take two weeks to get rid of Aurora in France, and after that, with negotiations finished the world would lie before him. Of course he would have to be careful for a year or so. People had long memories and revenge was sweet even to a man like Quayle. He shrugged his shoulders He was used to being careful. He knew he could look after himself

He finished the Martini; left the Palm Court; went into the telephone call box at the hall entrance. He dialled Callao's number. He thought when Callao spoke that the voice was tired and uncertain.

Kiernan said cheerfully: "Good morning, Vincente. I see you have been a good boy and done what you've been told to do. I'm so glad. When did you do it?"

Callao said: "Thees morning. The sooner thees business ees over the more pliz' I shall be."

"Why not?" said Kiernan. "You'll be pleased all right. Don't bother. In the meantime there's nothing for you to worry about—not so long as you do what you're told. Now listen to me. To-morrow is Thursday. In the evening hire a car; drive out beyond East Grinstead—on the main road. On the left hand side is a lorry drivers' shack—the sort of place where you get tea. Meet me there at nine o'clock. You can send the car back just before you get to the place. It's called the 'Ace of Diamonds.' You needn't worry about transport after that. I'll look after it. You understand?"

Callao said: "I understand."

Kiernan's voice became grimmer. "Sometimes people who get very scared try to be brave and start a little funny business. Don't do anything like that, will you—or else you know what'll happen to you?"

"I've tol' you I weel do what you say. I am seeck of thees business. Why should I do anything else?"

"Exactly . . . why should you?" said Kiernan. "I'll see you to-morrow night at nine o'clock. I'm looking forward to it."

Kiernan hung up; went back to the Palm Court.

Guelvada sat in the deep arm-chair in front of the electric fire in his rooms in the Brompton Road, his feet, elegantly encased in dark-red leather slippers, rested on the mantelpiece. He smoked cigarettes; drank coffee; ruminated on the pleasantries of life.

For Ernest considered life to be pleasant. It was pleasant provided it was eventful. Only monotony and routine were boring. These were the only things that made a man unhappy. And he was enjoying himself. He considered that once again he would prove to Quayle his efficacy as an operative. He—Ernest Guelvada—had put his finger on every weak and strong point in the matter of the missing lists. He—Guelvada—would bring the matter to an adequate conclusion. He thought the whole affair was most satisfactory.

He sighed; began to think about the future. One day, he thought, he would be too old to continue adventuring with Quayle. When that day came it would be an unhappy day. He would miss the sinister events which had brought life and colour into his existence. A kaleidoscope of pictures—throughout the war in Lisbon, France, Germany, Spain; everywhere where he had been—flashed through his mind. He remembered things. Situations from which he had thought there was no hope of extricating himself; situations from which—he smiled at the recollection—he had always managed to extricate himself. Because, he thought, he was Guelvada, which meant something.

The telephone rang. He moved quickly to the instrument.

"Yes? . . ." His voice was soft and pleasant.

The voice at the other end said: "I'm talking to you from Rye, Mr. Guelvada. I thought you'd like to know that you were right."

Guelvada said: "Listen, my friend, always Ernest Guelvada is right, hey? Tell me what you found."

"There is an inlet off the coast with deep water at high tide," said the man. "There is a boathouse which has been built at the end of it. It is about three miles from West of Amber, just off the main road."

"Yes? Then what?" asked Guelvada.

"It is a lock-up boathouse," the man went on. "There is a sixty-foot cabin cruiser in it. She's been looked after by a firm called James Fording & Sons. She was serviced a few days ago. The tanks are full and she's ready to put to sea."

"Excellent . . ." said Guelvada. "Tell me something. . . . To whom does the boat belong?"

"The owner hasn't been seen," said Goddard's operative. "But his agent has looked after the business. The boat appears to belong to a certain Señor Callao—a Spaniard who is resident in England. But he's never been down there. The instructions have always been received through someone else—a Mr. Mannering."

Guelvada smiled. "Thank you very much. Now you can come back to London."

He hung up. He went back to his chair; sat down. He lighted a fresh cigarette. He was smiling. He felt very happy. Kiernan, he thought, was the supreme artist. He had informed the people at Rye who looked after the boat that it belonged to Callao. This was clever. Guelvada foresaw that, when Kiernan decided to leave England, Señor Callao—the owner of the boat, would be leaving with him, so that if anything went wrong Kiernan was still doing his job and sticking to the man who had the lists.

Guelvada thought that it was a great pity about Kiernan; that a man whose brain was so facile, so intelligent, should have made the small mistake of leaving the account for the repairs done to the motor boat against his shaving mirror in the bathroom. But, thought Guelvada, always the cleverest man made one small mistake; always the cleverest criminal did something which gave him away. Everybody did things like that—except himself, Guelvada, who never made a mistake.

He got up; stretched. He went to the telephone; dialled a number. He asked for Colonel Goddard.

He said: "Good afternoon, mon Colonel. This is Guelvada. I expect you've had some instructions about me."

"Yes . . ." said Goddard.

Guelvada went on: "I want two very good men—or better still, one man and one woman. From this moment they will not leave Miss Aurora Francis who lives at No 21 Lowndes Square. She must be tailed all the time. Start off with these two; put fresh people on every two or three hours. She must suspect nothing."

Goddard asked: "Have you any idea what she proposes to do; where she proposes to go?"

"No. . . . Except that I think she is going to book herself an airplane passage. It is important that I should know where she intends to go and when she leaves, but she must not suspect. I should hate the mind of the lady to be disturbed."

Goddard said: "We won't disturb her mind. Directly I have anything definite I will call through to you."

"I am much obliged to you. One day I hope to do something for you. I am so pleased with life that I have a great respect for you, mon Colonel. Good afternoon."

He hung up. He stood in the middle of his sitting-room, one finger in the armhole of his waistcoat, considering the situation.

He began to walk up and down the room. He realised that Quayle, having left everything in his hands, would have utter and complete confidence in him. Guelvada remembered the dozens of assignments he had had from Quayle during the past six years.

Each one of them had been satisfactory. This, which might easily be the most important, must produce the finest denouement. He searched back in his mind for any possibility of error. He tried to find a flaw in his own reasoning; could not do so. He thought of the personalities concerned—their minds, their characters. He thought about Callao. He stopped walking. He stood immobile in the middle of the floor, thinking.

Callao was a coward. He was afraid. Always Callao had been afraid. So, as he, Guelvada, had said from the start, he was being used. He was the person who was to cover up for Kiernan; the person who was to suffer if Kiernan was caught. Both he and Aurora Francis were tools of the clever Kiernan, but of the two Guelvada guessed that Callao was the most stupid and the most afraid.

If Callao would do what he was doing because he was afraid of Kiernan, then he must be made to talk because he was more afraid of Guelvada. If, at this last moment, Callao could be made to talk because the climax had been reached; because now something desperate must happen, then he, Guelvada, would know that he was right; that there would be no possibility of an error.

He shrugged his shoulders. It seemed to be a matter merely of whom Callao was most afraid.

Guelvada continued his pacing up and down the room. He considered that in his heart he was a little afraid of Vincente Callao. He was a little afraid of Vincente Callao because the man was a coward; because he was frightened and because you never knew what a frightened man would do. Supposing he, Guelvada, took the bull by the horns; scared Callao even more than Kiernan had done. There was still no guarantee that the Spaniard would not talk. He might tell Kiernan.

Guelvada thought that it was a great pity that the war was not still on; then it would have been so easy to dispose of Callao.

He went back to his arm-chair. He smiled. He had nothing to bother about. The solution of the enigma of the missing lists was in his hands.

He admitted that he was pleased with himself. Only one thing remained to be done. He must tell Quayle. He must tell

Quayle all about it. It was time that Quayle realised how clever he, Guelvada was.

Frewin was seated at Quayle's desk checking reports when Guelvada came into the room. He laid down his pencil, looked at Guelvada for a long time.

He said: "Sit down, Ernest. I'm glad you came in. I wanted to talk to you, anyhow."

Guelvada sat down. He pulled up his trouser legs carefully, inspected the creases. He asked: "Where is Mr. Quayle? I desire to talk to him."

Frewin said sarcastically: "Desire will have to be your master. He's gone."

Guelvada raised his eyebrows. "Gone? But where? Just at this moment when everything reaches its climax. Just at the time when—"

"When the one and only Ernest is to achieve his usual success," said Frewin cynically. "Well . . . he's gone. Where and for how long I can't tell you. Is it something important?"

Guelvada shrugged his shoulders. He lit a cigarette; offered his case to Frewin, who refused with a shake of the head.

"Not particularly," murmured Guelvada. "I merely wished him to know that everything was in order; that success is certain. I thought he would like to know that."

Frewin grinned. "He probably knows it."

Guelvada smiled. He blew a smoke ring and watched it sail across the room. "It is nearly six o'clock," he said. "Time that you and I went somewhere for a cocktail. But first of all you wished to speak to me." His smile broadened. "There is something on your mind, my Michael," he said cheerfully. "I observe that you are slightly perturbed. I observe that something worries you. Worry is not so good. I never worry . . . hey?"

He blew another smoke ring. He felt that somehow the process annoyed Frewin.

Frewin got up. He began to pace about the office. He said: "Sometimes I think you are just a bloody fool, Ernest—a fool who is inclined to be childish. When you're not killing someone you like to annoy people. I suppose it satisfies your sadistic instinct."

Guelvada spread his hands. "Nobody is less of a sadist than Ernest Guelvada," he said smilingly. "Merely I have an overdeveloped sense of humour. Always I am one jump ahead of the game. And why? Because I have an extremely elegant and agile brain which invariably flings itself to the correct conclusions. It is for this reason that I will tell you exactly why you are annoyed with me. I will tell you exactly what it is you wish to talk to me about."

He continued to smoke. He watched Frewin. He was almost laughing.

Frewin went back to the seat behind the desk. He felt angry with himself. Angry and with a peculiar sense of frustration. Angry because Guelvada possessed some strange ability to dominate a situation, and frustrated because, in the circumstances, he, Frewin, felt unable to do anything much about it.

Guelvada said: "You are angry with me because of Antoinette Brown. For some reason which has not yet been made apparent to any one you consider that you have some proprietary interest in this baby . . . hey? You think she belongs to you. So you are annoyed with Guelvada because he uses her to do a little piece of work which results in her getting her face smacked by the beautiful Aurora, who cuts the delicate cheek of Antoinette with her diamond ring."

Frewin began to speak. Guelvada held up his hand and stopped him.

"If you please," he said. "I desire to finish. My Michael, you are so obvious that you creak. Have you ever before objected to the Brown girl doing work which has been dangerous? Not at all. Many times during the war this girl did things of the most extreme danger and you said not a word. Now, because you are in love with her, you object to anything at all."

"Don't talk damned nonsense," said Frewin. "I'm not in love with her."

"No?" said Guelvada. "Hear me laugh. And so, last night because I knew that she had missed an appointment with you the night before, because then she was working for me, I tell her that you wish to take her to dinner, and she appears and you do not know anything about it. So you wonder what the hell I am playing at . . . hey?"

"Exactly," said Frewin. "What the hell are you playing at?"

Guelvada sighed heavily. "Listen, my friend. . . . I know a great deal about you. You are an extremely brave and intelligent man. You are an organiser of the first class. As an agent in the war you were superb. There is only one sort of thing with which you cannot deal adequately. I'm telling you! Mr. Quayle also knows this. He knows that you are not very good at dealing with women. Because you do not know a great deal about them. Because they are very elusive and sometimes so intelligent that they are almost stupid."

He smiled again. "I remember a girl I once met in Nantes. . . ."

"Damn the girl in Nantes," said Frewin.

"All right," said Guelvada. "Let us damn the girl in Nantes and continue. You are head over heels in love with the girl Brown. But you cannot do anything about it because the girl Brown has an elusive personality. She is elusive because she does not even know what she wants. I know what she wants. She is in love with the stupid Michael, but because she has a certain antagonism for him—which is the result of annoyance at feeling as she does—she does not show it. I, Guelvada, desired to bring this matter to a head. So I told her you wished to dine with her and I will bet my bottom dollar that you did nothing about it—except take her to dinner!"

Frewin asked: "What in hell did you expect me to do?"

Guelvada raised his eyebrows. "What did I expect? You asked me, Guelvada, that? You have the effrontery to ask me that? You amaze me! That a man of your intelligence should ask such a goddam stupid question . . . hey?"

He stopped for want of breath. Frewin said nothing.

Guelvada continued: "I expected you to give her an excellent dinner. I expected you to congratulate her on her frock; to tell her that she looked marvellous; to say that she was the only woman who had ever really made you dissatisfied with life. I expected that. Then, after dinner, I expected you to take her back to your rooms on some excuse or other—either to see your etchings or, if that excuse is too old, to make some notes about something you wished her to do. Then you should have made love to her. But outrageously. The girl Brown expects to be made love to outrageously."

"What the hell do you mean by that?" asked Frewin.

Guelvada threw his cigarette into the fireplace. He crossed to the desk, leaned on it towards Frewin. His voice was almost intense.

"Consider to yourself, my friend, the girl Brown . . . They call her the Practical Virgin—as if a Virgin could ever be really practical. They call her that because she is good at her job, and because beyond her job she is so afraid of life and all the things that life really means that she surrounds herself with a mental barbed wire entanglement. An entanglement which, I tell you, she desires ardently some man—you—to attack and decimate. That is what she hopes all the time, but doesn't know it. She has never put the thought into words. When I speak your name to her a strange look of antagonism comes into her eyes. I noticed it immediately. And it was followed by a look of softness which made her eyes—which are beautiful—almost luminous. I tell you the girl is for you. She loves you. But you are going to have one hell of a goddam job to make her admit it."

Frewin began to speak but Guelvada interrupted him.

"You are a fool, Michael. But because I am your friend I will give you some good advice. If you say to this girl 'Antoinette, I love you,' she will probably say to you 'So what!' which is not what you desire . . . hey? She will repulse you because of this mental barbed wire entanglement which surrounds her. So what do you do? You use other means. You must attack the citadel. You must take her in your arms and get cracking . . . goddam it. You must make this girl Brown realise that you, Michael Frewin, are no ninny, but a man!"

Guelvada removed himself from the desk. He stood in the centre of the room; lighted a fresh cigarette. Frewin thought that always Guelvada posed as if he were about to have his picture taken.

He said: "You're nuts, Ernest!"

Guelvada smiled. He picked up his hat from the chair. "So I am nuts . . . very well. . . . Listen to me, my Michael. At the moment, as you know, I am engaged on important business. I am about to bring this affaire of the missing lists to a satisfactory conclusion . . . but satisfactory! I am about to do that. But when I am finished . . . when I am finished . . . if I discover then that you have done nothing about the girl Antoinette, it will be necessary for me to reconsider this matter . . . and how!"

"What exactly do you mean by that?" asked Frewin.

Guelvada strolled casually over to the door. He opened it; stood with his hand on the knob.

He said: "If you have done nothing about her I propose to do something myself . . . hey? Maybe she'll react to the Guelvada technique . . . and how . . . damn it!"

Frewin opened his mouth to speak, but before he could do so Guelvada had gone.

Frewin lighted a cigarette; got up from his chair; began to walk about the office.

After a little while he picked up the telephone. For a moment he hesitated; then he told the girl on the switchboard to put him through to Miss Antoinette Brown.

The nearby church clock struck ten-thirty. Guelvada, who was sitting in the arm-chair by the fire, opened his eyes; got up; stretched.

He said to Plimley—the M.I.5 man who had been loaned to look after the telephone: "Realise, my friend, that in one hour and thirty-one minutes it will be Thursday—a most important day."

"Yes, Mr. Guelvada. . . ." Plimley thought what the hell did he care whether it was Thursday or raining! He was bored. Sitting by a telephone waiting for calls that never came was not Plimley's idea of life. Besides which he knew nothing about the job in hand. He supposed it was too big, too hush-hush for him to be in on.

He wondered about Guelvada. Vaguely he had heard of him. One of the real people—the "cloak and dagger" boys. Rumours about Ernest Guelvada had permeated even into the innermost recesses of M.I.5. Stories of his amazing exploits during the war, of his narrow escapes, of his lingual ability, his versatility, his charm and success with women.

Plimley mentally shrugged his shoulders. To him, Guelvada seemed a little mad. But then most of these clever bastards were mad, thought the M.I.5 man. If they weren't they would never have done the things they had—and got away with them.

Guelvada began to walk about the room. He said: "The fact that it is Thursday means nothing to you, but to me it's almost the end of an epoch." He lighted a cigarette. "I think I shall go for a walk, Plimley. You will stay here in case the telephone rings. I don't expect it will, but it might. Life is full of pleasant surprises . . . hey?"

"If it does ring and something comes through where do I get you?" asked Plimley.

"Ah . . ." said Guelvada. "That is yet another point. I shall be back by twelve. I know that nothing important will happen by then. In fact," he went on, with a smile, "I expect nothing to happen to-night. Au revoir, my Plimley." He went out of the room.

Outside, the Brompton Road was bathed in moonlight. It was a lovely night. Guelvada thought that this was the sort of night for adventure. He remembered other nights when the moon had been shining. He walked down the Brompton Road, through Knightsbridge, along Piccadilly. For some reason he began to think about the Cockatoo.

Here, he thought, was an extraordinary place—a spot which had formed the meeting ground for some odd personalities. It was here that Callao, Aurora Francis, Kiernan, Nielecki, Antoinette Brown had all encountered each other. Only he, Guelvada, had not met any one or done anything of note in the Cockatoo.

He turned down the side street; walked towards the entrance. He thought it was time that he visited the place. He went in. The cocktail bar at the end of the passage was still open. Guelvada ordered a liqueur brandy; stood, leaning against the bar, sipping his drink.

Nothing, he thought, would happen until to-morrow morning. Then things would begin. Of that he was certain. He finished his drink; walked back to the main entrance; turned left; went into the restaurant. The lights were subdued and Guelvada could only vaguely distinguish the faces of the people sitting at the tables round the dance floor. On the band platform a new band—the successor of Callao's played hot music. Guelvada's eyes wandered round the room. They stopped suddenly at a table against the wall—a table occupied by a solitary figure whose chin was resting in its hands; whose eyes were turned towards the band platform.

Guelvada grinned happily. It was Callao. No less a person than Vincente Callao. Here, thought the Free Belgium, was the hand of fate. And very understandable. Here was Callao listening to the music of the band that had followed his own, living a little in the past, thinking over what had happened during the last few days. Guelvada shrugged his shoulders cynically in the half-darkness. This, he thought, was definitely the hand of fate. This was an indication.

He walked quietly round the side of the room, keeping near the wall. He came up behind the table. He said in Spanish: "Good evening, Señor Callao. How delighted I am to meet you once again. It seems there is no end to the pleasures of life."

Callao turned his head. Guelvada could see the small piece of sticking plaster on one side of his mouth. He thought: So he cut himself while he was shaving. He is as nervous as that. The stupid fool. . . .

Callao looked at him with large, brown, soulful eyes. He said in the same language: "You have the advantage of me, Señor."

Guelvada sat down. He beckoned a nearby waiter with his finger. He said to Callao: "Do me the honour of drinking with me, Señor Callao, whilst I refresh your memory." He ordered drinks.

"If I remember rightly," he continued, "you were in Lisbon during the late war. You were supposed to be running a band at the Astoril. It was there that I met you."

Callao said: "Yes? I do not think I remember you, Señor."

"I am sorry for that," said Guelvada. "Permit me to refresh your memory. My name is Ernest Guelvada. Does it mean nothing to you?"

Callao shook his head. "I'm afraid not. I regret it very much."

There was a silence. The waiter appeared with the drinks.

Guelvada said: "I hope, in spite of the fact that you do not remember me, you will not refuse to drink with me."

"I am honoured," said Callao. He drank a little of the brandy. His eyes, unhappy, harassed, moved from Guelvada about the room, as if he were seeking some means of escape.

Guelvada went on: "I heard your band here was superb. I expect you have come to listen to the indifferent music of your successor. I am extremely fond of music—of good music, of beautiful women and adventure. You also, I believe, Señor Callao, are fond of adventure."

Callao shrugged his shoulders. Guelvada sensed that all the Spaniard wanted was to be left alone; that his, Guelvada's appearance had scared him more than ever.

He went on: "I have been having a most amusing time. I know you are a discreet person, Señor Callao, because I know that during the war you worked for your country; you carried documents which were confidential from place to place. I have even heard it said of you that you were a secret agent, but I never believed that. You are too good a musician to have the resourcefulness of a secret agent."

Callao said: "You are perfectly right. I am merely a musician."

Guelvada looked at him. He was smiling. "I have been engaged on a business which is interesting and adventurous. I have been looking for some missing documents. Possibly I shall find them That will be most amusing."

Callao said wearily: "Señor, what has this to do with me?"

"Nothing very much," said Guelvada, "except—and this is the question I wish to ask you—I know that you are a friend of an individual called Kiernan. You have been seen together, believe it or not. I am interested in the man Kiernan—very interested Are you interested in this gentleman, Señor?"

Callao said: "I have met him—as I meet other people. I know nothing of him."

"I am very glad of that," said Guelvada. "If you desire to know why, I will tell you. This man Kiernan is a dangerous man. He is strong, resourceful. He can be very difficult. He is the sort of man of whom one should beware."

Callao asked nervously: "Why do you bother to tell me all this, Señor?"

Guelvada spread his hands. He said with the most amiable expression: "Because in my heart I am rather fond of you. I have listened to your music in different places. I think it is most attractive. There have been times when I have been inspired—in Lisbon for instance—by the music you have played, to make the most supreme love to some beautiful woman—a woman possibly as beautiful as Miss Francis. I expect you have never met the Señorita Aurora Francis?"

Callao nodded. "She was good enough to admire my music. As you say she is very beautiful."

"Beautiful but unlucky," said Guelvada. "Here is a woman who has everything. She has beauty and charm. She has that strange and lovely thing called allure. She is attracted by this man Kiernan. I consider it most amazing that he has the power to attract all these intelligent people."

Callao turned his hands flat on the table. He looked utterly hopeless. Guelvada could see that there was sweat on the palms of his hands.

The Spaniard said: "Señor, what does all this mean? What are you trying to say to me? What do you wish of me?"

Guelvada raised his eyebrows. "I wish nothing of you, Señor. I saw you here and merely desired to exchange greetings by expressing my admiration for your music; to renew an acquaintanceship which I regret to say you seem to have forgotten."

He drank his brandy. "Señor Callao, I believe it is written in the stars that we shall meet again. I, Guelvada, who am supposed to be an excellent prophet, believe that this is merely the beginning of a friendship. In the meantime, Señor, adios . . . may God go with you. . . ."

He got up; walked slowly back to the doorway. Halfway through he turned and looked at Callao.

He was grinning.

Callao's damp fingers gripped the tablecloth. He was obsessed by fear. He waited a few minutes; got up; hurried to the cloakroom for his hat and coat.

He began to walk to his apartment in Clarges Street. What, he thought, should he find there? Perhaps Guelvada . . . the grinning fiend whom he had pretended not to remember, but about whom he knew so much. Guelvada . . . who had captured and handed over Antonio Streltz; who had knifed Madrilles in Lisbon. Guelvada, whose name had been a legend in every country hostile to the Allies.

Perhaps, thought Callao, Guelvada would be waiting for him. With his knife. The folding Swedish knife that he threw with such deadly accuracy.

Or Kiernan, or Aurora Francis, or someone else. People came to his apartment and threatened and beat him. They forced him into terrible situations. He, Vincente Callao, who desired only peace and sometimes a little love.

When he arrived at the door of his apartment house his hair was dank with sweat. He opened the door; went up the stairs. Almost he could hear his heart beating.

He opened the door; switched on the lights. He looked fearfully about the apartment. It was empty. He went into the top rooms. They too were empty.

He returned to the sitting-room; picked up a bottle of brandy; put the neck of the bottle in his mouth and drank. He sat down in the arm-chair by the unlit electric fire. He continued to drink brandy; to commiserate with himself.

When he had drunk enough brandy he began to cry.

THURSDAY

At seven o'clock in the morning the telephone in Guelvada's sitting-room jangled harshly. Plimley, who was asleep in the big arm-chair, his fingers folded about his ample stomach, his mouth opened, got up from the chair slowly; walked across to the telephone. He hoped this would be the call; that now he could go back to his normal routine and see his wife in the evenings.

He took the message; went into the bedroom. Guelvada was asleep. Plimley thought he looked like a cherub. His round face was relaxed, and a little smile played about his lips. The M.I.5 man thought that for a man who was reputed to be so handy with a knife Guelvada's conscience troubled him very little.

He said: "Wake up, Mr. Guelvada. Colonel Goddard's on the line. He wants to speak to you. It's urgent."

Guelvada opened his blue eyes. They were quiet and untroubled.

"My Plimley," he said, "you are a joyous and welcome messenger. I like you, Plimley. In spite of the fact that you are inclined to be gross and your breath is occasionally extremely fiery, I am, on this occasion, well disposed towards you, hey? Tell the good. Colonel I shall be with him."

Plimley went away. Guelvada got out of bed and put on a scarlet dressing-gown with black fleur-de-lys sprinkled about it. Then he went into the sitting-room, treading delicately on well-shaped, bare feet.

He took the receiver from Plimley. He said: "Now you may go, my beautiful Plimley. Return to the bosom of your family. I shall always remember you with pride and gratitude. I consider you to be the cat's whiskers."

Plimley went. Now he was quite certain that Guelvada was mad.

Guelvada spoke into the telephone. "Good morning, mon Colonel," he said amiably. "I feel that you have good news for me."

"How should I know?" said Goddard. He also felt, for a reason which he could never determine, a faint sense of irritation when he spoke to Guelvada. He had a vague impression that his leg was being pulled. He went on: "Here's your report. I hope you like it. As I don't know what you're at, I don't know whether it's good or bad."

"Don't worry, mon Colonel," said Guelvada airily. "But tell me about my girl friend."

"I've had a bunch of tails on her since yesterday morning," said Goddard in his quiet, official voice. "Also I had a man on the switchboard at the apartment house where she lives in Lowndes Square. And another on the other side of the square, and another—a woman this time—in the apartment above. I'd have rigged a microphone, but I hadn't time to fix things with the other tenant."

"What admirable organisation," said Guelvada. "Continue, mon Colonel."

"Yesterday morning, at ten-thirty," said Goddard, "the woman Aurora Francis was telephoned by a foreigner, a man named Callao. He said that he had thought about what she had said; that she was right; that he would do what she said. He told her he would bring the package round to her in half an hour. She said no. She said it would be better for him to meet her at the Hyde Park Hotel in half an hour's time."

"Excellent," murmured Guelvada. "So they met?"

"Yes," Goddard replied. "He handed her a package and went off. She returned to Lowndes Square and went to her apartment. Ten minutes later she telephoned the International Charter Company and chartered a plane to take her to Le Bourget, France, to-day. She's leaving this morning at twelve o'clock from London Airport. D'you want anything done about that. Do you want her picked up?"

"Good God, no . . ." said Guelvada. "I would not interfere with the lady for worlds. Who is going to be pilot? Do you know?"

"Of course," said Goddard. "He's one of the usual pilots on the International Company's list. A man named Farn—an ex-squadron leader in the R.A.F."

"Good," said Guelvada. "Well . . . just for the sake of this and that get him taken off the job. Get in touch with Mr. Frewin and arrange that an R.A.F. pilot—a man with intelligence—flies the plane. You understand? In plain clothes, of course. If the pilot is able—and he should be able—let him find out to what destination she goes after she leaves Le Bourget. That should be easy. Then let him return at once to London and telephone to Mr. Frewin and inform him. Is that clear?"

"Perfectly," said Goddard. "I'll fix it."

Guelvada said: "I cannot tell you how grateful I am to you, mon Colonel. I shall always remember you with pride and gratitude. You enchant me!"

Goddard said a trifle wearily: "You're not being funny with me, are you?"

"You outrage me," said Guelvada with passion. "You outrage me to such an extent that I am practically speechless. To suggest that I am being funny with my good friend Colonel Goddard. What do you take me for—a rude Englishman?"

"I don't take you for anything," said Goddard. "But I've been up all night and I'm tired. Perhaps your method of expression is a little peculiar. But perhaps you like that."

"Of course!" said Guelvada cheerfully. "Me . . . I speak English like a native . . . but also I endeavour to improve on the vernacular on occasion. And how! Well . . . I'll be seeing you, my friend. In the meantime, I entreat you not to do anything that I would not like to see photographed in the public press. Au revoir! I kiss you on both cheeks!"

He hung up the receiver. He went back into the bedroom, lighted a cigarette; returned to the sitting-room; searched in the telephone directory for a sports' outfitters. He found the number he wanted.

He told himself that he was very happy.

A mile beyond East Grinstead on the Eastbourne road Callao tapped on the window behind the driver; signalled him to stop. He got out of the car. In spite of the cold night air he felt hot and excited. Yet, for the first time for days, he had a feeling of relief that this business which had caused him so much trouble and anxiety was nearly over.

He paid off the driver; began to walk down the winding road, his hands in his overcoat pockets. After a few moments, illuminated in the moonlight, he saw the sign of the Ace of Diamonds. The place was a double shack, set off the road, used by lorry drivers. Callao walked along the path, pushed open the door and went in.

He found himself in a large room with a counter at one end. The place smelled of smoke and greasy cooking. Behind the zinc-topped counter a fat man with a quiff and a dirty apron, fiddled with the coffee urn. He looked thoroughly miserable. Callao thought that everything looked like and smelt of misery.

Kiernan was seated at a table in the far corner. He smiled when he saw Callao. The Spaniard went over and sat down.

"Good evening. . . ." His voice was soft as usual, and he looked at Kiernan with his large brown eyes. Kiernan thought that he looked rather like a whipped dog. For a moment he felt something like a pang of sorrow for the unfortunate Callao. The feeling was strange and momentary.

He said: "Have some coffee? And cheer up. There's nothing for you to worry about. Your troubles are nearly over."

Callao said: "I am glad. I theenk it ees mos' wicked that I should have to suffer so much for something that I have never done. I theenk you are the cruellest—the mos' unkind—man I have ever met in my life."

"Maybe," said Kiernan cheerfully. He signalled to the man behind the counter; ordered him to bring two cups of coffee. He went on: "The trouble with you, Callao, is you are used only to dealing with women, and the sort of women you pick are easy for a man like you. But what have you to bother about? You had to leave England, anyway. To-morrow you'll be in Paris. You'll have some money. You can take a train and join your band in Barcelona and be happy. In a week's time you'll have forgotten about all this."

Callao said: "In a week's time I shall know how I feel. Now I am mos' unhappy."

Kiernan lighted a cigarette. The man brought the coffee. Kiernan picked up his cup, but Callao sat silently looking at the brown liquid. He was thinking that it was not very good coffee. He was remembering the coffee which he made, which was always good.

Kiernan asked: "What's been happening to you—anything exciting?" His smile was cynical.

"I telephoned Aurora," said Callao. "I met her at the Hyde Park Hotel. I gave her the package."

Kiernan asked: "Do you think anybody saw that? Do you think any one was watching?"

Callao shrugged his shoulders.

"Not that it matters," said Kiernan amiably. "Nothing really matters. And since then you've been having a quiet time?"

Callao nodded. "I suppose so . . . although times have no' been quiet for me during the last few days. Last night a theeng happened that disturbed me greatly."

"What happened?" asked Kiernan.

Callao said: "I went to the Cockatoo. I wanted to hear the new band. I wanted to say good-bye to the place. I was happy there at the beginning. I liked it. When I was there a man came and spoke to me. He was a man whom I had met in Lisbon during the war—a man I did not like. His name was Guelvada."

Kiernan raised his eyebrows. "So . . . Ernest Guelvada's at work. Well . . . well!" He laughed shortly. "And what did the enterprising Ernest want?"

Callao said: "He came to my table. He asked me if I remembered him. I thought it best to say that I did not. He reminded me that I had met him in Lisbon. He bought some brandy."

"Well, that's all right," said Kiernan. "What is there to worry about?"

Callao went on: "Then he told me that he was very interested in some missing leets. He told me that he was interested in you. All the while he was talking he was looking at me and laughing with his eyes. He reminded me of a cat playing with a mouse. I felt jus' like a mouse. I was ver' unhappy. He talked to me of Aurora Francis and asked if I had met her. I said she had admired my music. That was all. Then he got up and went away. When he went away he was grinning. He looked like a wolf."

Kiernan said: "Ernie Guelvada always looks like a wolf when he grins. But you don't have to be afraid of him. Was that all he said to you? He didn't ask any other questions?"

Callao shook his head. "He asked no questions at all that mattered. He was telling me. It was as eef he was giving me some sort of warning; as eef he knew something."

Kiernan laughed. "I'll bet he does know something. Guelvada is a clever one. I know his methods. So they've put him on to this job and he's come to certain conclusions. Well, that's all right. That suits me."

Callao asked: "What are we going to do?"

"When you've finished that coffee," said Kiernan—"it's not very good, but it's the best they have—we're going to take a motor drive. We're going to the place on the coast where I have that motor boat. You'll find that all arrangements have been made. To-morrow, before twelve o'clock, you'll be in Paris, Callao. To-morrow night, if you like, you can be on your way to Spain."

Callao said: "I don' want the coffee. I'm sick in your stomach."

"All right," said Kiernan. "Let's go. Don't worry about feeling sick in your stomach. It's a fine night. I don't expect the channel will be very choppy and if it is—well"—he laughed—"you'll have something to be really sick in your stomach about. Come on. . . ."

Callao said: "I am so cold. And eet's going to be colder. Thees overcoat is not very good."

"Don't worry, I have a couple of duffle coats aboard the boat and she's a cabin cruiser. You won't be too cold." He laughed. "You always have cold feet, anyway. I've never known such a fellow."

He went to the counter; paid for the coffee. Callao followed him. Outside they walked silently away from the Ace of Diamonds down the road. Parked in the shadow of some bushes was Kiernan's car. He opened the door politely.

He said: "Get in, my friend. We're going to drive fast. It'll do your stomach good."

He got behind the steering wheel; started the engine.

It was a few minutes after midnight when Kiernan bypassed Amber Village and drove on to the secondary road that led towards the coast. Ten minutes afterwards he stopped at a gate, got out of the car, opened the gate, drove through into the field beyond. He stopped the car; leaned out and closed the gate. He looked sideways at Callao.

The Spaniard was slumped in the passenger seat, his head sunk on his chest. He might have been asleep . . . or brooding. Kiernan thought with an inward grin that it would be brooding. Callao was too scared to sleep.

He re-started the car and began to drive slowly along the cart track that bisected the field. On the other side he drove through a gap in the hedge, turned on to a narrow dirt road; accelerated. He drove for another ten minutes; then pulled the car into the shadow of a deep coppice. He switched off the engine.

He said to Callao: "Here we are, Vincente. Now your troubles are nearly over. Get a ripple on."

He got out of the car. Callao followed him. Kiernan led the way through the coppice, along a narrow path. On the other side they came out on to shingle. Before them lay the little cove, leading out of the small inlet that formed a miniature bayou. A few yards away Callao could see the boathouse.

The wooden structure was reached by a wide gangplank that ran over the water. Kiernan, with Callao behind him, crossed the plank; produced a key; opened the double doors at the back of the boathouse. They went in. Kiernan closed and locked the doors; switched on a shaded electric light.

Before them lay a cabin cruiser. She was a fine boat. Callao, in spite of himself and his misery, admired her graceful lines.

Kiernan said: "See what she's called, Callao. Look at her stern."

Callao looked. The name was Vincente.

"I thought you'd like her named after you," said Kiernan, with a grin. "She's registered in your name, anyhow. In case you don't know it, she's supposed to be your boat. Get aboard, my friend, and go into the cabin. You'll find a duffle coat there. You'll need it."

Callao went forward into the cabin. It was roomy and comfortable. There were two sleeping bunks and between them a table. At the end, beside the small door leading forward, were two duffle coats hanging on a hook. Callao took one, put it on. He pulled the hood over his head; sat down on one of the bunks, his body hunched forward, his head on his chest. Already he was beginning to feel sick.

In the stern he could hear Kiernan busy with the engine. Then, in a few minutes, he heard the sharp staccato hum as Kiernan swung the motor over. The boat began to throb. Callao lay down on the bunk and closed his eyes.

In the stern, Kiernan stood, smoking a cigarette, listening to the rhythmic hum of the motor. He checked over the controls, the oil and petrol gauges. Then he jumped ashore and worked his way round the narrow platform that led round the sides of the boathouse. He pushed over the lever on the wooden wall, and the entrance doors swung open.

Kiernan jumped aboard; went back to the stern. He threw in the gear lever; smiled as the engine picked up. The boat glided slowly out of the boathouse. As the stern came out Kiernan revved up the engine; noted with approval the backwash closing the entrance doors of the boathouse.

The boat gathered speed. Kiernan's sharp eyes looked forward; scanned the cove and the sea beyond. Everything was quiet. Nothing else disturbed the silence.

Now they were almost out of the inlet. The Vincente began to roll a little as the wash of the sea met her bows. Kiernan noted with approval that it was a quiet night, with a small shore wind and an easy sea running against him.

He threw his cigarette stub overboard; lighted another. Then he gave the motor the gun; noted with approval how the boat pushed her nose forward into the swell.

Only when he was a mile off shore did he switch on the navigation lights. A minute or so afterwards the light was switched on in the forward cabin. Kiernan grinned. Callao, he concluded, had tired of sitting in the dark. Maybe now that they were well away from the coast the Spaniard was feeling a little more cheerful.

Kiernan called out: "Vincente . . . how are you feeling? Nobody could be sick on a night like this—not even you. Come out here and look at it. And bring out my coat."

There was no reply. Kiernan shrugged his shoulders. After a minute he reduced speed; set the automatic control on the steering wheel to keep the boat head on. He went forward to the cabin. Callao, he thought, was in the throes of sea-sickness. Probably making a hell of a mess.

He opened the cabin door; went in. The door closed behind him, and Kiernan stood, his back to it, grinning.

Callao was sitting up on the starboard bunk looking at him. On the other bunk at the far end next to the forward door, smiling cheerfully, was Ernest Guelvada.

Kiernan said: "Well . . . if it isn't Ernest. Fancy seeing you." He looked at the Luger pistol in Guelvada's left hand.

Guelvada smiled. He said: "It's good to see you again, Kiernan. The last time we met was in occupied France. Then you were a man and not a traitor . . . hey?"

Kiernan shrugged. "Don't jump to conclusions, Ernest. You know damned well that I've been doing the same thing as you. Trying to find those lists. Well . . . I've found 'em. I'll bet you any money you like they're in the locker over there."

Guelvada's smile became more childlike. "How delightful! How hunky dory. Tell me some more, Kiernan. Let me hear how good it is."

Kiernan laughed. "It's good because it's true," he said. "I knew damned well that Callao brought the lists into England; that he was trying to do a deal with them. I knew that he had to get them out somehow. Well . . . I found how. This boat is registered in his name. I put a woman—Aurora Francis—he had a yen for her—on to him and she got the story out of him. I came down here after him to-night and came aboard with him. I knew that Quayle wouldn't want any sort of show-down with a Spanish national in England; that he would prefer me to get the stuff on him in France—nice and quietly. . . ."

Guelvada shrugged his shoulders. "It's a nice story . . . a very nice story. You ought to have been an author, my Kiernan."

Kiernan said cheerfully: "It's my story and I'm sticking to it and nobody can disprove it. Not even the very clever and most charming Ernest Guelvada."

Callao's eyes went from one to the other as they talked. His hands were trembling.

"You're a liar," said Guelvada, with an amiable smile. "You have been very good, my Kiernan. But you made one mistake—the usual mistake that every crook makes . . . hey? You left the account from the motor marine engineers in Rye on the shelf in your bathroom. The sharp-eyed Antoinette Brown saw it. Then I was on to you, my friend. Then I knew what you were at. I saw everything. Guelvada always sees everything—eventually! "

"Nuts," said Kiernan. He threw his cigarette stub on to the floor, ground it out; fumbled in the pocket of his coat; produced another. He lighted it. Guelvada watched him like a cat.

"You ought to get your brain examined," said Kiernan. "You're slipping, Ernest. Of course I had the account from the Rye engineering firm. How the hell do you think I discovered that Callao had this boat down here? I went over to his rooms one night when he was playing at the Cockatoo and found the account there. That's when I first began to get wise as to how he was going to make his getaway."

Guelvada sighed. He thought that it was time he brought things to a head. He thought that the time had come to try out his scheme for the tying-up of the ends of this affair. The time had come for him to try out the bluff he had thought out that afternoon.

He spoke slowly. "My good Kiernan, I know you are no fool. From the first to the last you have covered yourself admirably in this business. You have covered yourself so well that if you were brought to trial you were certain that on your record and on Callao's you would get away with it. Nobody would believe Callao. Everybody would believe you. Unfortunately, you made one mistake . . . one very big mistake."

"Such as?" Kiernan asked the question easily. His voice was smooth.

"Such as believing that this Callao would be more frightened of you than of me," said Guelvada smilingly. "Last night I met him at the Cockatoo . . . very frightened, very miserable." Casually Guelvada put his right hand into the pocket of his raincoat. The Luger pistol, in his left, pointed in the direction of Callao.

"I thought that the time had come to work on him," continued Guelvada. "I scared him. I scared the pants off him. So he was petrified. So he talked. And how! Eventually I took him away and persuaded him to make a complete statement. It was all properly done. It means the end of you, my friend. Callao's statement—whatever happens to the lists—means the end of you. At best you will get fifteen year's hard labour—and all because you thought that this man was too scared of you and not scared enough of any one else."

Kiernan looked at Callao. He put his hands in the pockets of his coat.

He said slowly to Guelvada: "What did he say in the statement?"

Guelvada raised his eyebrows. "Wouldn't you know?" he asked. "Do I have to tell you? He told of everything that you and Aurora Francis had said and done to him; from the night you arrived and beat him up until yesterday. He told your story of the fake lists; how you had threatened him. He told of this boat; how you were to take him away so that if anything went wrong you could accuse him. This man, I tell you, my good friend Kiernan, is going to get you fifteen years!"

Kiernan looked at Callao contemptuously. The Spaniard still sat with his head sunk on his chest, but Guelvada thought he saw something like a gleam come into the dead eyes. His mind worked quickly. If the Spaniard could be sufficiently goaded; if he could lose his temper for once, Kiernan, even if he had not fallen for Guelvada's story of the night before, would prefer Callao out of the way. It would be more convenient—much more convenient.

Guelvada looked at Kiernan who stood, leaning against the cabin door, his right hand still in his pocket. There would be an automatic in that pocket, thought Guelvada. Kiernan was taking no chances.

Kiernan said to Callao: "You cheap Spanish bastard . . . so you talked! So you hadn't even enough sense for your own sake to keep your stupid mouth shut!" He began to speak in Spanish. He called Callao unutterable things. His obscenity embraced Callao's mother, his sisters, his wife—if there ever should be a wife. Even Guelvada, whose ability in obscenity in five languages was unique, listened with a certain admiration.

Kiernan stopped speaking. Callao said nothing. But he raised his head. He ran his tongue over his dry lips.

Guelvada said suavely: "My Callao, you are something less than a worm. You allow this cheap-jack to talk to you like that. He talks to you like that because he is frightened himself . . . goddam it, he is scared. I'm telling you! He knows that he has come to the end of his story; that you can put him where he belongs—in prison. So he abuses you. He says unspeakable things about your women. If I were you, knowing what you know, I would crack his thick skull with the iron stanchion on the locker, I would tear him to pieces. I would . . ."

The Spaniard spoke. He spoke quickly, the words tumbling out of his mouth. His eyes glittered. He seemed half-mad. He looked at Kiernan, his face twitching.

He said: "He ees right. What he says ees the trut'. You feelthy scum, I hate you so much. How I hate you! You have made out of my life a misery. I who was happy and asked so little. You have done all these theengs to me. You have taken my woman away from me, and now . . . you insult me!"

He got up. His mouth was working. Guelvada thought: Here it comes. . . .

Kiernan laughed. He said: "Nuts . . . bastard! . . ."

Callao said thickly: "I am going to keel you! Damn you, I am going to keel you! I am going to tell everything about you and what you did to me and what you made me do. I am going to sell you out, and you will rot in prison. You—"

Callao moved quickly forward. He was slobbering with the insensate rage of the habitual coward who, in spite of himself, acquired the courage of a desperate rat. He sprang for the iron stanchion that lay on top of the locker.

Kiernan let him get his fingers on it. Then, as Callao leapt towards him, he fired through his pocket.

The Spaniard slumped against the table. The stanchion fell from his nerveless fingers. The bullet had smashed through his breastbone and penetrated the side of the heart. His eyes, dilated with fear, looked wildly about him. He slithered to the floor. He jerked spasmodically; then lay still.

Guelvada sat motionless. His left hand, holding the Luger, hung by his side. His right hand was in the pocket of his raincoat. He watched Kiernan.

Kiernan shrugged his shoulders. He said casually: "You are witness, Ernest, that I killed him in self-defence." He grinned at Guelvada. "In any event, it makes it a great deal more convenient for every one. Incidentally, I think you were lying. I do not believe that he talked to you last night. If he had done that he would never have met me to-night. His nerve would have been finished entirely. He would have asked you to look after him."

Guelvada said amiably: "Maybe I didn't want to look after him. Maybe I didn't even like him."

"This thing can still be easily worked out," said Kiernan.

Guelvada said: "So? . . ." He was smiling.

Kiernan shrugged. "You lose your only witness. Quayle will be glad to do a deal with me. Any one will be glad to do a deal with me. Do you think Quayle wants publicity about this—about the lists—about anything? He wants the lists. Well . . . he can have them at my price."

Guelvada got up. He threw the Luger on to the table. He yawned.

"You are a tough proposition, my Kiernan. But tough! You are one of the toughest eggs I have yet encountered. So you wish to make a deal. Listen . . . let me, Guelvada, tell you the sort of deal that, is possible for you."

Kiernan leaned back against the door of the cabin. "Tell me . . ." He was smiling.

Guelvada looked serious. "I will tell you what is possible," he began. He looked down at Callao. "I observe that our friend is dead. Perhaps it is well for himself and every one else . . . hey?"

Kiernan looked at Callao. As his eyes went down to the floor, Guelvada's right hand came out of his pocket. As Kiernan's head came up he threw the knife. . . .

The knife flew across the cabin like a silver streak. It took Kiernan in the throat just above the Adam's apple. The force of the impact smacked his head back against the cabin door.

His hands moved upwards towards his throat. A hoarse, choking sound came from him. His knees buckled. He crashed against the side of the cabin; hit the end of the bunk; fell sideways across the cabin floor. His legs threshed and writhed for a moment. Then he lay still. The blood began to stream from his mouth.

Guelvada waited. After a minute he got up. He moved quickly and systematically about the cabin. He went to Kiernan; opened his jacket; searched the pockets.

He moved over to the locker; forced the top drawer with the thin end of the stanchion. He opened the drawer. He smiled. Inside the drawer lay the long parchment envelope, heavily sealed over the red tapes. He threw the packet on the table.

Now he moved to the top of the cabin. He put his hands under Callao's shoulders; drew him towards the prone body of Kiernan. He took Callao's right wrist; pressed the fingers about the hilt of the knife in Kiernan's throat. Then he moved the Spaniard's body back to its original position.

He thought about Kiernan. Kiernan had been clever. Clever enough to leave the lists aboard the boat. Aboard the boat registered in Callao's name. Up to the last he had kept up his bluff. A bluff which in any normal circumstances must have worked.

Kiernan had been almost brilliant. From the first he had been one jump ahead of Quayle. He had known that he was suspect. But he had also known that the important thing in Quayle's mind was the securing of the lists. Anything else—even the ruin of Kiernan—was of secondary importance. And he had played on that. He had worked out what Quayle would expect him to do. He had done it up to a point; but all the time he had covered himself.

The only definite evidence against him would come from Callao—or the woman. Well . . . Callao was dead—killed, as Kiernan had said, in self-defence. And the woman was out of the country. Guelvada thought, with an inward glow, that but for him Kiernan would have got away with it.

He took off his raincoat and the gumboots he wore beneath it. He had unclothed except for the royal blue swimming trunks he had ordered from the sports' outfitters that morning. He placed the Luger pistol in the pocket of the raincoat; rolled up the gumboots inside the coat; fastened the coat with its belt.

He took the parchment packet from the table; rolled down the top of his swimming trunks. Inside was sewn a large oilskin sponge bag. Guelvada put the packet inside the oilskin case; fastened it; secured the belt around the top of his swimming trunks. He took the duffle coat from the hook behind the door; put it on. He picked up the bundle.

He moved round the left side of the table; stepped over Kiernan's body. He switched off the cabin light; opened the door. He looked back into the cabin. He said: "Bon voyage, mes amis!"

He closed the door; stepped into the cockpit of the boat. The Vincente chugged rhythmically forward into the sea.

Guelvada threw the raincoat overboard. He watched it sink. He moved to the controls. He took off the steering control; brought the boat about; headed back towards the shore. He pushed up the speed control; switched off the navigating lights.

He stood in the cold night air, his hands on the steering wheel. He was contented. His eyes scanned the empty, moonlit sea.

In twenty minutes he saw the line of the coast. Another ten minutes showed him the mouth of the inlet. He steered the boat carefully for a hundred yards; brought her about, headed out to sea; set the steering control; regulated the engine. He switched on the navigating lights.

Guelvada threw off the duffle coat; climbed out of the cockpit on to the stern. He stood there for a few moments regarding the scene, watching the moonlight play upon the water. He took a purchase with his bare feet; raised his arms above his head. He posed for the dive almost as if a camera was turned on him.

As he hit the water he thought that diving into the sea was like the embrace of an extremely cold woman.

He struck out steadily towards the shore.

Chapter Five
CONGA

FRIDAY

Frewin was sitting behind Quayle's desk when Guelvada came into the office. He looked tired and worried.

Guelvada said cheerfully: "I am delighted to see you, mon vieux! Once again, Ernest is with you—and all in one piece, goddam it! But why are you looking so worried?"

He put his head on one side. He said whimsically: "Don't tell me that you took my advice about the charming Antoinette . . . and that you were unsuccessful. I cannot believe it!"

Frewin said wearily: "Why don't you mind your own damned business, Ernest? But I suppose you're feeling expansive. You've pulled it off again. I congratulate you. It must have been too cold for swimming early this morning. But I suppose you liked that too?"

Guelvada said modestly: "At sports I am very good. I have always been an excellent swimmer. One day I should like you to see the new swimming trunks I wore—most attractive, I think."

Frewin said: "The boat was picked up by a trawler early this morning. They reported to Rye. It got through to Scotland Yard at seven o'clock. I'd given them an instruction to let me know about it after your phone call last night. There must have been quite a time on that boat."

Guelvada shrugged his shoulders. "It was shocking," he said dramatically. "A most appalling scene. Actually, of course, immediately Kiernan saw me on the boat he wished Callao out of the way. With the woman in France the only person who could have testified against him was the Spaniard." He smiled, almost whimsically. "Actually," he continued, "I had myself come to the conclusion that Callao was redundant. He was of no use to any one—and he knew too much."

Frewin nodded. "Of course he did."

"So," Guelvada went on, "I thought that the time had come when I might endeavour to bring about a little activity. So I bluffed the good Kiernan. I told him that I had met Callao the night before at the Cockatoo and that Callao had talked; had told everything. I don't think that Kiernan believed this, but he could not be sure about it and he was taking no chances."

Guelvada paused to light a cigarette.

"He insulted Callao," he said. "Mon Dieu, but how he insulted him! Never have I heard such a beautiful conglomeration of words. I was lost in admiration. Kiernan was so good that the Spaniard who was so frightened forgot, for one moment, to be afraid. I think it must have been something that Kiernan said about his mother and the peculiar method of his birth—an impossibility, I assure you, this method . . ."

Frewin smiled. "So he went for Kiernan?"

Guelvada nodded. "He went for Kiernan with a knife," he said glibly. "And Kiernan shot him. Of course it was self-defence. But even so Callao managed to kill him."

"That was very clever of him," said Frewin. "After he was shot he managed to stab Kiernan through the throat. Pretty good, must say. It was an extraordinary coincidence that he should have used a five-inch Swedish folding knife—the sort of knife you used to use. . . ."

"Most extraordinary," said Guelvada. "I thought at the time that it was a most peculiar coincidence. Of course I would have stopped it if I could. But I had no time. Everything was over so quickly."

Frewin grinned. "I bet it was. So that's how it happened, Ernest?"

Guelvada raised his eyebrows. "Of course. I'm telling you. I was there. I saw it."

Frewin said: "It's a good story. It'll do. Well, this looks like the end of the business."

"But of course," said Guelvada. "Where is Mr. Quayle? I wish to speak to him."

"He's at his place in the country. He said he'd be back either to-night or to-morrow morning."

Guelvada said: "I see. I think it's a great pity. I wished him to be here to receive the documents. I felt it would be a fitting end."

"I think you've done pretty well, Ernest," said Frewin admiringly. "But then you always do."

Guelvada sat down. He lighted a cigarette. He pulled up and arranged his immaculate trousers. He admired the knife-edged creases, and his polished shoes.

He said: "My friend, always I notice the small things. There were two mistakes that Kiernan made in this business—two mistakes which told me everything I wanted to know. First of all he proposes to this woman Aurora Francis. That is not like Kiernan. I tell you it was entirely unlike him, hey? This man would never marry any woman. He is what you call the great big cat who walks alone. Never would he tie himself to a woman. But figure to yourself, not only does he propose marriage to her, but he makes her his confidante. He tells her things—important things. That also is entirely unlike Kiernan. He never talks to anybody unless he wishes them to spread what he says. So he knows that Aurora Francis will tell Antoinette Brown. He knows that the information he wishes to get back to Quayle will be got back to him."

Frewin nodded. "I see that. . . . You've suggested that before."

"Precisely," said Guelvada. "Also he uses the woman Aurora Francis to work on Callao. Maybe Callao brought those lists into England for Kiernan. Remember that Kiernan knew him before and Callao scares easily. He uses the woman to get the lists back from Callao. This meeting of all these people at the Cockatoo . . . that also was arranged, partly by Kiernan and partly by fate. From the first he played this thing very well. But he made the mistake of leaving the marine motor engineers' account on the shelf in the bathroom. That was stupid. It enabled me to make inquiries about the boat. You will understand of course that Kiernan had even covered himself about that. Up to the last moment he had the story that he was sticking to the Spaniard because the Spaniard had the lists. He knew that Quayle wouldn't want any sort of public inquiry. He knew that if Quayle got the lists back and if he, Kiernan, had any sort of possible story, he would still get away with it.

"Figure to yourself that if he had reached France he could have done a deal with anybody about those lists."

Frewin said: "I suppose you're right."

Guelvada opened the document case he had brought with him. He opened it with a flourish. He threw the parchment package on the table.

He said: "Once again Ernest Guelvada brings home the bacon! There is the bacon."

"Quayle will be pleased about this," said Frewin. He opened a drawer; took out a steel knife. He slit open the tapes about the packet; cut beneath the seals.

Guelvada watched him. Frewin opened the parchment envelope; put his hand inside; brought out the documents.

Guelvada said: "My God! . . ."

In Frewin's hands were six folded copies of the Evening News!

Frewin said in a low voice: "So he double-crossed you. He double-crossed all of us. The woman had the documents."

Guelvada sat down in the arm-chair. He put his face in his hands. He said: "My God! . . . So he was cleverer than even I thought. He even let the lists go out of his possession to get them out of the country. It wasn't a double-cross; it was a double double-cross. Maybe he did love this woman. Maybe he did mean to marry her. He knew that we would let her go. . . . He gave her the real lists." He looked at Frewin. He presented a picture of misery.

"This isn't so good," said Frewin. "You're not to blame, Ernest, but it's an awful pity you didn't have that woman picked up."

Guelvada spread his hands. "How could I? Mon Dieu . . . how could I? If we pick the woman up, and the lists she has are fake, Kiernan does nothing. Don't you understand that? And I knew that she must have the fake lists. Never for one second had it occurred to me that Kiernan could have been as subtle, as clever, as this."

Frewin said: "There's nothing to be done. We'll wait for Quayle."

Guelvada got up. His face was grim. "I wait for nobody. Where has this woman gone? Did the pilot report?"

Frewin nodded. "When she landed at Le Bourget she got a hired car. She was to be driven to the Hotel Plaza Athénée, on the Avenue Montaigne in Paris."

Guelvada's voice was tense. "Listen to me, my friend. Get me a plane quickly. It is five o'clock. I can be in Paris by seven. You'll remember I have yet another knife. If I find her she will give me the lists . . . I'm telling you."

Frewin said: "If you find her and if, when you've found her, she's still got them. . . . Do you think she's going to stay around in an hotel, waiting to be picked up with those lists on her?"

Guelvada said: "I must do something. Get me the plane. If I find the woman by all the devils in hell she talks to me. She tells me where the lists are. I shall find a way of making her talk."

Frewin shrugged his shoulders. "O.K. . . . ." he said. He reached for the telephone.

It was eight o'clock. Guelvada sat in the little cafe at the end of the Rue Jean Bottin waiting for the boy to come back.

He was impatient. For once in his life a sense of disappointment obsessed him. His record was at stake. He, Guelvada, who had never yet failed, had been ditched, left in the air, frustrated and helpless—and by Kiernan. Kiernan, whom he had merely considered to be intelligent, cunning, courageous and nothing more. A man without inspiration or brilliance.

And Quayle? What would Quayle say? He would shrug his shoulders. He would say: "Hard luck, Ernest. I thought you were good enough to pull it off. But I expect you did your best."

Was this to be the end of the Guelvada tradition? He lighted a cigarette; sat, staring at the glass of vermouth-cassis on the table before him. For the first time in his life he was a little annoyed with Guelvada—a process as unique as it was unexpected.

The boy came into the cafe. He approached the table.

Guelvada said: "Well? . . ."

"She is there, M'sieu," said the boy. "She has a suite—No. 274—on the second floor. She arrived this afternoon. Whilst I was in the foyer there was a gentleman asking for her. They were waiting for a page to show him up."

"Ciel!" said Guelvada. He threw a fifty-franc note to the boy, put another beneath the saucer on the table and made for the door. He hurried across the Avenue Montaigne; turned into the entrance of the Plaza Athénée.

A heavily built man was following a page boy towards the lift at the back of the foyer.

Guelvada crossed the foyer quickly; got into the lift with the man and the page. The lift stopped on the second floor. The page boy and the man got out. Guelvada also.

They walked down the corridor, Guelvada half a dozen paces in the rear. Outside the door marked 274 the boy stopped and knocked. Guelvada continued to walk down the corridor; turned off to the right and stopped. He waited for a few moments; then turned back into the corridor.

The page boy was walking towards the lift. Guelvada waited until it had disappeared; then he moved quickly.

There was no one in the corridor. Outside suite No. 274 he stopped and listened. He could hear nothing. Inside the doorway, he thought, would be the usual hall with the bedroom on one side and the sitting-room on the other.

He felt in his pocket; produced the "spider" key. He inserted it in the lock. He turned the spiral; felt relieved as he felt the wards engage. He turned the key. The door opened.

Guelvada stepped inside. He had been right about the hallway. There was a door to his left; another to his right. That on his left was slightly open. He could hear voices.

Guelvada opened the door on his right very quietly. Inside, the light was on. He was in the bedroom. He closed the door behind him; moved to the door at the upper end of the room on the left, leading into the sitting-room.

It was ajar. Guelvada looked through.

The man was standing inside the door leading from the hall into the sitting-room. He was tall, heavily built. He had a strong, thin face, with a short moustache. He might have been anything or anybody.

Facing him, in the middle of the room, with her back to Guelvada, was Aurora Francis. He thought that her back view was superb. She wore a pink lace negligée, lined with pink georgette, with wide flowing sleeves caught at the wrists with blue velvet ribbons.

Guelvada thought he would like to take a very long look at Aurora Francis. He thought that if her front view was as good as that from the back she must be very, very good.

She said to the man facing her, in French: "M'sieu, I am extremely sorry, but I have no authority to negotiate with you. I regret this very much. I can do nothing until the arrival of Captain Kiernan."

He shrugged his shoulders. "I am sorry, madame, but my instructions are explicit. A large sum of money has been placed to the credit of Captain Kiernan, as arranged. I am to collect certain documents from you or from him. He is not here so I propose to collect them from you. You will understand that time is pressing; that there is no time to be wasted in useless argument. If the papers are not handed over it will be not very good for madame. I shall carry out the instructions I received in the event of there being some delay about handing over the documents. The instructions are definite."

Guelvada began to smile. He thought: This is excellent. So nothing has been handed over.

He stepped into the room. As he passed the woman he said: "Pardon, madame. . . ." He faced the man. His hand in his overcoat pocket.

"M'sieu," he said, "I have to inform you that I am Chief-Detective-Inspector Antoine Leclerq of the Sûrété Nationale. I have also to inform you that you have been under observation since your arrival in France. I have also to tell you that you will immediately leave this hotel and will make arrangements to leave French territory within the next twelve hours. During that time, I assure you, you will be under close observation. If you have not left France at the end of the stated period you will be placed under arrest."

The man shrugged his shoulders. He said to Aurora: "Very clever, madame. Perhaps you will be good enough to inform Captain Kiernan that we shall remember. That it will go hard with him."

He turned on his heel. Guelvada followed him into the hall; closed the apartment door behind him.

Guelvada stepped back into the apartment. The woman was standing in front of the fireplace. She had her back to him. She was taking a cigarette from a box on the mantelpiece.

Guelvada threw his hat on to a chair. He produced his cigarette lighter; lighted her cigarette.

He said: "Miss Francis, please to sit down and listen carefully to me. I am Ernest Guelvada, and I am an extremely angry man. But angry. I have been made a fool of by your boy-friend Kiernan. I have been made a fool of by you. The fact that Kiernan has made a fool of you and also one of himself is of little use to me. It does nothing at all to console me . . . I assure you."

She sat down in a high-backed chair by the fireplace. Guelvada thought that the glow from the electric fire reflected attractively on her dark hair.

She said coolly: "I've heard of you, Mr. Guelvada. What can I do for you?"

"I shall tell you," said Guelvada. "And I shall tell you very clearly so that there is no possibility of any misunderstanding . . . hey? First of all, your friend Kiernan is no more. He is very dead, which I think is a good thing. Secondly, he was extremely successful in leading me on a wild goose chase whilst you got out of England with those lists. I congratulate you. But, madame, the story is not yet over. Guelvada is not yet entirely defeated. Please listen to me."

She moved a little. "I'm listening, Mr. Guelvada."

"Quite obviously, your recent visitor—the gentleman who has just left us—was the person who was to receive the lists—the real lists—for Kiernan. He came here by appointment. He came here because Kiernan had already arranged that he should come here and take delivery of the lists against the money credit which he mentioned just now. So you have the lists. And you will get them—wherever they are hidden—and give them to me. I will tell you why."

He put his hand in his pocket and produced the knife. He held it out across his open palm.

"Madame," he said, "I can throw this knife unerringly. I can put its point through the ace of hearts on a playing card at twenty yards. Just as easily I could put it through your so beautiful throat. And I would not like to do that, madame, because you are a very beautiful woman and it would be a great pity if your beauty were to be spoiled."

He threw the knife into the air; caught it as it fell.

"No one has seen me come into this room," he went on. "When your body is discovered it will be supposed that the alien gentleman who just left is the person responsible for your death. And you will be dead, madame. Very dead. Where are the lists?"

She smiled. "I'm awfully sorry, Mr. Guelvada, but I haven't the remotest notion. There is a heavily sealed parchment package in that drawer over there, but to the best of my knowledge it contains some folded copies of newspapers. Perhaps you'd like to look at it."

Guelvada's mouth tightened. "I admire your courage and your sense of humour, madame." He laid the knife across the palm of his right hand. "I ask you for the last time . . . where are the lists?"

She got up. Guelvada heard the door behind him open. He spun round.

Quayle stood in the doorway. He said: "Hallo, Ernest, I thought you'd finish up somewhere in the vicinity. I'd like you to meet Miss Francis officially. Aurora, this is Mr. Guelvada—a most superb operative. Ernest, you'll be glad to know that Miss Francis has been working for me for a long time—since Nuremberg in fact."

He came into the room. Guelvada shut the knife with a click. He replaced it in his pocket. He sat down on the settee behind him. He put his head in his hands.

He said: "Oh, my God! This is too much . . . even for Guelvada."

Quayle refilled the champagne glasses.

He said: "There was only one way to play it, Ernest. I played it just like that. When the lists first disappeared I checked on everybody who'd had access to them. That included Kiernan. I put Aurora Francis on to him. She was his type, and he fell for her. But he was clever. When he thought she'd fallen for him he arranged to meet her at the Cockatoo in England; told her about Callao; imagined he'd whetted her curiosity about the Spaniard. Aurora had rather given him the idea that she went for men in a big way; that she was curious. So he fell for the idea of using her to make Callao into a stooge for him."

Guelvada nodded. "And then you used all of us as stooges. . . . But all of us . . . except the beautiful Aurora."

"There was nothing else to be done," said Quayle. "My one idea was to push Kiernan into action. To make him do something. Something that would enable us to find where he had the lists; how we could get them. You helped a lot in that."

Guelvada raised his eyebrows. "I helped. . . . But how?"

"By putting Antoinette Brown in to search his rooms," said Quayle. "When Frewin told me what you had arranged, I telephoned Aurora Francis and suggested that she appear and 'discover' Brown. I knew when she told Kiernan he'd get a ripple on. As a matter of fact he'd expected to have his rooms searched He left the Marine Engineering Company's account so that it could be found. He guessed what you'd think, Ernest."

Guelvada said: "And you knew that someone would come here to contact Kiernan to-night. You knew that you'd be able to find out who it was wanted to buy the lists?"

Quayle nodded. "Now we know." He looked at his watch. "It's time to be moving. The plane goes in forty-five minutes, and I have an appointment in London at midnight."

The morning sun was shining as Quayle walked down the corridor on the way to his office. As he passed the door of Antoinette Brown's room he paused; retraced his steps. He opened the door; went in.

She was sitting at her desk by the window. Her face was buried in her hands. She was sobbing bitterly.

Quayle said: "Well . . . well . . . Antoinette! On such a nice morning too. What's it all about?"

He went over to her.

She looked up at him; then away. She said in a voice strangled by sobs: "It's terrible, Mr. Quayle. . . . I don't know what to do. . . . I don't know why I ever said yes. . . ."

"Good heavens!" said Quayle. "You don't say so! That's too bad. What did you say yes to?"

She indulged in a fresh outburst. "I've promised to marry Michael Frewin! And that isn't the w-w-orst, Mr. Quayle."

"No!" said Quayle. "Well, tell me what the worst is."

She began to dry her eyes. "I think I rather like the idea . . . and I never intended to be married. I didn't think I'd want to be. . . ."

Quayle patted her on the shoulder. "Cheer up, Antoinette. I think it's rather charming." He stopped at the door and turned. He said, with a smile: "Now I suppose they'll call you the Impractical Virgin." He went out to the office.

Frewin was at work at his desk when Quayle entered. He said: "Congratulations. . . . It was a marvellous idea. The odd part is that Kiernan will never know that Aurora Francis handed the lists over to you immediately she got them from Callao."

"It is rather funny," said Quayle. "However, it saved him a certain amount of annoyance."

He went to the door. "You'd better go along and have a word with Antoinette. She's in a bit of a state. I think she needs a little moral support."

Frewin smiled. He got up from his chair. "O.K. . . . Anyhow, it's time we had a marriage in this rather peculiar organisation."

Quayle went away. Frewin walked down the passage. He went into Antoinette Brown's office. He stood just inside the doorway.

She got up from her desk.

Frewin asked: "What's the matter, honey? What are the tears about?"

She said: "I don't know how I ever let you talk me into it. I don't think I want to be married. I don't like men. I don't think I like you. . . ."

Frewin said softly: "Don't talk nonsense, darling. Come here. . . ."

"I don't want to," said Antoinette Brown.

But she went just the same.

THE END

Printed in Great Britain
by Amazon